DESIGNATED
SURVIVOR

Also by John H. Matthews

The South Coast

Ballyvaughan

Red Grace: A Grace Short Story

JOHN H. MATTHEWS

DESIGNATED SURVIVOR

Bluebullseye Press

DESIGNATED SURVIVOR
Written by John H. Matthews
Copyright © 2016 by John H. Matthews

ISBN: 978-0-9897233-5-0

Bluebullseye Press
www.bluebullseyepress.com
A division of Bluebullseye LLC

Edited by Ginger Moran

Cover design copyright © 2016 John H. Matthews

For Brennan,

I tried to write the kid's book you asked for but things kept blowing up.

DESIGNATED SURVIVOR

CHAPTER 1

The weapons and gear were heavy, but Jared Long was used to it. He'd been a Marine for six years before being accepted into the Secret Service uniformed division, then another two before joining the tactical team. His training had been hard and long and brought him to this point in his life, standing in the lobby of the United States Capitol building with an FN P90 compact assault rifle loaded in his hands, a Sig Sauer P229 on his side, and extra ammunition for both.

On either side of him lined up at fifteen foot intervals through the hallway were a dozen other members of his team, all armed and ready. Jared kept looking at his watch and each time tried to stop, to not draw attention to himself. He still wasn't sure he could go through with it, in case what the man on the phone had said was a lie. But he also didn't know if he could take the chance it was true.

A bead of sweat worked down his brow, coming from

under his helmet, across his forehead and into his right eye. The words would come soon and he'd have to decide what to do, if he could do it. He wasn't even sure he was capable of it. He hadn't been home since before sunrise that morning when he left to prepare for tonight's assignment, when he left quietly his wife was sleeping in bed, their daughter in her crib inches away.

The doors began to close along the hallway, locking the chamber behind them. It was going to come soon. He had to choose. Was the threat against his family real? The calls had started weeks ago, getting worse each time until the vile words spoken today.

The cheap white speakers were spaced out throughout the hall, clumsily mounted to the old stone columns and defying the architecture. They began to transmit the proceedings happening in the large closed room behind him. Jared's stomach tightened. He moved his right hand to check the safety on the automatic weapon he was holding and glanced to both sides to see his team members.

Each word that came through the speakers made him jump for fear it was the signal he was waiting for. He wondered if he was the only one or if others had received similar calls, the same abrupt and vulgar threats. Capitol Police lined the outside of the building and inside there were enough Secret Service officers to stop anything, he thought.

He'd tried calling home three times in the short gap between the last phone call he'd received to his unlisted and secure work cell phone and when they were entering the Capitol building. She hadn't answered, but in normal situations it wouldn't have been a cause for concern. She might have taken the baby out to do some grocery shopping, or had simply turned the ringer off so they could both nap.

The applause coming through the wall behind him began to fade as the sound from the speakers grew and he knew it was time. He thought of his wife and their beautiful little girl, Lila. The baby would be asleep by now but Sarah would be watching on television as she always did.

And then the gentle but assertive woman's voice came. "Mr. Speaker, Mr. Vice President, members of Congress, my fellow Americans…"

Jared Long paused for only a moment and gripped the assault rifle tightly. He closed his eyes and spoke to himself.

"I'm sorry, Sarah."

He raised his rifle as he turned to his left. He began firing in short, three round bursts as his training as a Marine and a Secret Service tactical officer had taught him. He knew to aim at a target further away first, that it would distract those closer to him as they turned to identify the threat he was firing his weapon towards. The first cluster of bullets hit Officer Timothy Strong thirty feet away and the man's body fell to the ground. Just to his left, Sergeant Bobby Martinez stood frozen. Unsure of what to do as he looked at the body on the ground then back at Jared, he began to raise his rifle. Jared took aim and squeezed his trigger for a second burst of bullets that struck the man in his head and chest and he watched Martinez fall to the ground. It had only been seconds since he'd first pulled his trigger. He heard more gunfire behind him and turned to engage.

Some officers weren't even raising their weapons, confused why one of their own was firing on them. Others reacted more quickly and returned fire in self-defense. It took only moments and nobody knew who had begun the fight or who was on which side. Yells for cease-fire were heard throughout the hallway and through the earpieces they each wore.

He stepped back to the wall and let himself slide down to the floor until he was sitting, his rifle still in front of him. He'd killed four men in a matter of seconds and nobody was left standing. The magazine in his rifle was empty and when he tried to reach back with his right hand to grab a new one his arm didn't respond. Though there was no pain he was sure he'd been shot in the shoulder. There was little movement in the room as most of the officers were dead or seriously injured. Protocol had the doors to the House chamber locked from inside and the exterior doors were secured by Capitol Police protecting the perimeter for the State of the Union address.

The speakers were overloaded with the sounds of the commotion inside the chamber, reacting to the barrage of gunfire outside its doors. By now the president should have been pulled down from her podium and moved to a secure location, if there was such a thing at this point. He knew from the extent of the firefight that others must have been forced into killing, that he hadn't been the only one.

Glass shattered and more gunfire erupted from down the stairs and hallway to the outside. Moments later three armored Capitol Police rushed in and spread out through the hall. A sense of relief rushed over Jared Long. He'd done what he was told to do and he'd survived. He watched the first policemen use their feet to kick the downed Secret Service officers to see if they were alive. With one kick came a grunt, a moment of silence, and a single shot from the Capitol Police officer's rifle.

Jared sat there, realizing survival wasn't to be and his time was limited, but hoping he would be missed, as he watched the methodical extermination of any survivors in front of him. He held still and closed his eyes. Even if he could have moved his arm and put his fingers around the grip of his Sig Sauer pistol, he didn't know if he had the energy to pull it and fire.

"Over there," he heard.

An officer in full gear, his face covered with the black balaclava used for secretive missions walked up to him and he tried to hold still and hoped he could avoid reacting when pushed or kicked to see if he was alive.

Something struck him in the side of the head, a blunt object against his helmet, and his reflexes defied him and kept him from falling over, his head returning back to an upright position.

A single bullet entered his forehead and everything was gone.

CHAPTER 2

Grace's face was pressed into the dirty carpet of his one bedroom apartment in Arlington, Virginia. The empty bottle of Tito's vodka was still clutched in his right hand, his left arm trapped underneath his own body. The cellphone began to vibrate and ring in his jeans pocket. On the tenth ring he let go of the bottle and gradually pulled the phone out and swiped his finger across the glass surface to answer.

"Huh," was all he could get out.

"It's Arrington. Are you there? Grace?"

"Uhh Hhhuhh."

"Grace, we need you," Arrington said. "Have you been watching the news?"

"Unh uhh."

"Shit. Sober up. I'm coming to get you," Arrington said. "We need to get to Herndon."

"Nhuu," Grace pressed the button to hang up and passed out.

His phone began to ring again then someone was banging on the door to his apartment. He rolled himself onto his back and everything inside his head kept moving even though his body was still. Something large smashed against his door and it swung open, slamming against the wall.

"Shit," he tried to sit up. "That was loud."

"Dammit, have you even moved since I called ten minutes ago?" Arrington said.

"What?" Grace said. "Ten minutes?"

Four men were with Derek Arrington, wearing dark suits and tiny receivers in their ears with clear curly cords running down into the perfectly starched white collars of their shirts.

"Okay, guys, stand him up," Arrington said.

The men struggled to hoist Grace's body to a vertical position. His slight build was deceiving as to how much muscle mass he actually had. As they lifted, he adjusted his weight to slip to his left. As his 190 pounds began to fall, one of the agents moved to catch him. Grace's right hand slid up under the man's jacket and pulled the agent's weapon out of its holster.

Just as the agent realized what was happening, Grace stood and spun around behind with his left arm tight on the agent's neck and raised the Sig Sauer .45 caliber pistol at the other three men.

"What the hell is going on here," he said.

"Jesus Christ, Grace," Arrington said. "Quit fucking around and give the man back his gun. We have a situation."

The black Chevrolet Yukon's windows were blacked out to keep anyone from seeing inside the customized and heavily armored vehicle that carried the director of the National Security Agency. Grace sat in the middle of the back seat facing his boss, the back of the SUV fitted out like a limousine rather than a standard Yukon's. At Arrington's order he'd taken a quick shower after the director got too close to him and smelled the two days and nights of drinking Grace had been through with his team after the successful mission.

He'd put on clean khakis and a striped dress shirt with the tails out and the sleeves rolled up to just below his elbows. His exposed forearms displayed the tattoos that began at his wrists and disappeared beneath the shirtsleeve, the face of his oversized silver Breitling watch striking a strong contrast against the inked skin. His hair was still wet from the shower but didn't look much different than when it was dry, light brown and almost to his shoulders, flowing down around his head. A hint of silver was coming in on his temples. On operations he would pull it into a tight, high ponytail.

"So why am I not unconscious on my floor right now?" Grace said. "I just got back from the Soviet Union two days ago." The mission had taken his team eighteen hours to carry out after four weeks of planning and training at a compound in South Carolina.

"It's not the Soviet Union anymore and you know that," Arrington said.

"You been there lately? They sure as hell act like it is," Grace said.

"Watch this," Arrington sat facing him.

A television screen was mounted on the wall behind

Arrington that separated them from the driver's seat. The two men watched the live coverage from CNN through a satellite feed to the vehicle. No media helicopters were being allowed in the air in D.C., so all of the views were zoomed in from any vantage point the reporters could find from blocks away. Blurry shots of the United States Capitol Building filled the screen as the reporters kept repeating the few things they thought to be true or had guessed about the situation.

"What the hell?" Grace said.

"State of the Union," Arrington said. "Gunfire began just after President Abrams began speaking."

"I didn't vote for her," Grace said.

"I know," Arrington's charcoal grey pinstripe suit jacket was hung on a chrome hanger attached to the dividing wall, his white dress shirt still crisp from the dry cleaners, as it always was. His light brown skin never showed signs of being shaved and no stubble was ever visible on the man's chin or the top of his head.

"How do you know that?" Grace said.

"Because we're the NSA. The last time you voted was for Ross Perot when you were eighteen years old because your father hated him."

"Shit," Grace said. "You guys are good."

"Yes, we are," Arrington said. "Capitol police began to enter the building after the initial gunfire stopped, but then the emergency barricades were activated from inside, effectively locking everyone in."

"We have anyone inside?" Grace said.

"A few radio transmissions have come through, usually followed by gunshots then lost signals," Arrington said. "We believe all of our people are being systematically eliminated, if they haven't been already. There's no cellphone activity so we think there's multiple jammers in place."

"So someone has the president, vice president and all of Congress held hostage inside the United States Capitol?" Grace said.

"That's the short answer, yes," Arrington said. "Don't forget about all of the Supreme Court justices and cabinet members and the hundred distinguished guests in the gallery."

"Who's running the country?" Grace said.

"Precautions are taken during the State of the Union," Arrington said.

"You mean the designated survivor?" Grace said. "Whatever low level cabinet member drew the short straw and is eating a five-star dinner in a bunker somewhere? That's the leader of the free world right now?"

"Yeah," Arrington said. "Aren't we lucky."

"Who has the football?" Grace asked about the black suitcase that travels with the president that contains the launch codes for the Nation's nuclear missiles.

"The president has it inside the Capitol," Arrington said. "The designated survivor has a backup. The pentagon can delete all active launch codes and replace them with new ones as soon as we tell them to."

"And you haven't yet? We think that's the target? Is someone trying to get our nukes?" Grace said.

"It's our primary assumption. Changing the codes brings the system offline for an hour and we can't be left with our pants down right now in case that's what they want. Russia alone has 1600 warheads pointed at us. 60 minutes gives them time to land quite a few of those," Arrington said. "If we knew who the hell was behind this it would help us narrow down their end game."

"How does something like this happen?" Grace said. "There are hundreds of agents and officers from half a dozen agencies protecting that building."

The SUV turned sharply then slowed as it approached the gates to the newly constructed building in Herndon, Virginia. The gate opened without the car stopping and they sped through the dark parking lot to the front of the building.

"We're trying to figure that out," Arrington said. "And we should find out more soon. Early reports are that it was friendly fire."

"Seriously?" Grace said. "Our men just started shooting at each other inside the Capitol?"

"Again, it's early reports," Arrington said. "We'll get an update as soon as we get inside."

Grace looked out the window. "Why aren't we going to Beltsville?" Grace said. Beltsville, Maryland is home to the Special Collection Service, a highly classified joint operation between the NSA and the Central Intelligence Agency. Their primary mission is to infiltrate and insert eavesdropping equipment in foreign territories, though specialized teams such as Grace's were often used for more proactive missions.

"This fits our immediate needs better," Arrington said. "We're flying by the seat of our pants to get a leadership team together. The secretary of defense, the FBI director and the Attorney General are all in the Capitol. There's no guidebook for this."

"Whose building is this?"

The generic building stood out from others in the area only by the row of large boulders that were placed around the perimeter of the compound, outside the fourteen-foot tall fences with razor wire stretched along the top. The boulders became standard at all new and updated federal buildings housing intelligence agencies in the wake of the bombing at Oklahoma City, after a homemade fertilizer bomb in a rented U-Haul parked on the street beside the Murrah Federal Building and detonated.

"Homeland Security," Arrington said.

"Homeland Security?" Grace said. "Shit. They're like the neighbors who just moved in and start complaining about your grass being too tall before the moving truck even leaves."

"Trust me, I don't like it. The NSA isn't used to playing nice with anyone, I'll be the first to admit that. Hell, just sharing your team with the CIA annoys the hell out of me," Arrington said. "But right now we need all the help we can get. I haven't been here yet, but from what I hear they have everything we need right now to try to get ahead of this thing."

"Who's here? Are they read in on me?" Grace's status within the SCS was top secret and only known to a handful of people. His role within the agency was technically not even on the books.

"I sent word ahead that I'm bringing in a special operator from a cross-agency task force," Arrington said. "We'll give them the details when we need to."

"Nothing I like better than having a bunch of agency heads know my identity," Grace muttered.

They entered the building. Even at the late hour there were still people working on several floors. From the main atrium they took the elevator three levels below ground and exited into a lobby with cement walls and a steel door with two armed guards. An armed guard checked Arrington's credentials then turned and swiped an access card across a sensor. Once the sensor beeped approval the guard placed his right hand on a glass panel and a red light scanned his fingerprints, body temperature and pulse. The scanner turned off and after a moment the magnetic lock on the door released. The guard stepped over and quickly opened the door for the director of the NSA, his arm flying up into a salute.

"I'm not military," Arrington said. "You can put your hand down."

The circular room was large and lined with monitors wherever they could fit along all of the walls up to the ceiling creating a barrage of flashing images that rivaled Times Square. The entire room was a media display of every news channel covering the events at the Capitol from domestic and international news broadcasts. The desks surrounding the center of the area were mostly empty except for one analyst that had been hand picked.

"This is the new operations control center for the Executive Terrorism Task Force. It wasn't set to go live for another two months, but right now it's the best place for us to run this thing from," Arrington said. "From here they can access any satellite, any transmission from a United States or ally airplane or ship, and command a drone strike anywhere on the globe."

"But somehow somebody just stole the US government," Grace said.

Arrington grimaced at him as they approached the group sitting around a conference table in the middle of the room.

"You said Executive Terrorism Task Force?" Grace said.

"This different from the Joint Terrorism Task Force?"

"Yes," Arrington. "The JTTF is buried in paperwork, red tape and more than 5,000 employees. The ETTF was created by the president and answers only to her and the Joint Chiefs. It's streamlined and efficient, designed to be run with minimal staff and even less oversight."

"Cool," Grace said. "They hiring?"

Arrington again threw a frown at Grace then turned to the people at the large conference table in the center of the round room.

"Grace, you know CIA Director Bernard Leighton," Arrington said.

"Of course," Grace said. "How's Betsy?"

"She's doing wonderfully, good to see you Grace," Leighton said.

"Betsy?" Arrington said.

"The director's labradoodle," Grace said. "I dog sit for him occasionally."

Arrington turned and stared at Grace before continuing.

"This is Amanda Paulson, Assistant Director of the FBI," Arrington said.

"Pleasure to meet you, Mrs. Paulson," Grace leaned across the table and shook the woman's hand.

"It's Ms.," she said. "Pleasure's mine."

"And this is . . . " Arrington said.

"Admiral Vic Darby, of course," Grace said. "How's life in Florida?"

"Good, until today," Victor Darby had been confirmed as the commander of Special Operations Command, or SOCOM, six months earlier. Grace's SCS team worked closely and covertly with the Navy's SEAL teams under SOCOM command when they need assistance with infiltration and exfiltration beyond their normal means.

"We're in DHS's house but they have nobody here?" Grace said.

"The deputy secretary is at the Capitol," Arrington said. "Congress has yet to confirm the new secretary."

"Great. So where do we begin?" Grace said.

"Let's watch some TV," Leighton said. "If you will, Mr. Murray?"

The analyst sitting at a desk ten feet away stood up and tapped on a tablet with one finger until all of the screens surrounding the room changed. Video began to play showing the inside of the Capitol building.

"This was taken at 8:14, just as President Abrams was beginning her speech," the analyst said.

They watched a series of security camera footage of a line of Secret Service officers in tactical gear and holding assault rifles. One of the officers turned and began firing at his team, taking down two before any other shots were fired. More officers behind him began to fire until everyone was down. Capitol Police were seen entering and putting bullets into the heads of any survivors, until they reached the original shooter leaning against the wall. After the body fell over, the shooter turned and aimed up at the camera and fired. Then the feed went black.

"That's some shit," Grace said.

"Please, some respect," Arrington said.

"No, he's right, that is some shit," Amanda Paulson said. "And we need to get to the bottom of it. Our leaders are being held hostage and men in our uniforms are helping." Paulson was a rising star at the Hoover Building. Not only was she the first female assistant director, but also the youngest at 39 years old. Her Georgetown undergraduate work then Yale law degree had put her in contact with a circle of powerful people with any law firm in the country ready to hire her. She chose a life of civil service, starting in the Attorney General's office straight out of school then moving to the FBI when the new director pulled her over.

"Are we sure everyone is still alive in the Capitol?" Grace said. "Any communications?"

"We have no video from the building anymore, but we've moved an NSA satellite into position and are getting some infrared images that shows plenty of heat signatures," Arrington said.

"What about helicopters?" Grace said. "Can we get in any closer with a muffled Apache to try to get audio?"

"We can't take the risk," Admiral Darby said. "With what we saw from inside the building, we don't know who's been compromised, especially to send an armed bird in the air over the building. That could be exactly what they want."

"Exactly what who wants? Who are we dealing with? ISIL? Al Qaeda?" Grace said. "Putin? The ghost of Timothy fucking McVeigh?"

"We don't know. It's been 91 minutes since the attack. Nobody's claimed credit yet," Arrington looked over to the leadership sitting at the conference table then back to Grace. "That's why you're here. We need an operator. We have some of the greatest military and law enforcement minds at our disposal, but we're all useless without insight into the terrorist. No offense to anyone present, but we're the people who say 'go.' You're the person who goes."

"We still have a clearance issue," Grace looked around the table then back at Arrington. "Not everybody here is read in."

Arrington stared at Grace for a few moments then leaned over to CIA Director Leighton and spoke in hushed tones. After a short discussion Arrington stood and turned.

"In light of the events of this evening and our need for transparency and cross agency cooperation," Arrington said. "We'll be disclosing sensitive top-secret information." He paused to look at Grace then continued. "Grace is the lead operator in the Special Collection Service. His experience is greater than anyone else at either agency involved with the team. When I say that Director Leighton and I put our trust in him, it is with full confidence we do so."

"So that's out there. Any questions?" Grace said.

"The SCS is real?" Amanda Paulson said. "I thought it was just one of those Beltway rumors."

"It's very real," Grace said. "And the fact that the assistant director of the FBI didn't know we were real is a testament to how seriously we take our clandestine status."

Grace turned and looked at the darkened screens. "We need to establish who on the inside was compromised," he said. "Can you roll that back to the first officer who fired?"

The images began to roll backwards as the analyst controlled it from his keyboard. The screen froze on the moment just before the first shots.

"Zoom in, enhance, whatever you can do," Grace said. "Can we get his name?"

Moments later the video enlarged and the analyst scrolled until the patch with the officer's last name was visible.

"Long," Grace said. "Start with him."

CHAPTER 3

Jared Long's service record was displayed all around them on the screens, detailing his history dating back to high school, ROTC in college then straight into the military.

"Six years in the Marines, five years so far in the Secret Service," the analyst said. "Married, has a daughter."

"What's your name?" Grace turned to the analyst who stared blankly for a moment.

"Ben," he finally said. "Ben Murray."

"Who do you work for?" Grace said.

"Uhh . . . "

"CIA? Homeland Security? NSA?" Grace pressured the man. "Look around the room, Ben. You don't have to worry about your security training."

Employees of the top-secret intelligence community are trained and taught to not disclose their occupation or employer to anyone but those closest to them, and even then only with great discretion.

"Department of Homeland Security, sir," Ben Murray said.

"Great. We're getting somewhere," Grace said. "How long have you been with DHS?"

"Six years," Ben said. "I'm the lead analyst helping get the Executive Terrorist Task Force Command Center ready for operation."

Grace turned to the leadership at the conference table. "We need more like him," Grace pointed at Ben Murray. "We need them to go through the records of every officer on that assignment."

Arrington nodded.

"Ben, I need you to handpick six more analysts to get in here immediately," Arrington said. "The best, the fastest, most trustworthy."

"Yes, sir," Ben said.

"Get me a list," Arrington said.

"And what are they going to be looking for?" Admiral Darby said.

"Terrorists," Grace said.

"In the Secret Service?" Darby said.

"And the Capitol Police, and any other law enforcement that was in or around that building at 8:14 tonight," Grace said. "That's why we need a team of Bens in here going over the service records of every officer and agent in that building. We need Homeland Security analysts who are used to looking for profiles that are too perfect."

"Average grades in college, recently married or single, no kids, rented apartment, military then on to the Secret Service or Quantico," Arrington said.

"That sounds awful vague," Admiral Darby said.

"That's the point. It's supposed to be so bland you never

look at it twice," Assistant Director Paulson said. "Nothing stands out. They're clean enough to pass the background investigations to get hired."

"But Jared Long doesn't fit that profile," Darby said. "He has a long military record and a family."

Grace was looking up at the screens showing the Marine's record. "I know. I think there's something else at play here. I just don't know what yet. But if the Secret Service and Capitol Police were infiltrated, we start with the standard profiles. We'll figure out Jared Long as we go."

"I have some names for you," Ben said. "I know several of them personally and the others by reputation. All of them are assigned or are on the list to be assigned to the ETTF, so they have highest clearance and access."

"Thanks," Arrington said.

Grace stepped over and reviewed the list with him and they marked six of the ten names based on nothing more than gut feelings.

"Can we get a car to go pick them up without alerting them first?" Grace said.

"I've never seen you this cautious," Arrington said. "Sure. I'll get my driver to make the rounds and get them."

"Make sure no cell phones come with them," Grace said. "Who do we have on the ground at the Capitol?"

"I've activated all available agents, FBI SWAT and the Hostage Rescue Team," Assistant Director Paulson said. "HRT is actively trying to get communications up with whoever is inside the building but no land lines are being answered."

"We have SEAL Team Four at Quantico standing by," Admiral Darby said. "And a couple hundred troops ready to bring in."

"Great. What about CIA, Director Leighton?" Arrington said.

"We don't have anybody on site but can offer any intelligence assistance. Langley is on high alert," Leighton said.

"Fine," Grace said. "This may come down to finesse over firepower anyway."

"I hate to be the one to suggest it," Leighton said. "But should we retrieve the designated survivor?"

"What for?" Grace said.

"Accountability," Leighton said. "Deniability. We technically answer to him right now. If this all goes pear shaped, we can at least try to avoid standing in front of a congressional hearing if he gives the approval to move."

"You mean this hasn't gone pear shaped yet?" Grace said. "Who is the designated survivor anyway?"

"Richard Graham, secretary of transportation," Arrington said.

"Shit," Grace said. "Couldn't it at least have been somebody from education? So who knows where Graham is?"

Director Leighton looked around then raised his hand. "I've been briefed by the president," he said.

"What about security detail, do you know who's covering him?" Arrington said.

"Standard protocol for the designated survivor," Leighton said. "A couple dozen Secret Service, secure location outside the Beltway."

"Is the secretary's family with him?" Grace said.

"He's single, but I think he brought a, well, a companion," Leighton said.

"Great. America is being taken by terrorists and our acting president is holed up with his girlfriend," Grace said.

"Not exactly," Leighton said. "More like his boyfriend."

"Oh, okay," Grace said. "And is this public knowledge?"

"No. He maintains he's an available bachelor about town and has been seen with several high profile women in D.C.," Leighton said. "While he's been with the same partner for 12 years."

"All right. Good for him. So we need to get to Graham and bring him back here," Grace said.

"Here? Do you think that's safe?" Paulson said.

"I really don't know," Grace said. "I just want to get him moving to see if it puts anything else in motion. They may be watching for him to appear so they can attack again."

"We're going to use him as bait?" Leighton said.

"You have a better idea?" Grace said.

CHAPTER 4

The screens showed detailed maps and live satellite views of the countryside outside Charlottesville, Virginia and the Blue Ridge Mountains. Grace stared at them as he moved the maps slowly to see everything nearby.

"We have Darby ready with the SEALs," Arrington walked up to him. The rest of the group was talking at the table.

"I want my own guys for this," Grace didn't move his eyes from the maps.

"Definitely not. This is the acting president," Arrington said. "We can't have your group of shooters going in to get him."

"They're the only ones I trust to go with me," Grace said. "You saw those Secret Service guys turn on each other."

"I've given you free run since this started. You're the best asset the NSA has. Hell, you're better than anyone the CIA and FBI have combined. But this requires a bit of diplomacy. Plus there's a dozen Secret Service agents protecting him. How do you think they'd react to your long haired goons knocking on the door?" Arrington said. "SEALs need to be first in."

Grace turned to Arrington.

"Fine. But let Darby know I'm in charge," Grace said. "And make sure the SEALs know that."

CHAPTER 5

It had been barely two hours since the attack on the Capitol as Grace and Arrington rode the elevator up from the sublevel of the Homeland Security building to the sixth floor, then climbed a set of stairs and opened the door to the roof. Grace stopped and looked to the west as the glow of Dulles airport lit the sky. A Boeing 777 airplane dropped down behind the trees to land on the nearest runway.

"Stick to the plan, Grace," Arrington said. "It'll be clean and simple."

"You know me, Derek. I like simple."

"Since when?" Arrington said.

The downdraft of a helicopter coming to land on the roof hit them as the sound of the engine drowned out any more conversation.

"Just stick to the plan!" Arrington yelled.

Grace put his hand to his ear then motioned like he

couldn't hear his boss and turned to board the Bell 407 helicopter that had touched down.

As he pulled the seat belt on in the back seat of the chopper Grace turned to see Master Chief Petty Officer Murphy beside him.

"Are you it?" Grace said.

"No sir, I'm SEAL Team Four leader. I came ahead to pick you up. The rooftop pad couldn't handle the larger birds," Murphy said. "We have a short hop to a secured runway where my team is waiting with the larger aircraft. If you'd like to brief me then I'll convey orders and get us airborne again as quickly as possible."

"Sounds good," Grace said.

Murphy tapped the seat in front of him and the pilot lifted the white helicopter off of the roof and began to move forward.

Arrington watched as they lifted up off the building and headed south to loop around the busy airport. He turned and closed the steel door behind him.

Grace gave MCPO Murphy only the details he needed to know as they flew across Route 28. They barely got a thousand feet up and the pilot was bringing them down again to the private runway outside the Udvar-Hazy Smithsonian Air & Space Museum. No runway lights were on and Grace barely made out the blinking taillights of a pair of helicopters in the darkness. As they landed at the north end of the museum, two Blackhawks sat with their engines running. Grace watched the black machines and the five SEALs checking them out.

"Looks like our rides are ready," MCPO Murphy said.

"I thought you guys used Seahawks and Chinooks?" Grace said.

"Our birds are on the ground at Little Creek, sir." SEAL Team 4 operates out of a base near Norfolk, Virginia. "We were up here for some training and didn't have any helos with us. The Marines are giving us a lift today."

Grace nodded to the SEAL team leader and followed him out of the small helicopter and across the tarmac to the large Blackhawks.

"This is Mr. Grace. He'll be with us tonight and we'll be taking our orders directly from him," Murphy announced to his team then turned to Grace. "They'll get you geared up."

"It's just Grace," he said. "Honored to work with you guys tonight. I've spent a bit of time with Team 6 overseas."

Grace stepped beside one of the choppers and pulled on the bulletproof vest and helmet provided to him. The SEAL helping him reached to hand him a Sig Sauer P226-Navy 9mm pistol, the standard issue SEAL sidearm.

"Thanks, but I brought my own," Grace lifted his shirt to expose his Glock 19 on his side.

"May I check it?" the SEAL said. "We're very particular." The patch on the man's vest said Hendricks.

Grace handed Hendricks his weapon and the man looked it over, released the magazine to see it filled with 17 nine-millimeter bullets in the optional oversized magazine and one in the chamber.

"You ready, sir?" Murphy walked up and Grace turned to him to hear over the rotors spinning above them.

"Not my first rodeo, as they say," Grace said.

"Very well, sir," MCPO Murphy said.

Hendricks handed the Glock back and Grace holstered it then climbed up into the helicopter. The interior of a Marine Blackhawk helicopter is bare and uncomfortable. The seats are metal frames with canvas stretched between them to save weight and to be easily removed if needed.

The team split up and loaded onto the two aircraft, Murphy on one with two other men, Hendricks and the remaining two men of the six-man SEAL team boarded with Grace. Each chopper had a single Marine pilot up front. Straps were barely pulled down and connected to hold the men in their seats when the helicopters lifted straight up off of the ground then turned and went full throttle.

"Flight time of 32 minutes, sir."

"Thanks," Grace said.

Grace looked out the window to see the lights and buildings only a few thousand feet below them. He pulled his personal phone out of the front left pocket of his khakis, checked for a signal, then typed in a message and put the phone back in his pocket.

He leaned his head back in his helmet against the steel wall of the aircraft and closed his eyes. A little more than two hours earlier he was drunk and passed out on his floor after celebrating his return from a mission with his team. He'd been pleased that they hadn't fired one bullet in the exfiltration of a high level member of the Russian government that had been turned and used as an asset for the United States for nearly a decade. Intel had come in that put the man's life in danger and the team retrieved him. After the mission Grace went back to follow through on a promise to an asset that had aided in the rescue, only to have a shootout with a dozen Russian mafia bodyguards. His team ended up on the winning side of the battle. The body count didn't bother him. When he first entered the game years earlier it didn't take long to accept that in any altercation, one of the sides has to win and more often than not in his business, the other side has to die. He'd rather be on the winning side than the dead side.

"Sir, we're four minutes out," one of the SEALs spoke through the microphone, the sound blasting into Grace's headphones, waking him from an uncomfortable nap. He sat up and grabbed the button to transmit to the helicopters.

"This is Grace. We're diverting from the scheduled flight plan. Circle wide to the west of the target and come in low. There's a clearing four clicks due west of the house. We're landing there."

He gave out the coordinates of the new landing location.

"Sir, our plan was to land outside the house for easy extraction," Murphy's voice came from the other helicopter.

"Change of plans," Grace said. "We need to land then proceed on foot to recon before making ourselves known. This is an order."

"Yes, sir."

The pilots made adjustments and the aircraft turned left to compensate for the new orders and coordinates. A few minutes later they were almost touching the trees near the foothills of the Blue Ridge Mountains outside Charlottesville then dropped below the tree line and the two helicopters landed thirty feet apart in the clearing Grace had chosen from satellite imagery he'd studied back at the ETTF. Engines were wound down quickly to cut noise. As the field became quiet the pilots turned out the lights, leaving them in almost complete darkness.

The clearing was half the size of a football field, surrounded by a tree line 40 feet high. The mountains were to the west, the low ridges barely visible in the dark. The January night was below freezing out in the country and there were few clouds in the sky. The moon was low on the horizon.

The SEALs were out of both aircraft and moving to converge in the area east of the machines. Grace followed far behind the three men he'd ridden with. He stopped walking when he saw one SEAL in front of him pause as the other two kept moving to meet with the three men from the other chopper. The lone SEAL raised his FN SCAR assault rifle and with three short, muffled bursts of bullets, fired on his own men, killing the two SEALs directly in front of him. Grace dropped to the ground and pulled his Glock out as the shooter faded into the darkness. Grace lowered the night vision goggles on top of his helmet and depressed the button that activated them, but the view through the goggles was black. He raised them and focused in the dark to track the men walking ahead of him. The other SEALs had lowered their goggles only to have them malfunction as Grace's did and were blind in the darkness. The man fired again and bullets hit them before they could figure out what had happened. One SEAL managed to fire off a series of rounds before being struck. All three men fell to the ground.

Firefights between trained experts don't last long. The rogue SEAL had hit his marks with ease while his team mates had their guard down, never expecting to be attacked from within their close knit group. He had known exactly what gear his teammates were wearing and where to put the shots to drop them.

Grace kept his head down as he lay on the ground. He was 20 feet back of the SEAL and tracked him in the darkness by hints of reflection from the dim moonlight and soft footfalls on the cold ground. The man turned towards him, his rifle raised as the shape moved in his direction. Grace followed the sounds with the sights on his pistol and adjusted in the darkness until the man was only a dozen feet away. With the gear and armor the SEALs wore, he had to make sure he could place the bullet properly in order to stop the man. He raised his aim to come in under the front of the helmet.

Grace pulled his trigger. The firing pin flew forward with a click without releasing the nine-millimeter bullet he'd tried to fire. His mind raced back to the moment he'd handed the weapon to the SEAL before taking off and then he knew who was coming at him.

"You don't have to do this, Hendricks," Grace said.

The SEAL walked towards him, his rifle still raised. "Nothin' personal," Hendricks said. "Just protecting my own."

Grace rolled to his right to get to his feet and away from the aim of the FN SCAR. Tracking a moving target with an assault rifle through night vision goggles wasn't an easy task, though any SEAL would be able to do it without hesitation. Grace was on his right knee preparing to charge at the SEAL when a muffled cracking sound came from the trees 50 yards to the east. Hendricks fell sideways onto the ground before getting a shot off.

Grace recognized the sound of the weapon as the Cheytac .408-caliber rifle used by his sniper Chip Goodson. He went to the SEAL to check his pulse and saw the man's helmet was split in two from the round Goodson had put into his head. He put his malfunctioning Glock into his holster and pulled the Sig Sauer from the dead man's side.

He reached into his own pocket and pulled out the earpiece he'd brought with him and placed it into his left ear.

"Good shot, Chip. Clear on the ground," Grace said. "Checking the pilots."

He checked the Sig with no intention of being caught

with a malfunctioning weapon again, then turned, gun raised and moved towards the first Blackhawk.

"Marine pilot, this is Grace. Please respond," Grace yelled.

He heard movement then a voice from the front of the aircraft.

"What the fuck is going on out there?"

"We had a situation, pilot," Grace said. "All is clear now. I need you to radio your partner in the other bird, then both exit slowly without your weapons."

After a few moments of silence he heard the radio click.

"We've been requested to come outside," the pilot said. "Leave your side arm behind. Claims to be a friendly."

"Copy," came from the receiver.

After a few clicks and thumps of the seat belt being released and dropped inside the cockpit, he finally saw motion as the pilot opened the door.

"Come on down," Grace said.

The man stepped to the ground and walked slowly over with his arms raised and Grace patted him down.

"No guns?"

"No guns."

"Okay, let's go get your buddy," Grace said.

He turned the pilot and used him as a shield, the P229 aimed over the pilot's right shoulder as they moved. They reached the other helicopter as the pilot was walking towards them. Grace stopped when he saw the Marine had his service pistol in his right hand.

"Drop the weapon, pilot," Grace said.

"They said they'd kill her," the pilot said.

"Kill who?"

"My wife. We've only been married six weeks," the pilot said.

"Look around us," Grace said. "There's nobody else here. Nobody knows what you are or aren't going to do right now. Put the weapon down."

"But my wife . . . " the pilot said.

"Your wife will be fine," Grace said. "Let's think through this."

Grace saw the gun begin to rise.

"Don't do it," Grace said.

The pilot's arm extended and just as the weapon was aimed at him, Grace fired and the Marine spun to his right and fell to the ground. The pilot that had been shielding Grace doubled over from the blast of the pistol beside his right ear.

"You know what he was talking about?" Grace said. "Who was going to kill his wife?"

"No sir," he said. "No idea."

"Come on in, guys," Grace said.

"What?" the pilot said.

"Not you," Grace said.

Out of the darkness four men appeared with rifles aimed at the remaining pilot and Grace stepped back. He tucked the Sig into the back of his khakis with the safety on.

"I think he's clean," Grace said. "He's had plenty of opportunity to do something since we landed. I only winged the other pilot. We need him alive. Check his wound and tie them both up."

"Can somebody tell me what's going on?" the pilot said, his hands still holding his ears.

CHAPTER 6

Grace's men secured the two pilots after putting gauze on the gunshot wound and injecting a shot of morphine for the pain as well as to knock him out. They gathered their gear, ready for directions though they didn't need them. The team had worked together for the better part of ten years, covering four continents and dozens of countries. The number of kills credited to their team by the NSA was far lower than the actual body count they'd left behind.

"Chip still in the trees?" Grace said.

"Yeah. Probably napping now," Holden said. "Lazy ass snipers."

"I hear you," Chip's voice came through the earpieces.

Chip Goodson was their sniper and all-around weapons expert, coming from the Army Rangers where he destroyed every record that had existed before him. He was short and stocky and could carry more gear than most two men combined.

Always near Chip when they weren't on a mission was Holden Evinger. Grace had tapped him for the team when Holden was kicked out of SEAL Team 6 for punching his commanding officer for taking his parking spot on base. The parking spot actually belong to the C.O. Holden just liked parking there because it was closer to the gym. He stood six feet four and won most fights before a punch was swung. His shaved black head was always covered by a stocking cap, no matter how hot it was outside.

"We have about four clicks to cover," Grace said. "Corbin, you're here with the birds. Pick one and check it for bullet holes."

"Copy that." Corbin was a former Navy pilot who'd spent three tours on the USS Abraham Lincoln aircraft carrier. He'd flown every fixed wing and rotor he could get his hands on, sometimes without permission. Grace never bothered asking him if he knew how to fly something anymore.

The remaining men grabbed their gear and headed for the woods.

"How many targets we looking at when we get there?" Avery said.

"They aren't targets. They're Secret Service," Grace said. "Chances are everything is copacetic. We just need to be ready after what went down in the Capitol."

"But we can hurt 'em if we need to?" Avery said.

"Only if we need to," Grace said. "I know we aren't used to ops on U.S. soil, so keep your heads."

Avery Miller was the only one of the team other than Grace with no military background. He had been a mixed martial arts fighter in Dallas until he accidently killed a man in the ring. He was never charged, but no promoter would touch him after that. Having grown up on a ranch in Texas he knew guns well and could fix any motor that wasn't running.

The last member of the team was Levi Teehee, a full-blooded Cherokee Indian from Oklahoma. He'd graduated near the top of his class at OU and had played college football his first three years until he decided to focus on the academics. After college he went into the Marines as an officer. He liked to thicken up his accent and play the stereotyped Native American role even though he was a decorated Marine and a former operator in the elite MARSOC unit, the Marine Special Operations Command. He had three years of linguistics training and spoke four languages and could understand several more.

The team moved out across the field to the east and into the woods. As dark as the field had been, no light at all found its way into the trees. The four men moved as quickly as they could through the woods with night vision goggles in place. The thick canopy of trees overhead kept much from growing on the ground, leaving a clear trail. Only once did Grace think he heard their sniper Chip a few dozen yards off to his left, staying concealed while moving to be in position when his team left the safety of the woods on the other side.

Many of their missions took place in darkness. They were all used to the void around them and had learned to know what sounds to listen for. With the commotion of five men carrying heavy gear moving quickly through the trees, it's easy to obscure the sounds of the forest or of enemies tracking you. They had a system they'd used for years. At irregular intervals the lead man would give an audible signal to the rest of them then they'd all give a ten count in their heads then come to a stop. If anyone were following them their footfalls would easily be heard before they had a chance to stop. Through the three-mile trek in the woods, Holden had four times brought them to a stop only to hear the normal sounds of the trees.

They reached the edge of the woods and each of the four men took cover behind large trees. He couldn't see him, but Grace knew Chip was already there, probably 15 feet up in a tree and his rifle ready and scanning the target.

"I see six men on the front porch," Grace said.

"At least two inside," Chip's voice came from his earpiece. "I have the front and west sides covered. Three vehicles in back, all look to be government SUVs."

"Those might come in handy," Grace said.

"What's that on the porch?" Avery said.

Grace scanned the porch with his binoculars then lowered them. "Looks like a body," he said.

"So would that be a good guy or a bad guy?" Holden said.

"My guess is bad," Grace said.

"I hope you're right," Holden said.

"Me too," Grace said.

Grace lowered his binoculars and pulled his secure radio out of his combat vest and turned the dial to the frequency CIA Director Leighton had given him then punched in the secure identification number. Once the code was accepted he pressed the button that sent a signal to the Secret Service officers.

He raised his binoculars and watched. The men on the porch maintained their positions.

"We have movement inside," Chip said. "Someone's coming out."

The front door opened and another man in a suit came

out onto the porch, a radio similar to Grace's on his belt. Grace transmitted.

"Secret Service detail this is your ride calling, do you read?"

"We read you," he could see the man talking into the microphone more than a hundred yards away, his eyes on the sky over the trees. "Why aren't you wheels down by the house?"

"There's been some complications," Grace said. "We had to ensure everything was secure on your end. We're coming in on foot."

"The situation is secure now. We've had a casualty here. I'll require further confirmation before I can allow you to approach," the man was scanning the tree line.

"Understood," Grace expected the extra caution. He pulled a card from his vest with a series of letters Director Leighton had scribbled down. "Quebec. Uniform. Echo. Sierra. Tango. Three. Nine. Seven."

"Confirmed. Who am I speaking with?" the Secret Service officer said.

"This is Grace. I'm with Homeland Security. I have a team here to extract the package. We'll have a bird ready once we've cleared the area." His cover as an NSA operator was to be protected. He carried credentials and badges for every government law enforcement organization including the CIA, FBI, Homeland Security and even INS. He'd use whatever he needed to get people to comply.

"Move in slow. I'll meet you," the man said.

Grace watched the man take the four steps off the porch and began walking into the field. His weapon remained on his side, the strap fastened.

"I like this guy. He's cautious but ballsy," Grace said.

"I'd have my gun out and ready to drop anyone if they blinked wrong."

"Maybe you should ask him out," Levi said.

"Not my type, too tall," Grace said. "Okay, let's move out. Standard spread, weapons lowered but ready. Look twice before you react, we don't need any more blood on the ground than we already have."

Grace stepped out from behind the tree and started walking through the field. He didn't need to turn his head to know that on his left was Levi thirty feet away and on his right were Avery and Holden with the same spacing. The man in the suit had come out to the middle of the field beside the house and stopped with his arms hanging wide away from his side to show he was not holding a weapon in his hands.

The team stopped with Grace 20 feet from the man.

"Grace?" the man said.

"Yes, sir."

"I'm Special Officer James Foster."

"You in charge here?" Grace said.

"I am," Foster said. "We had an incident with one agent."

"Let me guess. He turned his gun on you or one of your men?" Grace said.

The man's head tilted.

"Yes," Foster said. "He pulled on me. I reacted quickly."

"You're lucky. Or good. That's been happening a lot lately," Grace said. "I'm sure you've been watching the news."

"No cable, no antenna," Foster said. "This is the secratary's private residence and he doesn't like to be disturbed by the outside world when he's here."

"Shit. And nobody's called you?" Grace said.

"No. We're on radio silence during the speech. We were

supposed to be called back more than an hour ago. What's going on? Where's the detail that was supposed to come for us?" Foster said.

"I hate to tell you, but you're not just protecting the transportation secretary in there," Grace said. "He's the acting president of the United States."

CHAPTER 7

Grace stood in the living room of the restored farmhouse facing Richard Graham for the first time. Graham was short with greying hair that not long ago had been blonde. He wore a blue and white flannel shirt that had been ironed and was tucked into flat front khakis. Grace figured the man thought the flat front looked more rugged with the flannel than pleats would. The room looked like a cross between a rustic cabin and a page from an Ethan Allen catalog. He finished describing what had happened less than two hours earlier at the Capitol and Graham turned and sat down on the end of a long, country plaid print sofa.

"Are they still alive?" Graham said.

"I've been out of contact since 2200 hours, sir," Grace said. "At that point we had no reason to believe they weren't."

Another man came and sat down beside Graham on the arm of the sofa.

"All our friends are in that building," Graham said. "What do you need me to do?"

"I need you to come with me and my men," Grace said. "We're taking you to a secure location to meet with the leadership staff that's assembled."

"Who?" Graham said.

"I'm not at liberty to discuss that right now," Grace said.

Graham turned to the other man then back to Grace. "William needs to come with me," Graham said. William was taller than his partner. He was slender but not slight. A snap to his gait contradicted his soothing voice.

"If Richard goes, I go," William said.

Grace paused while he thought then turned to Foster. "He was cleared to be here?" Grace said.

"He was," Foster said.

"That's fine," Grace said. "We'll sort it out when we get to the other side. You have three minutes to grab what you need then you're with me and my men."

"Whoa," Foster said. "You think you're transporting him without us?"

"I don't think that, I know that," Grace said. "This is our mission and it's under the command of the highest ranking people not inside the Capitol at this time. For the security of the mission and of Mr. Graham, it's how it has to be."

"I don't like it," Foster said.

"You don't have to like it," Grace said. "We'll have a bird land to pick us up. After we're gone, the second one will come in for you and your team. You'll follow us to our destination."

Grace turned and walked out of the room and onto the porch before the Secret Service agent could protest more. He tapped his radio.

"We're ready for you, Corbin," Grace said.

"Copy that. On my way," Grace could hear the engines begin winding up while Corbin was still talking.

"Chip, be ready," Grace looked out to the trees. "We're not sitting on the ground very long."

"10-4, good buddy," Chip said.

Back in the house Grace looked around.

"Okay, Mr. Secretary, you're with us," Grace said. "Bring no more than what you can carry, there's no overhead compartments on the helicopter."

Richard Graham stood and went up the stairs to pack. William followed him, trying to keep him calm.

"He's pretty rattled," Foster said.

"I know," Grace said. "Imagine you were just told you were president." He glanced over at the radio on Foster's belt. "Have your men ready."

The rumbling of the Blackhawk started growing from outside. By the time Grace had Graham out the door it was turning and landing in the yard in front of the house. Grace led Graham by the arm and began walking. Avery and Levi flanked them and Holden walked with William, watching all directions. The Secret Service officers spread out across the yard. Avery boarded first then helped Graham up. Holden followed then Grace stepped up. Once William was on board Levi took a look around then climbed on.

As the rotors began to speed up again Chip ran up to the other side of the helicopter and slid his gear in under the seat and sat down on the edge, his feet dangling out of the helicopter. Corbin pulled the stick back and the Blackhawk lifted off of the ground and turned as it flew back over the tree line. Grace looked around to make sure everyone was on board and saw the injured Marine pilot unconscious and tied up to a seat. Corbin had loaded him up to get him back for medical attention and interrogation. The other pilot was back with his helicopter to fly the Secret Service out.

Grace turned his radio back to the secure frequency.

"Foster, this is Grace."

"This is Foster."

"There's a field four clicks due west of the house. In that field is a Blackhawk with a Marine pilot tied to it," Grace said. "That's your ride. If you decide to drive back, would you at least go untie him?"

"You said the helicopter was coming to get us," Foster said.

"It's not," Grace said.

CHAPTER 8

Corbin had the Blackhawk at 10,000 feet and cruising 160 miles per hour on the way back towards Northern Virginia. Grace turned to look at Richard Graham.

"You don't look so good," Grace said.

"I don't like helicopters," Graham said.

"Better get used to them. If things don't go well you'll be riding in Marine One before long," Grace said.

"Don't even joke about that," Graham said. "Jill Abrams is still president."

Grace checked his watch. 11:32pm.

"Get some rest. You have a long night ahead of you," Grace said.

He wanted to sleep but couldn't. Getting back to Herndon was only the beginning of what he had ahead of him. After watching the darkness outside slowly fade into the glow of streetlights and shopping centers with empty parking lots he looked up to Corbin.

"How far?" Grace said.

"Two minutes out," Corbin's voice came through the headset.

Grace lifted his head and looked out the window and saw Dulles airport a few miles away, then dialed his cellphone.

"Big Daddy this is Hot Dog," Grace said.

"I told you we aren't doing that," Arrington's said. "Where are you?"

"Wheels down in less than two and should be back home within ten of that," Grace said. "Any change in the situation?"

"We'll update you when you're back with the package," Arrington said.

The chopper swung to the right and began to drop quickly as they approached the museum once again. The helicopter lowered to the ground at the end of the runway near the building. As the engines slowed down Grace opened the door on his side and jumped out then helped Graham down.

"What do we do now?" Graham said.

A black Mercedes Sprinter passenger van came speeding from around the corner of the building and pulled up to them. A moment later the side door slid open and the driver jumped out.

"Netty, good to see you," Grace said.

"Screw you," she said. "You're flying around in Blackhawks and I'm driving a fucking van."

"Someone needed to be here to pick us up," Grace said.

"I'm not a soccer mom," Netty said.

"You have the minivan," Grace said. "Where'd it come from, anyway?"

"Stole it," Netty said.

"Everyone needs a hobby," Grace said.

Everybody climbed into the van and they carried the unconscious Marine pilot over then Netty turned around on the tarmac, rear tires squealing, and sped away from the building. As they passed through the employee exit onto Route 50, Grace saw the metal gate lying on the ground to the side of the drive. He looked up to Netty and saw her looking at him in the rearview mirror and he nodded.

It took her six minutes to drive them to the Homeland Security building. When they pulled up to the security gate, Grace handed Netty his credentials and she slid them across the sensor and the gate opened in front of them. Arrington was standing in front of the building as they pulled up.

"Didn't know they had curbside service here," Grace stepped out of the van.

"Where the hell are the SEALs?" Arrington said. "I thought you agreed we weren't using your guys for this."

"And girls," Netty said as she walked past.

"I had them on site in case there were any problems," Grace said. "And there were problems."

"What kind?" Arrington said.

"One of the SEALs turned on us, shot the other five before they knew what was happening," Grace said. "Would have killed me if Chip hadn't had my back."

Arrington put both of his hands on his face and rubbed his eyes. As he lowered his hands he saw Holden and Avery carrying the shot Marine pilot past him into the building.

"Who the hell is that?"

"Blackhawk pilot," Grace said. "I had to shoot him."

"Is he—"

"No, just out cold," Grace said. "They're going to get

him comfortable. If you have a doctor you can bring in, that would be great."

"What did I do to deserve this in my life," Arrington said. "Okay, what about the Secret Service from the house?"

"Left them there," Grace said. "I think they were clean but didn't want to take the chance. They'd had a shooting but seems like they took care of the threat. We have Graham and that's all that matters right now."

Richard Graham was out of the van and walked up to Arrington.

"We've never actually met, sir. I'm Richard Graham," the secretary of transportation extended his hand to the director of the NSA.

"I know who you are," Arrington turned and walked towards the building.

"Well, that wasn't very friendly, was it?" Grace turned to Graham.

Grace and Graham followed Arrington into the building with the rest of the team behind them. They all stopped at the elevator.

"Seriously?" Arrington said. "Everyone is coming down?"

"Right now this is the only group of men you can trust," Grace said.

"And women," Netty said.

They all exited the elevator on the sublevel and entered the ETTF control room. Six new faces were at computers researching all of the Secret Service officers. Director Leighton stood and walked towards the group.

"Who the hell are all these people? This is a secure facility." Leighton said. He saw the bloody pilot being carried in. "Has that man been shot?"

"They're with me, and yes," Grace said. "Understand?"

Leighton looked past Grace at the group, shaking his head then turned and went back to his seat.

"Admiral Darby," Grace said. "I hate to ask, but may I search you?" The Navy SEALS and other special combat teams fall under Darby's command.

"Excuse me?" Darby said.

Grace walked up to him at the conference table and stood above him.

"A SEAL opened fire and killed the other five then tried to kill me," Grace said. "We just need to make sure you didn't alert anyone to their mission. Do you have a cellphone on you?"

"I conducted all of my communication over the secure lines right in front of everyone," Darby said.

"Still, just need to check," Grace said.

Darby looked at Arrington who just nodded at him. Darby stood and raised his arms while Grace patted him down.

"He's clean," Grace said. "Sorry, Vic, you know I had to."

Arrington brought the team up to speed.

"Since you left there's been little activity at the Capitol, and no demands have come in through any channels, including the media," he said. "Heat signatures in the House chamber are still strong."

"It's been almost four hours, what are they waiting for?" Grace said.

"If I may," Graham tried to speak.

"We have a perimeter set up around the building, again not knowing the condition of the troops and officers in use," Arrington said. "Stories are going around about the internal shootings, so everyone is jumpy."

"What if—" Graham said.

"Agents are going building to building around the Capitol," Paulson said. "We also have security details visiting the residences of the ranking members of Congress and working themselves down the list."

"What are they looking for?" Grace said.

"Anything at this point," Paulson said. "Any sign of incongruity."

"President Abrams once said to me—" Graham said.

"Langley is double checking chatter from the last two weeks to see if they missed anything," Leighton said. "Right now there's essentially nothing. Like everyone is asleep out there."

"Every terrorist organization in the world is watching and waiting," Grace said. "Nobody wants to take credit while it's still going on because they want to see how it ends first."

"Sir," Ben Murray said. "We've got something."

Grace turned around and looked at him.

"So show us," Grace said.

From his desk Ben displayed a series of photos and files up on the screens surrounding the room.

"We have four Capitol Police officers identified with suspicious backgrounds," Ben said. "First is Tom Redfield. His address is a rented apartment in Rosslyn, Virginia. He's lived there three years, since before he became an officer."

"Family?" Grace said.

"None on record, sir," Ben said.

"Call me 'sir' one more time and I'll shoot you, Ben," Grace said.

"Yes, sir, Grace, yes," Ben said. "Next is Charles Woodson, residing in Silver Spring, Maryland. Again a rented apartment for three years. No family either."

Ben detailed the other two officers with similar backgrounds.

"Good work," Grace said. "Get me print outs on all of them. Now I need you to go back through all of the officers on the scene and pull up cellphone records. Look for anything out of line. Anything fishy."

"How far back?" Ben said.

"Not far. Twelve hours to start," Grace said. "Start with Jared Long again. Compare all the numbers he received calls from with everyone else."

"Yes, sir. I mean, yes," Ben said.

Grace turned to the leadership at the table. "I want to go door to door at the four homes they identified."

"What will that give us?" Arrington said.

"Nothing, maybe, but if it provides one piece of evidence or a lead it's worth it," Grace said. "We need to find some connection back to who's behind this and so far, this is our only lead."

"Have you gotten anything from the Marine pilot?" Arrington said.

"No, he's been unconscious," Grace said. "We pumped him up with a lot of morphine. Once he's stable we'll talk to him."

"We need some kind of progress and we need it soon. The media is going crazy," Leighton said.

Arrington stared up at the four Capitol Police officers on the screens, his arms crossed and his right hand covering his mouth.

"Do it," Arrington said. "Keep it as low key as possible, we don't need neighbors calling cops for break-ins next door."

"Low key is what we do," Grace said.

"Really. Then why are there ten police cars at the Air & Space Museum trying to figure out how a Marine Blackhawk helicopter landed in the middle of the night and their security gate has been blown off?"

"The low key part is they haven't figured it out yet," Grace said.

CHAPTER 9

Grace left the control center and went to the elevator to go up and meet his team in front of the Homeland Security building. As the elevator door was closing a hand stopped it. When the door opened Amanda Paulson was standing there. She stepped in beside Grace and hit the button for the first floor.

"Think anyone suspects us yet?" she said.

"Nah, they're clueless," Grace said. "Plus I was impressed with your self control, not jumping across the table and ripping my shirt off."

"I figured I'd save that for later," she said. "So, SCS, huh? I knew you weren't some standard issue analyst like you told me."

"Yeah? How's that?" Grace said.

"Analysts usually don't have scars from bullet wounds on their backs," she turned to him and wrapped her arms around his chest and stood on her tiptoes and kissed him.

Grace looked up into the corners of the elevator. "Aren't you worried about security cameras?"

"The people who work down here don't like having their pictures taken," she said. "No cameras."

He grinned and his hand went to the small of her back and pulled her in tight. When the elevator stopped at the first floor she pulled away and stood next to him.

"Hiding this is killing me," she said. "But I guess it's not the best career move for the assistant director of the FBI to be screwing the NSA's top covert operative."

"I can see the headlines now," Grace said. "AD Paulson in relationship with some guy nobody knows."

He hit the button for the sublevel of the building and stepped out and watched the elevator door close. The stolen black Mercedes Sprinter was still parked at the curb, a security car parked behind it. Grace waved at the officer as his team finished loading into the van and pulled away as the officer was getting out of the car.

It was still middle of the night and Highway 66 was moving fast. The federal government had closed all non-essential offices for security concerns and many private companies had followed suit so when morning came rush hour would be light. Many roads within D.C. were closed around the Capitol and security checkpoints had been set up.

The van left the highway at Rosslyn and made three turns then pulled up in front of the apartment complex that had been military housing forty years earlier.

"The unit is in the bottom level of the building on the right, down those stairs," Corbin said. "How do you wanna play it?"

"You keep the van ready. Holden and Avery take perimeter, make sure nobody comes in on us and try not to draw any attention to yourselves," Grace said.

Avery looked at Holden then back at Grace.

"How is Holden not supposed to draw any attention?" Avery said. "He looks like an NFL linebacker and dresses like a homeless man."

"Chip, stay with the van and do your thing," Grace said. "Levi and Netty you're with me inside."

"Shit, you're actually letting me out of the van?" Netty said.

"I need someone to distract anyone who might come to the door and you have a better rack than Levi," Grace said.

"Hell yeah, I do," Netty lifted her breasts together with both hands.

Holden and Avery split up and went opposite directions while Grace, Levi and Netty moved down the long flight of stairs. The cement steps were old and cracked and the handrail was missing in several places. Where it wasn't missing, the paint was worn off from being exposed to the elements for several decades. The cold January air allowed them to wear coats concealing their weapons.

"Looks clear," Avery's voice came from the earpiece.

"Same here so far," Holden said.

Grace reached the door to the apartment and grabbed the doorknob with his left hand and slid a small metal tool into the keyhole with his right. The knob was loose on the door and the round plate that should be around the base of the knob was long gone. Three seconds later he opened the door.

"I love when people don't use their deadbolt," Grace said.

Levi turned a light on then pulled the shades closed. The windows faced out to a tall cement wall designed to block the building from the noises of Highway 66 and failed at it. Inside the apartment they spread out. Netty stayed in the front room while Grace went for the bedroom and Levi turned to the kitchen.

"Not much here," Levi said. "You sure someone actually lives in this dump?"

"Got a twin bed mattress on the floor in the bedroom," Grace said. "And a couple of Capitol Police uniforms in the closet, still in dry cleaner bags."

"Kitchen's empty except for an old coffee maker," Holden said. "Nobody's been shopping for a while. Or cleaning. Stinks like hell in the fridge."

"Whoever's been living here didn't plan on coming back," Grace said.

"I got something," Netty's voice came from the bathroom. "You two might wanna come in here."

The two men went to the bathroom door and looked in. Netty had the top to the toilet tank off and turned upside down. Taped to the bottom was a thick manila envelope.

"Open it," Grace said.

Netty pulled the tape off of the envelope and sat it on the counter then bent the metal tabs back and unfolded the opening. She tilted the envelope and poured the contents out onto the counter.

"Well, what do we have here?" Grace said.

"There's a stack of cash, $20's, maybe a grand's worth," Netty said. "And a passport."

"Bingo," Grace said. "Even if it's a fake, which it probably is, it gives us something to start with. Let's load up and hit the next address."

They left the apartment, taking the envelope and the uniforms with them. Back in the van they left the apartment complex, leaving the headlights off until they turned onto the main road. Grace plugged the next address into the GPS.

Netty took the G.W. Parkway along the Potomac with Washington D.C. to their left across the water. She continued onto Route 1 past National Airport and into Alexandria. After a right turn onto King Street and one more left she parked on the street in front of a four unit building. They sat and watched the quiet street.

"Here we are," she said.

"Okay, same drill," Grace said.

They got out of the van and followed the same plan from the first apartment. Netty, Holden and Grace got to the front door and were in within a few seconds. They searched the rooms.

"Another envelope with cash and a passport in the toilet tank," Netty said.

"Empty kitchen again," Holden said.

Grace came out from the bedroom.

"Pretty much the same in there except for this," he held up a thick work shirt with a logo embroidered on it. "Cunningham Construction. This was hanging beside a couple more uniforms."

They continued to the other two apartments, one in Mount Vernon and the other in Anacostia before returning to Herndon.

CHAPTER 10

Levi and Holden stood outside a locked steel door. The Marine pilot Grace had shot was on the other side, zip ties still on his wrists and ankles.

"He ready for me?" Grace walked up.

"Yes, sir," Holden said. "He just started waking up a few minutes ago. Arrington's doctor checked him out while we were gone."

Grace stepped in, carrying a folding metal chair and pulled the door shut behind him. Holden and Levi stepped into the room next door, a row of monitors and speakers showing everything going on in the room. Grace took two laps around the Marine pilot strapped to a chair in the middle of the room then came to a stop.

"Are we going to make this easy?" Grace said.

"As easy as I can," the pilot said.

"Good to hear. Name?"

"Captain George Arnold."

"Two first names, eh," Grace said. "So why did you try to fire on me?"

George Arnold looked away and stared at the plain white wall as he thought then shook his head then looked at Grace.

"I got a phone call," he said. "It was maybe ten minutes before we went wheels up at Quantico to come pick you up. The man knew we were going to get you, knew where we were going after that."

"Did you even know where you were going yet?" Grace said.

"No. We were ordered to get in the air then receive our orders en route to Dulles."

"What did he say?" Grace said. "And you're sure it was a man?"

"Wasn't a deep voice, but definitely a man. Sounded young. He said if I didn't do as he said then my wife would be raped and then her head cut off," George said.

"That's rude," Grace said.

"To say the least," George said.

"So you believed him? This mystery voice on a phone," Grace said.

"He knew my address, my phone numbers," George said.

"Could it have been a buddy playing a prank?"

The pilot slowly shook his head. "No. Nobody I know would do that. And even if they did they'd be smart enough not to do it to my work phone."

"And what exactly did he tell you to do?" Grace said.

"To ensure the mission fails, no matter what it took," George said. "No matter who had to die. He said that. No matter who had to die, including me."

"I'm guessing he didn't give you his name?" Grace said. "Did he have an accent? Anything distinguishing?"

"Not at all. Sounded very, well, normal. That's what made the threat seem so real," George said. "His voice, it was just so average. You expect something like that to be screamed, growled, grunted. But this guy was cool and calm. Didn't sound foreign or anything. Listen, can you check on my wife? Make sure she's okay?"

"I'll see if we can send a car over," Grace said.

He went out of the interrogation room and back down the hall to the control center. Netty and Avery were walking around and followed him.

"Ben," Grace said then looked at the new analysts. "And other Bens. Focus on the secure work cells. Start with the time of the first attack and work backwards. Start with Jared Long, the SEAL Hendricks and the Marine pilot, George Arnold. They're our only known shooters. If you have any problem getting access to the records for the secure phones, tell Director Leighton. Or just hack in."

"What are we looking for?" Ben said.

Grace stopped and turned to him.

"Whatever it is you guys look for. Anomalies, inconsistencies, freak occurrences, repeating numbers, whatever," Grace said.

He turned to the conference table to hear raised voices.

"Under no condition should we send troops in!" Arrington was saying.

"I think it's the right thing to do," Graham said. "It's been almost six hours since the Capitol was taken hostage and there's been no progress towards freeing our leaders. The media is tearing us apart. The people need to see some progress. We need to send troops in before the sun comes up."

"This isn't a goddamn movie," Admiral Darby said. "We don't just send in a bunch of troops to entertain the masses."

"What the hell is going on here?" Grace said.

Arrington stood calmly a few feet from the table listening to the argument.

"Graham wants to storm the Capitol," he said.

"That's stupid," Grace said.

"Yup," Arrington said.

"Excuse me?" Graham said. "I sure do appreciate what you've done so far, but you are not an executive leader of this country, Mr. Grace."

"It's just Grace."

"Whatever," Graham said. "You are a hired gun. A disposable resource. Not a strategist."

Grace stepped over to Richard Graham until he was looking down at him, nose to nose. "I've done more to protect this country and its citizens than you ever will, Mr. Transportation Secretary. Do you recall the American nuclear physicist recovered from the Iran last month? Or the six CIA officers that were rescued from North Korea three months before that?"

"No, I don't," Graham said. "There's been nothing about that on the news about a rescue for North Korea and Dr. Andrews was released by President Rouhani as an act of good will."

"Rouhani doesn't know what good will is," Grace said. "They lost him and tried to spin it. That was me and these men."

"And women," Netty said.

"We went in there. We brought those people back without the media ever knowing," Grace said. "Why? Because the media likes clean stories and neither of those were clean. There was bloodshed, but not one drop was American."

"I got cut in Pyongyang," Avery said behind him.

"That was a paper cut," Grace said. "I also managed to plan the mission to bring you back in without you getting shot, Mr. Secretary. Don't make me regret that."

"That doesn't make you a military expert, Mr. Grace," Graham said.

"For the last time, its just Grace," he said.

Derek Arrington put his hand on Grace's shoulder and pulled him back.

"It so happens that Grace has not only completed every course at the Army War College and the Navy War College, Mr. Secretary, he has aided in rewriting curriculum for both in this new age of military reconnaissance and combat, albeit under a pseudonym since his existence in our agency is classified. Reports on his missions are used as training materials for new operators at the NSA and the CIA," Arrington said. "He's been the NSA's top operator for more than ten years and has carried out more successful missions than any other man. That again includes the NSA and CIA."

Richard Graham held his glare with Arrington then turned to the conference table.

"Am I or am I not the acting president?" he said. "Director Leighton?"

"Yes, Richard, you are," Leighton said.

"Admiral Darby?"

"Of course you are, but . . . ," Darby said.

"Director Arrington?"

"You can stop the roll call. We all know. That's why we brought you in," Arrington said.

"So if I make an order, it is your jobs to make them happen, correct?" Graham said.

"When did he grow a pair of balls?" Avery said.

"Shut it, Avery," Grace said.

"It's up to us to take your orders and determine the best manner in which to carry them out, Richard," Darby said. "It's also our responsibility to give our opinions as to whether we feel the orders are sound."

"And it's my responsibility to ensure the safety of our people and our government," Graham said. "I want a working plan to retake the Capitol and free the hostages in front of me within an hour."

Graham turned and walked out of the room with William following close behind.

"What crawled up his ass and died?" Grace said.

"We kept ignoring him," Arrington said. "He finally snapped."

"I'll go talk to him, try to get him to calm down," Amanda stood and left out the door Graham had gone through.

"What recourse do we have to not take his orders?" Grace said.

They turned to Admiral Darby.

"None," Darby said. "He's the acting Commander in Chief. If he orders a strike, even against my advice, we have to find the best way to carry it out."

"Well shit," Grace said. "We can't just lock him in a room?"

"Even just saying that out loud can be considered treason," Arrington said.

"You think he wants us to fail, so he can become president?" Grace said.

"Graham?" Leighton said. "Are you joking? He's a weasel, but he's not a psychopath."

Grace shrugged. "I talked to the Marine pilot. He said he'd received a phone call minutes before they left Quantico threatening his wife's life if he didn't do what he could to stop the mission. What if that's what happened to Jared Long?"

"What, social engineering?" Arrington said.

"Exactly," Grace said. "There's no terrorist organization in the world large enough to pull off this kind of attack, especially one with enough members that can pass as Secret Service and Capitol Police. They'd had to have been in place for years to get enough people active for this event."

"You get this from the pilot getting a prank phone call?" Arrington said.

"It was a big enough prank that the man pulled a gun on me," Grace said. "And he isn't the only one. The SEAL who turned on us, Hendricks, when he was about to shoot me he said he was 'just protecting my own,' and that it wasn't personal. That sounds to me like he'd been told to kill us, or else someone else might be hurt or killed."

Grace paced back and forth as he spoke.

"You spend three years getting your select few people recruited to your cause, then get them into law enforcement if they weren't already there. These are your base, your inside men. They're bought and paid for and will do what you hired them to do." Grace looked up at the screen showing Jared Long. "Then you use threats against many more to get them to act for you, if only for a minute."

"How do you mean?" Paulson said.

"Look at Jared Long," Grace said. "Father, husband, owns a house in Wheaton, Maryland. Doesn't look or sound like a terrorist. I don't think there's any chance he was. What he was, though, was a decorated officer and a devoted family man. But what if shortly before he's on assignment for the State of the Union he gets contacted and his family is threatened. He's told to start shooting or his wife and daughter die. What would you do?"

"Report it immediately to my commanding officer," Director Leighton said.

"Right, but what if you don't know if you can trust your CO?" Grace said. "What if you're told you're being watched, and if you don't shoot, you'll be shot then your family will still die?"

Arrington nodded and spoke. "All it would take is a small percentage of them to start shooting, even just one in the right scenario, then the others fire back to protect themselves and the president. With highly trained officers, all experts with their weapons, you have a bloodbath on your hands in seconds and you never had to train one person."

"Insta-terrorist," Grace said. "Lethal. Disposable."

"Brilliant," Arrington said. "But we can't be sure."

"That's why I have Ben and his team going through phone records for all of the officers and agents in the Capitol," Grace said "We need something linking them."

CHAPTER 11

The screens around the room displayed the live satellite imagery over the United States Capitol. The sun was still down and the video was grainy. Flashing lights surround the building where police and military vehicles were stationed.

"We don't have SEAL Team Four anymore," Grace said.

"What about Special Forces?" Arrington said.

"The 1st battalion out of Fort Bragg landed over an hour ago," Darby said. "And the 3rd out of Birmingham should be on the ground anytime. We can get troops from Kentucky activated and in the air."

"That gives us roughly a thousand troops," Grace said. "We're going to need every last one of them for the recovery effort, but that's way too many for first strike."

Grace drew on a wireless tablet that sent his drawing to the screens above. He began making marks around the Capitol.

"I think we put as many men as we have ready on the ground, but the primary contact will be made by six-man teams of Special Forces," Grace said. "One team at each of the four main entry points."

"What if we come from below?" Leighton said.

"The tunnels?" Arrington said.

"Exactly," Leighton said. "They connect the Capitol to all of the congressional office buildings, the Supreme Court and even the Library of Congress."

"But that's putting all of our men in an enclosed space," Darby said. "If they've thought about that it could already be wired with explosives or have armed guards down there."

Grace continued drawing as he thought about the layout of Capitol Hill. "It's not one or the other, it's both," Grace said. "But one is only a diversion."

He turned to see if he had their attention then pointed up to his scribbles.

"We send in Special Forces on the ground, in a full circle around the building and the breach teams at the doors," Grace said. "This should draw out most of the enemy gunmen to prepare for battle. We put helicopters in the air. Anything we can do for a distraction. Then we have small groups come in through the tunnels from each direction. Fewer troops will be able to better watch for booby traps and explosives than sending hundreds of men through there."

"Draw them to the doors then attack from below," Arrington said. "It could work."

"It could also get every last one of them killed, including the president," Grace said. "We don't even know who we're dealing with here yet. If we knew it was Al Qaeda, we know how they work, how they plan. If it's the Russians, we know how they think. But we don't. Going in against an unknown enemy is dangerous."

"How do we find out? There's still no chatter, no one's taking credit yet," Leighton said.

"Before any full assault you need a recon team," Grace said. "We need to get an idea of some faces, manpower counts, weapons being used. From that we can better determine who we're up against and how to neutralize them."

"Let me guess," Arrington said.

"We'll do it," Grace said.

"Graham won't like it," Arrington said. "He wants something big."

"Then we don't tell him," Grace said. "Work up a full on assault plan and tell him that's what we're doing, it's just going to take time to get all the moving parts in position. Meanwhile, my team will already be underway."

"How do you think you can get in?" Arrington said.

The map above them all moved and a circle Grace had drawn centered on the screen.

"Anyone know what this is?" Grace said.

"Dupont Circle," Paulson said.

"Right. But do you know what's under Dupont Circle?" Grace said.

"The abandoned underground," Leighton said. "For an electric streetcar or something, right?"

"Give that man a banana," Grace said. "Around 1950 they used them to try to alleviate the already shitty traffic in D.C., but it failed. The ventilation couldn't move the air fast enough and it stank so bad down there nobody would take the underground train."

"How's this help? Dupont Circle is almost three miles from the Capitol," Arrington said.

"A lesser known fact," Grace said. "One line was built from Dupont to the Capitol building to allow congress to easily come and go, many residing in Dupont due to the abundance of housing and restaurants. The tunnel was sealed up for security in the 1970s."

"How do you know about it?" Paulson said.

"Because it also had an exit here," Grace drew another circle on the map.

"The Mayflower Hotel?" Paulson said.

"Exactly. The preferred host of congressional extramarital affairs," Grace said. "When congress approved the secret train line, they figured they might as well make it easier to sneak around on their wives."

"Have you been down there?" Arrington said.

"Once about five years ago," Grace said. "I used it on a covert mission. We can gain access below the hotel. It's easier than from Dupont Circle since there are a couple more walls between the two now. It's similar to the Capitol subway between the main building and the congressional office buildings, just a lot longer."

"You'll have a two mile walk in the dark between the Mayflower and the Capitol," Paulson said. "That'll take a lot of time."

"I have an idea about that," Grace said.

CHAPTER 12

It was one o'clock in the morning as Grace left the building in Herndon in an unmarked white Homeland Security car with Corbin in the passenger seat and headed towards D.C. He had sent the rest of the team with Netty in the van to their building to get the gear they would need. He had Highway 66 to himself and cruised the left lane at eighty-five miles per hour while Corbin stared out the side window.

He exited left from 66 onto E Street then swerved right towards the White House and used the lights in the grill of the car and his DHS credentials to get through two roadblocks. A few minutes later he pulled up on Desales Street beside the Mayflower Hotel and parked behind the black Mercedes van. The side door of the van slid open as he and Corbin approached and the team began spilling out onto the sidewalk.

"Get everything?" Grace said and heard only grunts and swear words back at him. He knew they were always prepared and expected the response. "Avery, get what we talked about?"

"Yup," Avery pulled the large canvas duffel out of the van and put it on like a backpack.

"Great. Access is from below the boiler room, a couple stories down from street level," Grace said. "The lobby should be empty at this hour, so we just have to get through to the service area then no one will care we're there. Let's do this."

They were all dressed in grey coveralls with a logo for Bugged Out, a fake pest control company, on the backs. Each grabbed a pair of large bags. They came around the front of the building, the side doors of the hotel being locked after hours. Two men in ornate uniforms opened the double gold doors and let them in.

As they stepped through they stopped and looked at each other then at Grace.

"Thought you said it would be empty," Holden said.

The lobby was packed with people from one side to the other. News crews had cameras set up in several places conducting interviews with people in suits and police uniforms and anyone else they could stop.

"This is a shit storm," Grace said. "We just have to get through to the back. Keep away from any cameras. Hats down."

The team headed out in a single line through the crowd, Holden leading the way to clear a path for the rest of them. Nobody who turned to look at him hesitated before they stepped out of the way.

They reached the back of the lobby and went through

the door to the employees only service area. After a long hall with white floors and walls they came to a locked door that Levi had open easily and they passed through. Grace went last, checking both ways down the hall before closing the door behind them. They moved through the darker area and down a flight of metal suspended stairs into the boiler room that provided all of the heat and hot water for the hotel.

"Where to, boss?" Avery said.

"All the way to the end then take a left," Grace said. "There should be an old door that leads to the sublevel."

After moving through the hot room they turned and stopped at a cement block wall.

"Well, this doesn't look good," Corbin said.

"Shit, they bricked over it," Grace said. "It was here five years ago."

They all stared at the wall. Holden stepped up to it and looked closer then reached into the bag he was carrying and pulled out a drill.

Avery looked down at the power tool and raised his eyebrows. "Why the hell are you carrying that around?" Avery said.

"Maybe in case there's a huge ass cement block wall in our way," Holden said.

He ran the power cord and Avery found a socket and he began drilling one-inch holes every six inches along the border of the newer cement blocks.

"We don't have time for this," Grace said. "We should already be a quarter mile down the tunnel."

"Levi, give me a block of the Semtex," Holden said.

"You want to let everyone in the hotel know what's going on?" Levi said.

"Trust me," Holden said.

He took the block of orange plastic explosives and cut thin strips off with his pocketknife then pushed one piece into each of the holes he'd drilled in the wall. Then he placed a blasting cap into each piece and ran the wire down to the floor.

"Just inside the door to the boiler room there was a cart with building materials on it," Holden said. "Someone go bring it here."

Avery turned and jogged off down the long hallway and returned a minute later pushing a large maintenance cart.

"Thanks," Holden said. "On the bottom of the cart there's a big can of spackle. Pull it out and open it for me but don't stir it up. I want it thick."

Avery knelt down and looked at the bottom level of the cart. Between a box of light bulbs and a broken plastic toolbox was the round tub of spackle. "How the hell did you see this?" He pulled the plastic container out.

"Know your surroundings," Holden said. "Never know what you'll need. I took inventory of that cart with a glance as we walked past it."

Holden took the spackle and a trowel and filled each hole then ran the wires together.

"Is that it?" Levi said.

"One more thing," Holden said.

"What's that?" Levi said.

"Get the fuck back," Holden said.

Everyone went around the corner as Holden ran the wires and attached them to the small black box with a hand crank on the side, a trigger he'd built that required no electrical power source.

"Fire in the hole!" Holden turned the handle a full

rotation. A metal cylinder spun inside a series of magnets, creating a small electrical charge that traveled down the wire to the detonators in the plastic explosives. A series of small explosions went off inside the cement block wall. The floor shook for a moment then everything was done.

They all went back around the corner to see the wall still standing.

"Any other ideas?" Avery said.

Holden walked towards the wall then stopped just in front of it. He ran his hand around the perimeter of the holes then stepped back and extended his right leg out in a kick, striking the wall with the bottom of his heavy work boot.

The wall began to crumble from the bottom, which allowed the top to fall away.

"Damn," Netty said. "That's some kick."

Holden and Levi cleared enough of the debris to let them climb over carrying their bags. Ten feet past the rubble was the decades old steel door.

Grace walked up to the door and turned the unlocked handle and pushed but the door was jammed in place.

"How about you bring your thunder boot over here again," Grace said.

"Thunder boot, I like that," Holden stepped to the door and repeated his kick and the door opened eight inches.

With a few more shoulders and kicks it was open wide enough for them to pass through with their bags. Following Grace they each wore night vision goggles. They came to a metal stairwell that went down twenty feet then found themselves standing on the wooden platform where the electric subway train used to pull up.

"You're standing where J. Edgar Hoover once stood, men," Grace said.

"And women," Netty said.

"And women," Grace said.

"So now we have two miles to walk in this tunnel?" Corbin said.

"Hopefully not," Grace said. "Avery, over here."

Twenty feet down the track sat an abandoned open-topped subway car. A tower came out of the middle and attached onto a grooved track in the ceiling. Electricity would have flowed through the elevated groove and traveled down the tower to the electric motors on each set of wheels on the subway car.

"It's an electric subway car from the 1950's. It was used to transport members of Congress back and forth," Grace said. "Can you get it going?"

Avery opened the large duffel he'd been wearing as a backpack and pulled out a two-foot square battery pack. "Let's give it a try."

"Give it five minutes, if you don't think it'll roll then we'll set out on foot," Grace said. "Everyone else, get ready. Either way we're out of here in five."

Bags were opened and gear spread out on the platform. Each person took off the grey coveralls to reveal their green combat pants. They pulled on the bulletproof vests they'd brought and strapped side holsters on and filled pockets with extra ammunition.

Chip opened his second bag and handed a Sig Sauer 516 tactical rifle to each person along with two extra magazines.

"I modified them myself," Chip said. "Sound suppression is better than anything on the market."

A clicking sound came from the small electric motor on the subway car followed by some swear words from Avery. He reached under the motor to check the wiring then tried to start it again and the motor came to life in a low hum.

"All aboard," Avery said.

Everyone sat along the edge of the narrow platform of the cart. Netty put two bags in the middle and was the last to climb on.

"Here we go," Avery shoved the handle forward to push the transmission into gear and the cart lurched forward almost throwing him off the back then steadied out and moved along.

"Not the fastest thing," Corbin said.

"Probably seven or eight miles per hour," Avery said. "Faster than we could make on foot through here."

CHAPTER 13

"You know if we have to leave in a hurry, this thing ain't gonna do the trick," Avery said. The electric subway car moved slowly within the tunnel

"These boots were made for running," Grace said.

"That's reassuring," Chip said.

The ride took 18 minutes through the dark tunnel. Avery turned the motor off as they neared the end point and they rolled to a stop and sat in the quiet to listen for any movement.

"Sounds clear," Grace said. "Let's just hope we don't have to blast another wall."

"Yeah, I'm guessing security in the basement of the United States Capitol is a little better than a hotel's," Levi said. "Shouldn't be a problem."

"Not helpful, Levi," Grace said. "For that you get to scout. Avery, you're with him."

"Just because I Indian, no mean I scout," Levi said.

"Can it and get moving," Grace said. "Okay everybody. Earpieces in, volume on low. Maintain radio silence as much as possible. We don't know what channels might be getting monitored. Even with our secure channels, we can't count on them unless necessary."

Levi disappeared down a dark hallway at the end of the tunnel with Avery right behind. The team sat in silence as they waited. It took four minutes and Avery returned.

"Door's still there," Avery said. "Levi ran a camera underneath. Looks like a clasp and padlock on the other side."

"Netty, you're up," Grace said. "Show me what you got."

"Sure thing, captain," Netty said.

She moved into the darkness. At the end she found Levi then opened the satchel she'd carried with her.

"Any movement?" she said.

"Nothing," Levi said. "We're in the basement still so they're probably all watching the ground level."

"Good." From her bag Netty pulled out a can of automotive air conditioner refrigerant and a short crowbar. "I need you to pry the door away from the jamb as much as you can. I need at least a third of an inch."

Levi took the crowbar and placed it just above the doorknob then leaned back and let his weight pull the lever back. A quarter inch gap opened up allowing Netty to see through to the back of the metal clasp. She mounted a brass valve to the can with a six-inch extension tube attached to it and pointed it into the jamb and began spraying.

"How long?" Levi said.

"Only a minute or so, hopefully," Netty said.

"Will it break the clasp?"

"No, it'll weaken the hinge," Netty said. "The clasp

is all one piece of metal. I'd need liquid nitrogen to get through that. The pin in the hinge is usually weaker. We just need it to get fragile enough to break apart with a little bit of pressure."

"Where'd you learn this?" Levi said.

"Girl Scouts," Netty said.

The can stopped spraying as it ran out of refrigerant and she set it off to the side.

"Keep the gap open," she placed a thin metal bar through the gap and put tension on the back of the clasp. "Still quiet?"

Levi looked down at the small screen attached to the fiber optic camera running under the door.

"Unless someone's around that corner, we're good," he said.

Netty took a rubber mallet and lightly tapped the end of her crowbar several times to make sure the end was resting against the back of the clasp on the other side of the door.

"Here goes nothing," she pulled back and gave one more hard hit.

The clasp broke free and the sound of metal hitting the outside of the steel door was followed by small pieces falling to the floor. She held still and watched Levi as he stared at the monitor. Ten seconds later he nodded.

"No movement," he said.

Netty put her tools into her bag and ran back down the dark hallway to get the rest of the team.

"We're unlocked," Netty said.

"Great work," Grace said.

With Netty leading the way they made it to the door.

"Holden, you're in first to the left. Avery to the right on point. Subdue over shoot. We don't want to alert anyone we're here and we don't know who might be actual tangoes or who's just been coerced. This is recon only. I repeat, this is recon only."

Levi checked the monitor one last time then nodded as he pulled the fiberoptic camera from under the door and stepped back. Grace pulled the door open as Holden moved in, rifle up and ready, and turned left as Avery turned right. Grace went through next followed by the rest of the team.

They moved down the hallway to the right, Avery taking the lead as Holden became the sweeper, walking backwards. Corbin was in front of him and made sure Holden never backed into anything or anyone. At the first corner Levi moved to the front and ran the end of the thin cable with a high definition camera mounted in the tip around the edge at floor level then nodded and stepped back. Avery went around the corner with his rifle scanning left and right as he cleared the way and everyone followed.

They were in the main congressional subway on the House end of the Capitol. Senators and Representatives used the private electric train cars to move between the office buildings, out of sight of the public. The team reached the stairs and escalator leading up to the first floor of the Capitol building. The escalator was still running in the silent and empty halls.

Once up to the first floor they fanned out to check all directions. The maze of hallways are home to the windowless private offices for members of Congress, usually the newly elected with less seniority to claim something with a window and perhaps a view in one of the office buildings surrounding the Capitol.

"This is freakin' me out," Grace said.

"How the hell is nobody here?" Levi said.

The level cleared, they moved to the stairs that would take them up to the second floor and the entrance to the House of Representatives. Holden led the way with the rest of the team behind him, their weapons angled out to cover all directions, fingers stretched across the trigger guards to avoid accidental firing.

They reached the landing for the second level and the floor was littered with the dead bodies of Secret Service and Capitol Police officers as well as more than a few civilians. Just to their left was the door to the main hallway that ran in front of the House of Representatives.

"Scope it," Grace said.

Levi stepped up to the corner and used the fiber optic camera once again. His head began to nod then stopped and he held a fist up. Grace looked over at the monitor and saw nothing but bodies on the ground. Levi pointed at a dark area at the far end of the hall. A moment later there was the slightest movement. Grace motioned for Levi to keep an eye on the monitor.

He scanned the rest of the team then stepped quietly to Netty and whispered in her ear. She gave him a confused look then shrugged. She took ten steps back away from the team and faced the other direction.

"Oh god, somebody help me," Netty cried. "Is anyone here? Oh my god it hurts. PLEASE! Somebody help! I've been shot!"

Grace was back at Levi's side watching the monitor. As Netty began her act the movement stopped for a moment then finally a shape emerged from the shadow.

The black uniform of a Capitol Police officer in tactical gear appeared as the person moved slowly towards them, still 50 feet away. Grace gave a signal to the team to be ready, that they only had one target sighted.

Netty cried in pain again. The uniform moved closer, becoming clearer on the small monitor. A black balaclava covered the face and an assault rifle was raised. The figure's steps were unsure and slow.

Grace leaned in to Levi's ear.

"He looks nervous as hell," he said.

Levi nodded then reached to his belt and handed Grace a six inch black canister. Grace looked at it and nodded. He glanced at the monitor and pulled the curved aluminum pin on the canister and waited.

Thirty feet. Twenty-five. The figure got closer. He held his hand with the black metal canister up so his team knew what was coming.

Twenty feet.

Grace tossed the canister around the corner. The sound of the metal casing echoed as it hit the marble floor. The team all covered their ears just before the nearly 200 decibel blast came from the non-lethal flashbang device as it exploded within its steel casing, the blinding light lit up the hall and the monitor turned white. Holden was through the door first with Avery and Grace right behind him. They covered the 20 feet before the smoke dissipated and found their target kneeling on the floor, hands over ears. Sounds of yelling and screaming came from the closed doors to the House chamber.

"Drop the weapon and lie down on the floor," Grace said.

"You don't understand," a man's voice came from the mask.

"What do I not understand except that we have six weapons pointed at your head right now?" Grace said.

The man's right hand move slowly away from his ear, the palm turning to show them the black trigger in his hand, his thumb on top of a red button. A wire ran from the trigger down his arm and into his bulletproof vest.

"And what do you have there?" Grace said. He motioned for the team to begin backing up while the man's vision was still obscured from the blast.

"It's everything," the man said. "I push this button and the whole building goes up along with everyone in that room." He motioned over to the door to the House chamber where Congress, the president and vice-president were all being held captive.

Grace glanced at Levi and tapped his vest to see if they were thinking the same thing. Levi nodded.

"I'm not sure what you think you have there, but I don't think it's gonna blow the building up," Grace said.

The man's finger twitched.

"Try me," he said.

"I'm pretty sure what you have is a common terrorist grade suicide vest," Grace said. "You press that button and the last thing you're not gonna see your own brain splattered against all four walls."

Everyone was around the corner of the doorway except for Grace and Levi who were back at the edge of the entrance.

"Why don't you slowly put the trigger by your side and drop your weapon and we'll get the vest off of you," Grace said.

"I can't," the man said. "They'll kill my family."

Grace paused. He ran the scenario through his head and thought of the Marine pilot.

"Not if they think you're dead," Grace said. "We'll keep you safe and take you out of here in a body bag. Once clear we'll get your family to safety."

Levi looked at Grace and raised an eyebrow. Grace shrugged.

"Can you do that?" the man said.

"We're with the FBI," Grace lied. "We can do anything. What's your name?"

"Laurence," he said. "Laurence Bradley."

"Okay, Laurence Bradley," Grace said. "I'm looking forward to having a long conversation with you, but not until we get that bomb off of you."

Laurence's right arm lowered to his side and he let the trigger fall. He lifted the strap to the rifle over his head and set it on the floor on his other side.

"All right, Laurence," Grace said. "We just need you to place your hands behind your head now."

They watched as the man's hands began to rise then stopped. "I can't. They'll know," his right hand dropped to the floor and grabbed the trigger. His thumb pushed the red button down.

Levi and Grace turned and dove through the door onto the hard floor as the rest of the team did the same to get further from the blast zone. After several seconds Grace pushed up onto his hands and looked back at Laurence kneeling, his thumb pushing the red button over and over.

CHAPTER 14

"That's a pleasant surprise," Grace said. "Looks like we were both wrong."

Laurence collapsed to the floor, his chest heaving.

"I can't tell if he's laughing or crying," Grace said.

"Actually I think he's puking," Levi said.

Levi rolled the man onto his back and pulled the man's pistol from the holster on his belt then checked him for other weapons.

"He's clear," Levi said. "But the hall is littered with weapons."

"Tie him up," Grace said.

The rest of the team came from the door and Avery helped Levi put zip ties on Laurence's wrists and ankles. Grace looked up and saw Netty headed for the door to the House chamber.

"Don't open the door," he said.

"Isn't this why we're here?" she said.

"We don't need 600 people rushing out to get on camera," Grace said. "This guy was nervous as hell about something, so I'm not ruling anything out. Let's split up and look around."

The team moved out in teams of two. Methodically they checked every office door and stairwell surrounding the House as well as the connecting Statuary Hall. Grace and Holden were clearing an office on the backside of the House when Avery's voice came through their earpieces.

"Boss, you should get down here."

"Where's 'here,'" Grace said.

"A level down, east hallway," Avery said.

"On our way," Grace said.

The two men went to the stairs, weapons always at the ready, and made their way down. They followed the center hall between offices and saw Netty standing at the far end.

"What do you have?" Grace said.

"In here," Netty said.

They followed her into an office at the corner of the east and central halls and found Avery in the small room, standing on a desk he'd pushed against the wall.

"What is it?" Grace said.

"In the stairwell on the other side of this wall I saw fresh plaster. Couldn't reach it without a ladder so I went to the office on the other side of the stairs," Avery said. "It was a pretty crappy plastering job and the paint on top of it didn't even match."

He was picking at the wall with his six-inch pocketknife blade and chunks of plaster were falling to the ground. He opened a foot long section running along the edge of the ceiling then pointed his flashlight into the hole.

"Yup, it's here, too," Avery said.

Grace climbed up onto the desk beside Avery and looked into the hole.

"Holy shit. That's C4," Grace said.

"And a lot of it," Avery said. "This is the third office I've found it in."

"Always at the ceiling?" Grace said.

"Yup," Avery said.

Grace looked up at the ceiling.

"Let's check the rest of the offices," Grace said.

Avery, Grace and Netty made their way through each of the offices, finding the fresh plaster along the ceiling of all the rooms and stairwells on the inner square of the floor. They came out of the last office and stood in the hall.

"I need you two to go up two levels and check some more, most likely at the floor instead of the ceiling," Grace said.

Avery and Netty moved out. Grace reached into his pocket and pulled out his cellphone and dialed. The phone just beeped at him, showing no signal.

Grace made his way back to the main entrance to the House Chamber. He went to the double doors and inspected the frame and hinges then took his knife from his belt and slowly slid the blade under the frame and pried it out.

"Shit," a line of C4 was running along the doorframe below the trim.

A voice came through his earpiece.

"Boss. More of the same up above," Avery said. "Not just the perimeter, but everywhere you could get access."

"You see any detonators or wires?" Grace said.

"I do, but no ends," Avery said. "No idea where it's originating. No way to disable it. Even if I pulled the detonators I can reach, there's many more I can't."

"Okay. Get back down here. We have work to do," Grace said. "Looks like the house doors are wired, too."

The rest of the team stood and looked at him.

"What now?" Holden said.

"Time for some construction work," Grace said. "Or destruction is more accurate. How much more Semtex you have?"

"Enough to take down a tank," Holden said.

"That should do it," Grace said. "Holden, Levi, Chip and Avery you're with me. Netty and Corbin, you're here to watch the door."

"Shit," Netty said.

"Don't worry. There's plenty more to come, Netty," Grace said.

Grace moved out with the three men and went back down to the first floor of the Capitol. They stood in the center hall that ran under the House Chamber.

"I need a few desks pulled from offices to give Holden enough height to reach the ceiling," Grace said. "After that we'll need more desks to stack up to use as stairs."

Holden looked up at the ceiling and grimaced. "Are we gonna . . . "

"Yes, we are," Grace said.

"Don't you think there's some bad guys in there?" Holden said.

"When terrorists go to all the trouble to wire an entire building they're really good at making sure they're out of the way of their own explosives," Grace said. "My guess is that the worst people in that room are members of Congress."

"You're the boss," Holden said.

"Pick your spot as close to the middle of the hall as possible. No C4 was found through here and we want to stay as far away from it as possible. We need at least a ten by ten square with clean lines. We should be dead center in the middle of the house chamber upstairs."

"How are we going to let people know that a huge fucking hole is about to be blown in their floor?" Avery said.

Grace looked up as he stepped to the center of the hallway. "How thick do you think the ceiling is?"

"Couple feet, probably," Holden said. "Maybe more. Also depends on what the floor above is made of."

"Start shaping your charge, Avery come with me," Grace said.

The two men worked their way up to the first floor and down the hallway that led to the center of the building. They entered the circular room below the great rotunda, weapons up, moving opposite directions to clear the large area. Once clear, Grace began scanning the dome above them.

"What are we looking for?" Avery said.

"The rotunda's been under construction for a few months. We're looking for tools," Grace said.

They walked around the room close to the walls to get a better viewpoint of the ceiling above.

"Nothing," Avery said.

"The stuff they're using is too big and heavy to haul out of here every day," Grace said.

He turned and went through the opening facing west into the stairwell.

"Bingo," Grace said.

Avery followed him in. The walls of the landing to the stairwell were lined with industrial carts covered with tarps.

"Uncover all of them, let's see what we have," Grace said.

Avery moved right and Grace left as they began to

pull back the thick canvas tarps revealing cans of plaster, brushes and ladders.

"Boss," Avery said. "Think this would work?"

Grace turned around to see Avery holding up the end of a huge drill with a four-foot bit that was thicker than you could wrap your hand around.

"I think it will," Grace said. "Let's get moving."

Avery and Grace took each end of the heavy tool and went back through the building until they reached the hallway where Holden was placing straight rows of orange plastic explosives on the ceiling in a clean square.

"Perfect," Grace said. "Now help us get this up there."

They lifted the drill up to Holden who picked it up like it weighed nothing.

"What do you want?" Holden said.

"One clean hole right up into the house chamber," Grace said.

Avery got the other end of the power cord plugged in around the corner in an office.

"What about all that C4?" Holden said.

"C4 doesn't mind a bit of vibration," Grace said. "As long as we don't send a signal to the detonators, we're fine."

Holden pointed the bit up and placed it onto the ceiling and paused then pulled the handle to turn the drill on. The noise was deafening as the spinning four-inch wide bit started spinning up into the ceiling. He was a foot in and they heard it hit something metal. He let go of the trigger.

"What was that?" Grace said.

"My guess would be pipes," Holden said. "If I push through them we might get rained on."

"Can you feel your way to see if you can go past it?" Grace said.

Holden pulled the drill back an inch and angled the bit then turned it on again. A sound of metal again, but not as loud, and he stopped the drill.

"I think I'm on the edge," Holden said. "I can't get much more leverage without starting over."

"Push through it," Grace said. "We're gonna get wet when the ceiling comes down anyway. This is a construction grade drill so water isn't going to bother it."

"Hope not," Holden said. "I don't really wanna become fried chicken here."

The drill started up and the sound of grinding metal got louder as he kept pushing up. Avery climbed on top of the desk to help push the heavy drill toward the ceiling.

Water began running down the drill bit then a loud crack came from inside the ceiling and the flow of water got heavier.

"Keep going," Grace yelled over the loud machine. "Just get through."

Avery and Holden had water coming down their arms when the plaster around the bit cracked and fell. Holden stopped the drill and both men turned their heads away as gallons of fluid poured over them.

"Shit!" Avery yelled. "It's a fuckin' sewer line."

The raw sewage fell on them as Grace stepped away, his arm coming to his nose.

"Whew, and that ain't fresh," Grace said. "You gotta keep going. Just get through it."

The drill wound up again and the bit moved more freely upward once it was clear of the sewer pipe. Holden had the handles at his chest as it kept moving, Avery pushing from below. The tip hit something hard and the two men lowered it a few inches then propelled it up to strike whatever was holding it back. Only six inches of bit were left before they'd run out of drilling length.

With a guttural scream, Holden lunged his left leg out and forced the drill up, his biceps stretched the material that tried desperately to hold his arms inside their shirtsleeves. The drill then moved with no resistance and the machine slammed into the ceiling. Holden released the trigger and pulled it back through then dropped the tool down to the floor.

Water had faded to a trickle coming through the hole as Holden dodged the drops to look up into the tunnel he'd just made. On the other end he saw light then dark then light again as people were moving to look down through the hole.

Holden jumped to the floor.

"I think I'll let you make first contact," Holden said. "I wouldn't want to scare one of those Southern senators too bad."

Grace climbed onto the desk and looked up through the hole. "Hello," he yelled. "Who's there?"

After a pause a voice came back through the void.

"This is Senator Jack Thomson."

"Pleasure to meet you, Senator," Grace said. "But I need President Abrams."

"We can't do that until we know who you are," Senator Thomson said.

"The name's Grace. I'm with Homeland Security."

There was commotion above then another voice came.

"Grace, it's Jim Monroe," the director of the FBI said.

"Director, good to hear your voice," Grace said. "Is everyone okay up there?"

"We are. The president is secure," Monroe said. "We've

had no contact from anyone since the doors got barricaded. There's no cell service and we're completely cut off. What the hell's going on out there?"

"Long story," Grace said. "Let's just say we have a lot of cleaning up to do. We need to keep communications limited. Can anyone else hear me right now?"

"There's a few Congressmen nearby," Monroe said.

"Move everyone back so we can talk."

Grace saw light from the other end of the hole and the faint sound of FBI Director Monroe ordering people to move away from the hole.

"Okay, I'm back," Monroe said. "Far from secure on my end, but it's the best we can do right now."

"That works," Grace said. "The Capitol was taken by an unknown terrorist force. We believe we have the building secured but there's complications."

"Such as?"

"The entire House is wired with C4 and we don't know who has the button," Grace said.

It was quiet as the director took this in, knowing he couldn't ask too many questions without alerting everyone around him to the situation.

"What's our play?" Monroe said.

"We have a plan in place to get everyone out," Grace said. "It's not gonna be pretty, but it's all we got right now."

Grace continued to explain the plan.

"Sounds risky," Monroe said. "But you know more than we do right now, so let's go."

"One more thing, sir," Grace said. "We can't have any communications from the evacuees. We need to make sure nobody outside the building knows a rescue is underway or the explosives might get triggered."

"What do you want me to do?" Monroe said.

"Collect every cellphone in the room," Grace said. "Turn them off and leave them there. No exceptions."

"That's going to be tricky," Monroe said. "This gang is eager to get in front of the cameras."

"It's a non-starter. If they want out, they need to leave all phones," Grace said. "Do it however you need. Have every last one of them searched before they come through the hole."

"Will do," Monroe said.

CHAPTER 15

"This isn't going to be easy, and each of you will be on your own," Grace had his team gathered in the hallway below the House. "We need to keep everyone secure and away from outside communications."

"How are we gonna do that?" Avery said.

"FBI Director Monroe has identified a few friendlies to help. There's a few Secret Service officers in there as well," Grace said. "I've worked with Monroe before and I trust him. We'll spread his people out through the group to move everyone along and watch for cellphones."

"We know we can trust them?" Chip said. "Looking at the floor upstairs, there's a lot of 'friendlies' that ended up not being so friendly."

"We have to trust them. It's our only chance," Grace said. "Just do your best. Everyone know where you're going?"

Nods, yes's, one "screw you" and other methods of affirmation were given.

"Okay then," Grace said. "Be safe, be vigilant, and I'll see you all at the other end."

He looked at Holden. "You ready?"

"Damn straight," Holden said.

"Then let's do it," Grace said.

The six men and one woman divided and went around the corners away from the square of explosives lining the ceiling. Holden held the black box with the hand crank and looked back down the hall for a moment then ducked around the corner.

"Fire in the hole!" Holden said.

He gave a quick crank to the handle on the black box. The spark travelled down the thin wire and crossed the fifty feet to the detonator stuck into the burnt orange plastic explosives on the ceiling.

The blast sent a wall of smoke, plaster, wood and sewer water both ways down the hallway. While the dust was still thick in the air, Holden ran down the hall to check the opening he'd made as the rest of the team began pulling the desks they'd gathered from all of the offices down towards him.

"Everyone okay?" Grace looked up into the hole.

"All present and accounted for," Monroe said. "That was impressive."

Grace began to see the edges of the hole, a perfect ten-foot by ten-foot opening.

"Great. Get your groups queued up and keep them orderly," Grace said. "We don't have room for anyone to rush us."

"We're all ready as soon as you are," Monroe said.

The desks were stacked and stabilized as Holden

climbed to the top and stood up into the chamber of the House of Representatives.

"Hey there," he said. "I'll be your tour guide today."

Director Monroe stepped forward and down into the hole, forearms connected to Holden's. Once down one step he turned back up and watched as Holden helped a man and a woman through the hole then Monroe helped them down the next two desks until they reached the floor. The woman dusted her dark blue jacket off then looked up at the man standing in front of her.

"Madam President, this is Grace," Director Monroe said. "He's responsible for getting us out of here."

"Then let's get the hell out of here, Mr. Grace," President Abrams said.

Grace grinned and decided not to correct her. He looked up at Holden on top of the desks and nodded then turned and headed west through the hall, President Abrams behind him with her lead Secret Service agent Rick Haggard at her side and Director Monroe following.

"This way," Grace said.

Holden continued to grab arms and help people down through the hole and the rest of the team guided them to the floor.

Grace reached the stairs and went down a level, his Sig Sauer assault rifle raised as he cleared the way. Haggard and Monroe followed ten feet behind with the president.

They approached the door to the closed off railway they'd entered the Capitol through then moved into the dark tunnel and reached the electric subway cart. On board, Grace turned on the battery pack they'd used hours earlier and pushed the lever forward to put the transmission into gear and it lurched and began its slow trip back to the Mayflower

Hotel. With fewer people on board it moved slightly faster.

"Your team was first into the Capitol?" Monroe said.

"We were," Grace said. "Richard Graham is in the middle of planning an all out raid on the building and we went in to recon but ended up pulling you out."

"How many people were holding the Capitol?" Monroe said.

Grace looked at the president then back to the FBI director.

"One," Grace said. He continued to fill the president and FBI director in on what had taken place. Sixteen minutes later the subway cart reached the platform at the Mayflower Hotel.

"When we came through here before, the lobby was packed," Grace said. "We need to extract without being seen. Madam President, I'm going to need you to put this on," he picked up the grey pest control coveralls Netty had worn when they entered the building. He handed two more pairs to Monroe and Agent Haggard.

Grace dropped his backpack and opened it and pulled out two air filter masks he'd taken from the pile of tools in the Rotunda.

"You two are a lot higher profile than me, so wear these. Keep your eyes down and keep moving," Grace said.

"Do you have a hat?" President Abrams said.

He reached back into his bag and grabbed a dirty Washington Nationals baseball cap and handed it to her. She pulled her shoulder length hair back and tucked it up inside the hat and pulled the brim down low.

"At least it's the Nats," she said. "Let's go."

"That hat is so going on eBay when we're done here," Grace said.

They moved through the boiler room and to the door

into the service hall. Grace turned to head towards the lobby.

"Hold on," President Abrams said. "This way."

She started walking the other way down the hall, Agent Haggard right beside her.

"This isn't the plan," Grace said. He began to chase after them down the hallway, Monroe behind him.

"Trust me," President Abrams said.

They reached the kitchen and Abrams moved quickly through the maze of equipment. At the back of the kitchen was a door with a crash bar and a red sign informing them an alarm would sound if the door opened. She pushed the crash bar and swung the door open into an alley that ran between the hotel and the office building next door. The cold blast of air hit them from the winter darkness outside.

"How did you . . . " Grace said.

"I speak here at least once a month," she said. "This is how they bring me in and out. The kitchen staff uses the alley to smoke so the alarm was disconnected years ago."

"If the president thing doesn't work out for you, I can make room for you on my team," Grace said.

They moved through the alley and hit 17th Street and turned left. At the next corner they turned left again onto Desales Street. The black Mercedes Sprinter van and Homeland Security car were parked midway down the block.

It was still an hour until sunrise and Grace had the van on and was getting ready to pull out of the parking space. He reached over and hit the button for the car stereo, already set to the local news station WTOP.

"It appears at least a hundred troops are on the steps of the building facing the mall and even more on the backside. According to our military consultants we should expect to

see blasts come from each of the doors at the same time as Special Forces attempt to breach the Capitol for the first time since the siege began at 8:20pm last night."

"Shit, they're breaching the Capitol," Grace turned it louder as his passengers moved closer to hear it.

"There they go! All the doors blew within a second of each other and the soldiers are going in. It appears they're wearing gas masks— "

Grace hit a button on his cellphone and listened to it ring once then Arrington's voice come through on the other end. "Where the hell are you?" Arrington said.

"We just left the Capitol," Grace said. "You have to call off the attack."

"We can't, it's--" The sound of the explosion came through the stereo speakers and from outside the van as they felt the ground shake below them. The cellphone went dead.

"Oh god, the roof of the Capitol has collapsed. Special Forces are retreating but many were caught in the explosion."

"Did they get out?" President Abrams said. "Did everyone get out?"

He hit the button on the radio on his belt and began calling out names. "Holden, Avery, Chip. Anyone there? What's your status?"

Nothing came back.

"Netty, Corbin? Anyone? Levi?"

"What's wrong?" Monroe said.

"I don't know yet. I can't get hold of my team," Grace said. "Hopefully they're all in the tunnels and far enough away from the building. Right now we just need to get you out of the city."

Grace threw the van into gear and began working his way through the streets. He turned right onto 17th then again onto K Street to see several police cars racing down the road with lights and sirens on. The van made the turn to head to the ramp behind the Kennedy Center that would put them on the bridge to 66 West out of D.C. when the police cars turned and began blocking the road.

"They're going to shut the bridges down," Grace turned right and hit the gas.

"Where are you going?" Monroe said. "They'll let us through."

Grace was shaking his head while watching the rear view mirrors as he drove. "We can't risk it. You haven't seen what's been going on out here."

"At least let someone know we're out," Monroe said.

"Cellphones are dead," Grace said.

"It's procedure in case of a terrorist attack," Haggard said. "All cellphone signals are shut down to keep any bombs from being remotely detonated and so the terrorists can't communicate with each other."

Grace turned on the radio clipped to his belt and continued to call out the names of his team members, waiting for responses, but only heard static. He moved through the city to get to Canal Road running along the Potomac to the Beltway.

CHAPTER 16

Arrington walked back into the control room to see Graham and William talking in the corner and went to the conference table.

"What's going on over there?" Arrington said.

"No idea," Leighton said. "Getting pretty heated, though."

"Anything from the news about survivors yet?" Arrington said.

"Nothing. All stations are reporting the Special Forces breach teams are likely all dead," Darby said. "That's all they know how to report, death, whether it's confirmed or not."

Richard Graham walked back over to the table with William following behind him. He put his hands on the back of the large leather chair at the head of the table and stared down at the floor then looked up to the group.

"I need to be sworn in," Graham said.

"What?" Arrington said. "You don't want to wait until teams can get in to look for survivors?"

Graham looked up at all the screens showing the different news channels' coverage. The sun was coming up over the city and the video feeds were clear and bright. The roof of the building over the House was gone and three of the four walls had collapsed in the explosion.

"I think we all know what they'll find," Graham said. "Our Nation needs a leader, and right now I'm all they have. William has already made some calls and a news crew will be here anytime now."

"Jesus Christ, Richard," Darby said. "Is this really what you want to do? LBJ at least waited two hours before being sworn in after Kennedy was killed. It hasn't even been ten minutes."

Graham looked over at William then back. "Yes, it is. And, Amanda, I believe you're an attorney?"

"Yes," Paulson said.

"Would you please find the oath of office," Graham said. "I'd like for you to swear me in."

"Yes, sir," she said.

"William will work with you to prepare," Graham said. "I'm thinking in the atrium upstairs would be good."

"We'll take care of it," William said. "You just prepare some remarks for the press."

Amanda Paulson and William left the room.

"I really don't think now's the time," Director Leighton said. "We have a country in shock from a terrorist attack that happened on live television. I don't know if throwing a new president at them within half an hour is the right move."

"It is. We need a reassuring voice to tell the Nation we are going to find who is responsible for this and bring them to justice," Graham said. "Thank you for voicing your concerns, director. Right now I need someone to contact Secret Service and get a detail out here immediately."

Fifteen minutes later the lobby of the Homeland Security building had the two dozen employees that had come in to work early and were brought down from their desks to watch the event. The sun was coming through the windows on the east end of the atrium. A single news crew arrived and set up a live shot with one camera and a reporter who was more accustomed to covering human-interest stories than major political events.

Richard Graham and Amanda Paulson walked to the front of the group. Amanda opened her leather notebook with the printout of the presidential oath of office inside. Paulson turned to the audience.

"May we have silence, please," she said. "We have no means to amplify and hope the few in presence will be able to witness this historic moment," she paused, looking down at her hands. "We've experienced a great loss and a tragic event. We are fortunate to have someone as qualified as Secretary Graham to take lead of our Nation. Before we continue, first a moment of silence for all those lost."

The audience went into a hush, the weight of the moment happening before them getting heavier and more real by the second.

Paulson continued. "It is my honor as assistant director of the FBI to swear in Mr. Graham," she turned to him. "Shall we begin?"

After a moment of mumbling, the lobby became quiet again. Paulson looked at Graham then down at the printed page in her leather binder.

"Please repeat after me," she said. "I, Richard Eliot

Graham, do solemnly swear that I will faithfully execute the Office of President of the United States," Paulson read.

"I, Richard Eliot Graham, do solemnly swear that I will faithfully execute the Office of President of the United States," Graham said.

"And will to the best of my ability, preserve, protect, and defend the Constitution of the United States," Paulson said.

"And will to the best of my ability, preserve, protect, and defend—"

"Stop right there," a voice echoed from the back of the lobby.

Everyone turned to see then they moved to create an aisle for the four people walking to the front of the room. President Abrams stepped up to Richard Graham with Agent Rick Haggard and Jim Monroe behind her. Grace had stopped at the back of the room, out of the line of sight of the camera and the people watching.

"Thank you for your service, Richard," Abrams said. "But I'm still able to fulfill my sworn oath as president."

"President Abrams," Graham said. "I thought you were, I never would have . . . "

"I know, Richard," Abrams said. "I know." She leaned in and put her arms around Graham and held him tight then leaned out. "Thank you for taking the lead and working with Homeland Security, FBI and the military to stage a rescue."

She turned to the silent and awed crowd.

"Today is a very dark day for America," she said. "We lost many good soldiers. Soldiers who volunteered their lives to serve their country. Soldiers who died doing just that," she paused and looked out at the faces that watched her. "But thanks to the work of a special group of men and women, I received word as I arrived here that all members of Congress, the Supreme Court and everyone else in attendance at the State of the Union were successfully removed from the Capitol before the explosion." The audience cheered and the president raised her hands for silence. "But that doesn't change the fact that there is a terrorist force out there, a force with such extensive resources and reach that they were able to carry out this horrible act of destruction. I vow we will find the people responsible and bring them to justice."

More cheers and a wave for quiet.

"So what the hell are you all standing around for?" she said. "We have some terrorists to catch and you're the ones who will catch them."

She waved at the crowd then turned to Monroe and Arrington.

"Let's go," she said.

Arrington led them to the back of the room and Grace met them and walked beside the president to the elevators. They exited on the sublevel and entered the ETTF control room. The screens lining all of the walls still showed every possible news station and all of them were replaying the speech she'd given moments earlier.

"That's disturbing," she looked up at herself on the huge screens. "I haven't showered in two days and high-definition is not my friend. Turn those off."

"Over here, Ma'am," Arrington walked to the conference table and pulled the chair at the head of the table back and the president sat down. Director Leighton and Admiral Darby were already at the table and stood as she was seated.

"Where are we?" she said.

"We haven't confirmed who's behind the attack, ma'am," Director Leighton said. "Nobody has claimed credit, and likely won't now that it's public knowledge that they didn't succeed."

"Didn't succeed?" the president spun on her heels to face the CIA director. "Have you seen the Capitol? What about the dead bodies of at least two dozen Special Forces? How about the scores of Secret Service agents and Capitol Police murdered at the onset of the attack?"

"Yes, ma'am. I just meant that they didn't succeed in, well, killing you," Leighton said.

"I for one am quite glad they did fail at that, but there is to be no talk of this tragedy as a failure. We lost good, American lives. Whoever did this succeeded in killing those men and women, and I don't want them getting away with it," she said. "We're working from here until further notice. Let's get the rest of the Joint Chiefs on their way so we can try to make some real decisions. Get to work."

CHAPTER 17

Grace went to his desk and stared up at all of the screens showing interviews with members of Congress who'd run straight to the media, all declaring their commitment to finding who was behind the terrorist acts and the deaths of dozens of Special Forces troops. Ben Murray came over to him.

"I have something to show you," Ben said.

Grace followed the analyst back to his desk.

"We've identified a few matching numbers received by both Secret Service officers and Capitol Police," Ben said. "It's slow going."

"Were the numbers all from disposable phones?" Grace said.

"They were," Ben said.

"Can you get GPS data on the last places they were used?"

Ben starting typing and going from one window to another. He compared lines of data coming through.

"This is weird," he said.

"Weird how?" Grace said.

"We only have four numbers identified and all of them were in the same place," Ben said.

"Where?"

"DC," Ben typed and stared at his screen then scribbled on a piece of paper and handed it to Grace. "Here's the address. All four phones appear to have been in that building."

Grace tapped the button on his radio. "This is Grace. Gear up and head to the van. We're moving out in two minutes."

He turned back to the analyst.

"You're a rock star, Ben," Grace said. "Get me a list of all tenants in the building. I want to know what office they're in before we pull up to the curb."

Grace grabbed Arrington on his way out.

"We have a lead to check out," he said. "Can you do something for me?"

"What?" Arrington said.

"We're still driving a stolen van," Grace said.

"I'll take care of it," Arrington said. "Just try not to destroy it."

"Another thing," Grace said.

"There's always another thing with you," Arrington said. "What is it?"

"I want to go to Buzzard Point," Grace said. "It's getting too . . . government up in here."

Arrington glanced around the room at the president and her cabinet and the dozens of assistants for various people.

"Yeah," Arrington said. "Probably best you stay out of sight. Just keep things clean. The Attorney General is here and we want results we can take to the people, not something we have to hide in the basement."

"I'll do my best," Grace said.

"Your best. Like in Tehran?" Arrington said.

"Hey, they shot first," Grace said. "Wasn't our fault. Oh, and I want to take Ben Murray with us."

"He's not NSA or CIA," Arrington said. "I have no say over him."

"He's ten times faster than any of us on a computer and we need that kind of speed," Grace said. "I have the systems back at my office. Anything I don't have access to, I have a feeling he can get in to."

"Enough said," Arrington said. "Take him if he wants to go. We'll clean up the mess with DHS later. And keep me updated."

"Likewise," Grace said.

Arrington left and Grace went back to Ben's desk.

"I'm working on the list of tenants," Ben said.

"Do you want to help end this thing?" Grace said.

"I'm doing my best, it's just that . . . "

"No, I know you are. Do you want to do more?"

Ben stared up at Grace from his swiveling desk chair.

Grace was out of the building as the van pulled up. Holden and Avery came from behind him, each carrying large black cases.

"Do I want to know?" Grace looked at the cases.

"No," Holden said.

"Great," Grace said. "I'll pretend it's a margarita machine."

The rest of the team was in the van and Netty had them moving as soon as everyone was in. Grace gave her the address and she made a left on Centreville Road and two miles later a right onto the entrance to the toll road that connects Dulles Airport with Highway 66. She worked up to 70 miles per hour in the middle lane.

"So team, if you haven't noticed, we have a new member," Grace turned in his seat. "At least for the short term. Everyone give Ben a warm welcome."

"Fuck you, Ben," Holden said.

"Run while you can. Grace is a jackass," Avery said.

The welcomes continued as Ben shrunk in his seat, his laptop open as he kept working.

"What's the load velocity of a Heckler & Koch .88 caliber pistol?" Chip said.

"That question doesn't even make sense," Ben said.

"You'll do just fine," Chip said.

Grace grinned and turned back to look out the front windshield and saw a red police light flashing in the middle of the dash.

"Where'd you get the cherry?" Grace said. Netty didn't answer.

Twenty minutes later the van crossed the Roosevelt Bridge and took the E Street exit on the left into downtown D.C.

"We're almost there," Grace said. He looked around the van at his team. Everyone had changed into black tactical pants and shirts and wore Kevlar vests with POLICE written across the front.

"Subtle," he said.

The van stopped in front of a building on Vermont Avenue and Avery slid the side door open. Grace stepped to the side door.

"Ben, what do you have?"

"Eight floors, 11 tenants," Ben said.

"Who's the newest?" Grace said. Ben kept typing.

"Sixth floor, a company called Neurotomy," Ben

said. "Seems to be some kind of psychological and social research firm."

"How long they been here?"

"Lease was signed six months ago," Ben said. "The company was formed right about the same time. Everyone else in the building has been there a few years at least."

"That's it then. You hang tight here," Grace slammed the sliding door shut and turned to the building. "Six up. Holden and Avery I want you on the stairs. Rest of us are on the elevator. I want everyone on comms, so check your volume now."

Grace tapped the button on his radio and spoke to broadcast into the earpieces everyone was wearing. They all nodded. Holden and Avery headed in to get a head start on the stairs. The rest of them followed. There was no front desk and Netty hit the button for the elevator.

"I'll go up first with Levi," Grace saw the cameras mounted on the ceiling as he spoke. "Get the other elevator as soon as we're gone. I don't want all of us bottlenecked in case we have a greeting party. They may already know we're here."

Grace and Levi stepped on the elevator and Levi hit the button for the sixth floor. On the short ride up they checked their rifles one last time then stepped to either side of the door before it opened.

After the sixth "ding" from the control panel the elevator stopped and the doors slid open. The men checked the angles then turned at the same time and stepped into the hallway with their rifles raised.

Holden's voice came in through his earpiece. "We're entering sixth floor now."

To their left Grace and Levi heard the stairwell door

open and the two men came out, Avery first to clear then Holden following. Grace motioned and they fell in line. There were two office suites on the floor and their target was at the other end of the hallway. Holden took up the rear, staying turned with his rifle pointed behind them as they made their way to the solid wooden door.

Grace signaled that Levi would be first in and he'd cover, then the rest of the men. With his hand on the knob, Grace slowly turned it to silently release the latch then nodded. Levi put his shoulder to the door and pushed through and brought his rifle up and turned left. Grace caught the door and followed, turning right.

There was one large room in front of them with desks spaced out in cubicles everywhere. They began to spread out and move through the maze, at least one man keeping eyes up at all times while the others cleared the spaces under the desks to make sure nobody was hiding.

"We're coming in," Chip said through the radio. The door opened behind them and the rest of the team came in and worked to help clear the room.

Holden was furthest into the room then stopped and put his left fist in the air, his right hand still aiming the heavy rifle. Everyone stopped. Levi was closest to him and moved up. Holden pointed at a desk in the far corner. The men worked different directions to come up on the desk from opposite sides. Holden looked up at Levi and gave a three count with nods then they moved in together, rifles aimed under the desk.

"Get out, face down on the ground, hands on the back of your head," Holden's big voice filled the room.

"Don't! Please don't kill me!"

A man lurched forward from his kneeling position and

complied with the orders. Holden placed his size 14 boot on the man's back and Grace came over.

"Who are you?" Grace said.

"Jason. Please don't kill me!"

"Don't give us a reason to, Jason," Grace said.

Holden patted the man down and nodded to Grace.

"Roll over," Grace said.

Jason didn't move.

"Roll over," Grace said. "We aren't playing Simon-Fucking-Says here."

Jason rolled over onto his back while trying to keep his hands on the back of his head.

"What is this place?" Grace said.

"Supposedly some kind of social research," Jason said.

"Supposedly?" Grace said.

"Yeah. We were hired to make phone calls," Jason said. "But I don't think they were legit."

"Get him up," Grace said. Holden leaned over and grabbed Jason by the left arm and easily lifted him up to his feet. He glanced over as Chip and Netty walked back to the desk.

"Rest of the office is clear," Netty said.

Grace looked at Jason. "One stupid move and there's a lot of bullets flying your way," he said. "You understand?"

"Yeah. I just want to get out of here in one piece," Jason said. "This place scares the shit out of me."

"How do you mean?" Grace said.

"You ever see that old film they showed in psych classes in college, the one where people were told to press a button and then they'd hear screaming on the other side of a wall?" Jason said. "It was something like that. A social and psychological experiment, they told us."

"The calls you were making," Grace said. "What

were they?"

"They were weird. We were given scripts and call lists. Started out with prank calls a few months ago, gauging peoples responses," Jason said. "Then the other day our scripts changed. They got . . . mean."

"Mean?"

"Very. We were threatening people's families. It was creepy," Jason said. "But all of us needed the money and we just did it. One girl complained about the scripts and she was taken out of here and we haven't seen her again."

"Who hired you?" Grace said.

"It was through the school employment office," Jason said. "They said a request came in for some students to do some research."

"What school?"

"The community college in Virginia," Jason said.

"Boss, take a look," Netty dropped a box full of smashed cellphones on the desk beside him.

"What's with those, Jason?" Grace said.

"Those are the phones we used. After we used them a couple times we were told to destroy them."

"And that didn't seem fishy to you?" Grace said.

"The whole thing was fishy as hell, man," Jason said. "We were all scared shitless by the end, especially after what happened at the Capitol. We started thinking it was connected."

"Ya think?" Grace turned to walk away. "Cuff him and bring him with us." Holden and Avery dragged the man faster than he could walk with his arms tied behind his back. Out the front door of the building they put him in the back seat of the van and used handcuffs to secure him to the seat post.

Netty worked the van through the city to avoid the

National Mall and the recovery efforts going on at the Capitol. She exited onto South Capitol Street and passed Nationals Stadium then took a series of turns into an underdeveloped area.

"Where are we?" Ben said.

Grace glanced back to see a blindfold over the eyes of the college boy and a pair of huge headphones undoubtedly blasting some of Avery's death metal into his ears to keep him from overhearing anything in the van. "Buzzard Point."

"It's . . . lovely," Ben said.

"Used to be, until the new stadium went up," Grace said. "Now developers are buying everything up. Not long and we'll get pushed out and replaced by a strip mall with three Starbucks and a Jimmy John's. I liked it when it was nice and run down. Nobody paid any attention to us."

The van turned on to a dirt trail that ran to a decrepit warehouse in the middle of a dusty field. A rusty garage door began to open and the van drove into the building and the door started closing behind them.

Out of the van, the team began to lay out all the weapons they'd brought with them and ones they'd acquired from the ETTF and the downed SEALs on a row of tables along the back wall. Several cars were parked along the side of the large open space. Grace continued through the run down building.

"Put Jason in a holding cell downstairs until I figure out what to do with him," Grace said. He turned and began walking.

Ben struggled to keep up with Grace. "So is this your headquarters?"

"It's where we are when we aren't anywhere else," Grace said. "It's here today but might not be tomorrow."

"Okay," Ben said. "Didn't know I was working with the Riddler."

They went up an old iron stairwell that hung off the brick wall. Up one level Grace walked to a door and tapped a series of numbers on a high tech keypad that didn't even try to blend in to the wall around it.

The door opened. Grace walked in and Ben followed. The lights began to come on one row at a time. Ben stood, his breath held, as the room was slowly illuminated by the dozens of LED bulbs hanging from metal structures suspended from the old wood beam ceiling. As the last row of lights came on Ben looked across the entire room.

"What a . . . " Ben exhaled. "Shithole."

"Yeah, we haven't done much with it," Grace said.

The floor was splintered wood left over from the building's construction in the 1950's. A few random folding tables were set up with computers on top, some still with large CRT monitors rather than the thin flat screen LCDs.

"I expected . . . " Ben said. "More."

"This isn't Homeland Security, Ben. This is the SCS," Grace said. "We're not trying to impress members of the Senate Intelligence Committee. Our existence was only made known when Ed 'Shitface' Snowden made it known. We run black ops with money hidden from the public through a dozen different shell companies. Every federal dollar we spend has the chance of landing us on the front page of the Washington Post, so we don't spend any. Most of this shit was borrowed or stolen. A majority of our funding comes from cash we confiscate on missions overseas. We aren't the first to operate this way, and we won't be the last."

"Do you get paid?" Ben said.

"We're all government employees of one sort or another,"

Grace said. "But our compensation wouldn't afford any of us a studio apartment with running water anywhere in the DC area. We have a system of supplementing our income without going overboard. Nobody's driving Ferrari here, but we aren't hurting either."

"What about me?" Ben said.

"Right now you're still an employee of Homeland Security," Grace said. "If we all get to the other side of this alive and my team thinks you would make a good permanent addition, and you're interested, then a similar arrangement would be made for you."

"They didn't seem to like me much," Ben said.

"That's because they're all assholes," Grace said. "But for a good reason. We rely on the person beside us everyday to get us home again. Anyone we bring into this circle has to be trusted like that. Netty's our newest and they're just warming up to her."

"How long has she been on the team?" Ben said.

"Almost a year," Grace said.

"Shit," Ben said.

"Your table is over there," Grace pointed. "It's the best machine we have. Check it out and get it set up to access anything we need. If there's anything specific you need, let Netty know and she'll acquire it for you."

"Is it a secure connection?" Ben said.

Grace turned and looked at him.

"It's like we're not even on the network here," Grace said. "We're masked from looking like we exist."

"Cool," Ben said.

"Now get to work," Grace said.

"What do you need first?" Ben said.

"I don't need anything first. I need everything now,"

Grace said. "But I need you to keep going through phone records and look into Cunningham Construction." He picked up the shirt he'd found while raiding apartments and tossed it to Ben.

CHAPTER 18

The lights in the motel room were off but the sun lit up the cheap, sheer curtains that hung in the window. Below the windows, hot, dry air blew out of the heater built into the outside wall, forcing the curtains to dance in the artificial breeze and causing bright January sunlight to flash into the room. Specks of dust and other materials floated in and out of the stream of sunlight, invisible to the eye when they weren't illuminated.

Arash Abbasi sat on the edge of the one queen sized bed with a cellphone in his hand, waiting on the call he knew was coming any moment. On the small round table by the window were several guns and a closed brown leather satchel that held a passport, a change of clothes and enough cash to get him out of the country. He stared at the bag, contemplating using it to get away. He had bank accounts in three countries and could disappear easily.

The contract had been lucrative but had now turned too dangerous and he wanted out. The client was pushing back on the final payment that would allow him to pay his team then disappear for another year until he decided to work again.

The phone rang in his hand and he waited until the fourth ring to answer. He pressed the button and raised it to his ear without saying anything and just listened. As the caller spoke, Abbasi nodded his head as if the person on the other end could see him.

"This was not part of the contract," Abbasi said. "We were not to meet again."

He listened more, still nodding.

"I understand," he hung up the phone and walked to the window. Pulling the curtain back he looked out over the drained kidney shaped swimming pool below, the strip mall lined with stores selling alcohol, hookahs and lottery tickets across the street and in the distance, the smoke coming from the United States Capitol Building.

Turning to the table, he grabbed the handle of the brown satchel and paused. He'd never backed out on a contract before. Going into it he knew the risks were great, but the client hadn't anticipated the failure. The meeting could only mean a change in the terms of the deal. It was rare to meet a client face to face once, and this would be the second time. The chances of being seen or caught on surveillance cameras increased greatly.

He considered going to the meeting and putting a bullet in the head of the client and walking away with the money he'd received, half of the contracted amount. There would be far less left after paying his team, but they would be done.

He released the satchel and picked up the two automatic assault rifles and a Beretta nine-millimeter and put them into a green duffle that hung on the back of one of the two chairs.

CHAPTER 19

The roof of the building in Buzzard Point was littered with debris from the former moving company warehouse below as well as with beer cans, fast food cups and bags, more than a few used syringes. There was a campfire that had been built and burned at one point before his team had added security to the building and surrounding field when they bought the land and structure through a small management company based out of Richmond that was owned by them.

It was the third building Grace had built up for his team over the years. Different factors weighed in to the decision to move, the biggest being getting discovered. The smallest being the paranoia that was always present in the back of his mind. He was protective of his team, his only family, and wanted to watch out for them.

Grace used the roof to clear his mind and work through details that he otherwise couldn't do with his team around to distract him. The view of downtown across the water was calming to him as well as a reminder of what he'd accomplished in 16 years.

He sat on the edge of the roof, his feet hanging off the side three floors up, and watched the smoke still floating over the Capitol. Occasionally a siren could be heard and police and military helicopters were a constant sight as the mess was getting cleaned up, the bodies of the soldiers, agents and policemen pulled from the rubble. Teams were using sonar to try to find any survivors from the Special Forces teams but none had been found.

He was 24 years old when Jeffrey Morton had first approached him and 26 before he decided to join the NSA. By then Derek Arrington's predecessor had died of a heart attack from the stress of the job as well as from the overdrinking and lack of sleep caused by the job. It was Arrington's calmness that sealed it, compared to the hyper state of Jeff Morton, showing him that you could be in that world without being overtaken by it.

Three days earlier he'd made the phone call that would change his life forever and now he waited for the man that would make that happen.

He had sat in the back pew of an old wooden Methodist church in Mississippi. The bench was hard and cold as winter air found its way into the building. It was only used for baptisms and special events now; the new church was down the road and made of brick, glass and granite, a monument to the money that flowed into the coffers every Sunday morning.

The tall black man walked in and sat beside him. He could smell the hint of expensive cologne worn behind the man's ears.

"So you've decided?" Arrington said.

"Yes, sir."

"You know what it means, all of it?" Arrington said. "The secrecy, the danger."

"I do."

"Any questions?" Arrington said.

"Yeah. What's next?"

"There's a car waiting outside for you," Arrington said. "It will take you to a private airstrip where a plane will transport you to the farm. You'll be there until you're ready for us." The Central Intelligence Agency maintains a large area of land called The Farm near Williamsburg, Virginia used to train its clandestine operators.

"And after that?"

"After that you'll work with several other teams to prepare you," Arrington said. "Then you'll come back to me. If at any time any one of the people training you informs me you aren't making it, you'll be dropped off at a train station with a one-way ticket wherever you want to go."

"Won't happen."

"I like your confidence," Arrington said. "You'll never come back here, you know."

"Fine with me. Nothing left for me here."

Derek Arrington nodded his head. He knew the young man's story well. His mother had died when he was only three and his father was doing a life sentence at Parcham Farm after killing a young mother and her children in a drunken car crash.

"Shall we?" The man stood.

They walked out the front door of the building. Two black cars were waiting out front with several men in black suits nearby. They stopped beside the first car.

"One more thing," Arrington said. "You're giving up

your identity. Nobody can be able to track you to your former self, starting right here, right now. You get to pick what you're called, unless you prefer we do that for you."

He looked around then up at the sign by the road then at the building they'd been in then back to the NSA director.

"Grace," he said.

"Okay. Is that a first name or a last name?" Arrington said.

"Just . . . Grace."

Arrington nodded. "I like it. Most of the guys go over the top." He opened the car door and let the newly named Grace in and closed the door. The window buzzed down.

"I'll see you soon," Grace said

"I hope so," Arrington said. "I have big plans for you."

Grace looked out the back window as the car pulled away. He looked at the tall man who'd just hired him to work as a spy for the National Security Agency and at the sign in front of the building behind him for Grace Emmanuel Methodist Church.

CHAPTER 20

Grace's phone vibrated and he glanced at the screen then turned and went back inside and down the stairs from the roof. He tapped the code into the keypad, and entered the room where Ben Murray was working.

"What is it?" Grace said.

"I'm going through call histories for the Secret Service officers while researching that construction company you found the shirts for," Ben said.

"Multi-tasking? You might have to show the rest of the team what that is," Grace said.

"I've found several more matching numbers," Ben said.

"You trace them?"

"Sure did," Ben said. "And one is still pinging."

"What?" Grace said.

"It's active and on the move right now," Ben said. He pulled up a map on the larger of the two flat screens connected to his computer. A red circle would update every few seconds as it moved through Washington DC. At it's latest refresh it was tracking down Massachusetts Avenue past the rows of embassies.

Grace pulled his phone, dialed then spoke when Netty answered. "Two fast cars, ready for anything, leaving in two minutes." He hung up.

He walked to a shelf on the other side of the room and grabbed some equipment and put it on Ben's desk.

"Gonna need you to stay here," Grace said. "We're going to go find that phone. Here's an earpiece and a radio. Be on with us to tell us where to go."

Grace walked out of the room and took the stairs down two at a time. As he reached the garage, Netty and Avery were already pulling a pair of cars outside.

"What's up?" Holden said.

"We're going hunting," Grace said.

Grace walked over to the red Cadillac sedan and climbed in the passenger seat beside Netty.

"You know I hate red cars," Grace said.

"Yup," she said.

Holden and Corbin were in the backseat. Netty hit the gas and started down the dirt trail away from the building. Behind her a Mercedes E350 with Avery at the wheel followed, Chip beside him and Levi in back. The cars hit the paved road, turned left and accelerated.

"Head to northwest, Embassy Row," Grace said. He tapped the button on his radio. "Ben, you get wired yet?"

"I did," Ben said.

"Is the signal still on the move?"

"It is," Ben said. "Took a right on Nebraska, headed north."

Grace glanced to his left to see if Netty heard. She

gave a slight nod and sped up.

"Ben, see if you can patch into the city traffic cameras," Grace said. "I want to know what car to look for before we're right on top of it."

"Will do," Ben said.

Grace's body slammed into the passenger door as Netty took a hard left, swearing out loud as she did.

"What the hell?" Grace said. "We need to be going the other direction."

"Everything near the mall is shut down because of the explosion," Netty said. "It'll be faster to cross the river."

"When is it ever faster to go into Virginia?" Grace said.

"Just trust me," she said.

"Stay up with us, Avery," Grace said.

"I'm right behind you, Chief," Avery said. "She's not gonna lose me."

The cars merged onto 395 and crossed into Virginia then exited and headed up the Potomac on the George Washington Memorial Parkway past the Pentagon and Arlington Cemetery. She led them onto Highway 66 and across the Roosevelt Bridge back into Washington DC.

"Through downtown, really?" Grace said.

She took the E Street exit on the left then turned right to get onto Rock Creek Parkway. A line of cars was stopped to make the difficult turn across traffic. Netty put the car far left into the empty oncoming lane, her right hand on the horn. Avery followed. At the front of the line she cut off a Miata and made the right onto the Parkway.

"Ben, where is it?" Grace said.

"Still headed up Nebraska in traffic," Ben said. "Just got into the cameras and am waiting for the phone signal to hit the intersection at Connecticut."

"Big intersection, might not be able to ID which car," Grace said.

"I'll compare to the cars at the next corner," Ben said.

Netty had them speeding up Rock Creek Parkway then took the right exit onto Beach Drive. The curving two-lane road kept them right through the middle of the long park. She would move left into the oncoming lane of traffic to pass cars that got in her way. Without notice she cranked the wheel and turned right onto Blagden Avenue

"Where are you going?" Grace said. "You're headed east."

"So are they. They're just going the long way around," Netty said. "They're probably following a GPS that keeps them on primary roads. We can close the distance using the secondary roads."

"Grace," Ben's voice came into the team's ears. "The cellphone signal turned right on Military. Comparing to the cars at the last light it looks like it's a white Range Rover with dip plates."

"Shit," Grace said. "Had to be a diplomat. What country?"

"Looking it up . . . "

"What are the first two letters?" Grace said.

"DM," Ben said.

"Double shit," Grace said. "Iran. Okay. Let me know if they turn. We're headed east on Blagden. You can tap into the GPS on my phone to track us."

"Already did," Ben said. "The Range Rover will hit 16th in a few minutes if they keep moving. You won't be far behind if you hang a left on 16th and get north as fast as you can."

Netty glanced at the Mercedes driven by Avery behind her then hit the gas and began passing every car. Cars swerved right to avoid hitting her head on, a taxi went off the road and up into the trees.

"Just got a visual at 16th," Ben said. "The Rover turned north, but I don't think it's alone."

"What do you mean?" Grace said.

"There were two other SUVs following when it made the right onto Military, and they're still in tow," Ben said.

"Dip plates on the SUVs?" Grace said.

Netty ran the stop sign at 16th and turned left to head north.

"Negative, running them now . . .." There was a pause as the analyst put the tag numbers through the computer to find the owner. "Rentals. Both dark grey Suburbans, tinted windows."

"Okay. We might have shooters," Grace said. "How far back are we?"

"Only a few blocks now," Ben said. "They're stopped at a red light at Holly. You should be almost on them by them time the light turns green."

Grace scanned the split four-lane road ahead of them that ran through an upscale neighborhood. Large colonial red brick and new construction modern homes lined the right side of the road facing Rock Creek Park.

"I see them," Netty said.

She let off the gas and moved into the right lane behind a minivan.

"Avery, back off a little," Grace said. "Don't want to look like we're together. Let's just hang back and see where this parade takes us."

Netty kept four to five car lengths behind the grey Suburbans and Avery another few cars behind her. The white Range Rover led them north into Maryland and turned right onto Colesville Road through Silver Spring.

They continued northeast for 15 minutes until they were into the outer suburbs where strip malls and neighborhoods were more spread out.

"Where are you going?" Grace said. He watched out the windows at the gas stations and box stores as they drove past.

"Chief, look," Netty said.

Grace turned forward and saw the trailing Suburban signal then turn right off of the main road.

"Want me to follow?" Avery said from behind them.

"No, let's stick together," Grace said. "Hopefully just means less people to deal with."

Another mile down the road and the Range Rover turned right, the remaining Suburban following it. Netty backed off and took the turn. There were far fewer cars to hide behind on the smaller road.

"See why I hate red cars?" Grace said. "Too easy to spot."

Netty hit the brakes as the Suburban in front of them stopped, leaving only thirty feet in between. The Range Rover kept moving.

"What the fuck," Grace said. He pounded his hand on the dashboard. "Okay. Go around. Punch it."

She did as she was told and put the pedal down on the powerful V8 engine in the Cadillac. Just as the car began accelerating and she started moving into the left lane to pass the SUV, all four doors of the Suburban opened and men climbed out and raised guns at the front of the Cadillac.

"Shit!" Netty stopped hard and everyone inside the car ducked as they worked to get their weapons out.

The first bullets hit the windshield and Grace covered his face in anticipation of the shattered glass. Instead of traveling through the windows, the gunshots caused a series of loud thuds. Grace looked up and saw the shots striking the glass and stopping.

"It's armored?" Grace said.

"How do you like red cars now?" Netty said.

"Go!" Grace said. "The glass won't hold much longer." The spider webs of cracks were already beginning to appear as more bullets struck them.

Netty sat up and pressed her foot to the floor. The rear tires of the sedan squealed as they took off. One of the gunman dove to the right to avoid being hit and she struck a second man square on, his body rolling over the top of the car. Holden turned in his seat and watched the man hit the ground behind them as the remaining men fired at the Cadillac.

"Avery, you back there?" Grace said.

"I'm a block over," Avery said. "We saw it start to go down and made a turn to get around in front to help. We'll be there in a minute."

"We got through," Grace said. "Let's just catch up to the Range Rover."

The sound of crunching metal and screeching tires came through the radio earpiece.

"Avery, what's going on?"

CHAPTER 21

As Avery watched down side streets to cut back over and help the rest of the team, the second grey Suburban came up behind the Mercedes he was driving, moved to the right, and then bumped the rear corner of the large black car. Avery spun his wheel left to try to compensate, but it was too late and the German sedan was sent spinning. As it came around to face the Suburban, the rear end crashed into a car parked on the side of the road and the airbags exploded open into their faces then collapsed.

The engine died and Avery was pushing the start button over and over to try to get the motor to turn over again. The Suburban stopped 15 yards from them.

"Everybody out," Avery said. "Let's take them down."

Chip already had his rifle up and aimed out the front window, squared on the driver of the large SUV ahead of them.

"Go. I'll cover," Chip said.

Avery rolled left out of the car and dropped behind his door as Levi went out the right side from the back seat and around to the other side of the car they'd crashed into.

"Okay, Chip," Avery said. "Get out."

"Nah, I'm fine right here," Chip said. "I have a bead on them."

"Chip, godammit, get out of the car," Avery said.

"I can't," Chip said.

Avery looked across the driver's seat at Chip Goodson. The sniper held his rifle up to his shoulder, the front supports resting on the dashboard of the Mercedes. His left hand was covered with a deep crimson liquid.

"Where's the blood from?" Avery said.

"Not sure," Chip said. "But I can't move. We gotta get through this first."

"Shit," Avery said. "Grace, you there? We've been hit. Chip is hurt. We need help."

No answer came from the radio.

"Looks like it's you and me, Levi," Avery said. "You ready for this?"

"Sure," Levi said.

"Sure?" Avery said.

"Yeah, sure," Levi said.

The doors of the Suburban opened and two men began climbing out. Chip squeezed the trigger on his rifle and sent a round off that put a small hole in the windshield right in front of him in the Mercedes and then into the black combat boot coming out of the driver's door of the SUV forty-five feet away. As the driver's foot hit the ground the ankle buckled and the man fell to the ground screaming. A second round to the head silenced him.

The front passenger was out and moving towards the Mercedes and began firing with an M-4 assault rifle. Bullets were hitting the door in front of Avery then the shooter turned right as he heard a pistol firing to his side. Levi was running down behind the row of parked cars to Avery's left. Avery leaned out with his Sig Sauer pistol and put a round into the neck of the shooter and watched the body fall.

"Two down," Avery said.

"I see movement in the back seat," Chip watched through the scope on his sniper rifle.

Men got out either side of the Suburban in full tactical gear and body armor, rifles raised, and began firing as soon as they were clear of their doors. One man turned to track Levi and the other moved towards the Mercedes. Avery could hear Levi firing at the shooters but every time he tried to get out from behind the door to take a shot, another burst of bullets struck the car.

"Chip, can you see him? Can you get a shot off?" Avery said. He turned and looked into the car and saw Chip's chest and head slumped over the rifle. Glass from the shattered windshield covered him.

"Dammit!" Avery stood up and jumped from behind the door and began running at the man shooting at him. His Sig aimed and unloading as he ran. The man tried to point his rifle at Avery, but his body was being thrown backwards by the force of the .45 caliber bullets striking him square in the Kevlar vest he was wearing. Bulletproof vests keep the shots from going through but don't do anything to absorb the blunt force of a large caliber round as it slams into you. As Avery got closer, the shooter fell backwards onto the ground. Avery ran up and kicked the M-4 away from the man and pointed his pistol into the balaclava covered face.

The other shooter saw what was happening and turned away from looking for Levi and aimed at Avery. Before he could get a round off, Levi stood from behind a pickup, aimed and fired. It took only a fraction of a second for the Federal .45 caliber 230-grain ammunition to travel from Levi's weapon into the side of the man's head. The hollow point round left a large hole on the other side of his skull before the man hit the ground.

Levi heard a car engine and turned his pistol toward it to see the red Cadillac speeding up the road then turn and slide to a stop. Avery still stood over the final gunman, his pistol aimed at the man's face.

Holden and Levi came up on either side and began to put zip ties on the man's hands.

"Put it down now, Avery," Grace said. "We have him."

"He killed Chip," Avery said.

Grace looked over at the Mercedes Benz then at the row of houses. He saw at least three people filming them with cellphones out their windows.

"Not like this, Avery," Grace reached out and put his hand around the still warm barrel of the Sig Sauer and held it until Avery opened his hand. Grace turned to step away and Avery brought his right leg back and kicked the man in the groin.

"Feel better?" Grace said.

"No," Avery said.

Grace pulled out his phone and dialed then waited for an answer then spoke, "We need clean up."

CHAPTER 22

Ben Murray stared at his computer screen, avoiding looking over at Grace. "The diplomat plates were stolen."

Grace sat in a chair in the far corner of workroom at their building in Buzzard Point. He was leaned back as far as the chair could go, tossing a football into the air, each time it flying up in a spiral then stalling and coming back down to this chest. He hadn't said anything in nearly half an hour.

"A friend at the State department just confirmed, and the burner phone went dark just as the shooting began," Ben said.

"It was all a set up to draw us out," Grace said, his voice barely audible over the hum of the fans from the large computers Ben had set up around his desk. "And it worked," he threw the football again then caught it. "What about the Range Rover?"

"Range Rover has had that body style for a few years. Twenty-four white vehicles of that model are registered in the District, another 40 or so in Maryland and Virginia," Ben said. "I'll check for reports of any that have been stolen, but don't know where it'll get us."

"Thanks," Grace said.

"What now?" Ben said.

"We keep looking," Grace said.

"What about Chip?" Ben said.

Grace leaned forward to look over at Ben then leaned back in the chair and threw the ball into the air. "Chip's dead. We keep working."

"Just like that?" Ben said.

"Yeah, just like that," Grace said. "It isn't that we didn't like him. We did. We were all friends with him. He was the best damn weapons person I've ever known. But you don't take time to grieve when enemies are out there. We're not running a damn daycare here, people get hurt and people die."

Grace's cellphone rang. He answered.

"What the hell happened?" Arrington said.

"We were targeted," Grace said. "Won't happen again."

"Well, thanks to your shootout, everyone here knows you aren't sitting around doing nothing," Arrington said. "If you show your faces in public again, it had better be to arrest or kill the people responsible for this."

The line went dead.

"Doesn't sound like that went well," Ben said.

"It didn't," Grace said.

The door opened at the far end of the room and Holden walked in. He looked over at Grace then turned and went to Ben's desk. "Here's the ten cards and photos." He handed

Ben the white cards with all of the fingerprints of the men from the ambush, including the one they'd apprehended.

"Thanks, Holden," Ben said.

Holden glanced back over at Grace then began walking to the door.

"How's everyone downstairs?" Grace said.

The tall man stopped short of the door and looked at the floor then finally over at his boss. "Shitty," Holden turned and left.

Grace looked back at Ben. "Run the prints. Tell me you have something, anything, else for me."

"Well, actually, I do," Ben said.

"Show me," Grace threw the football into the wall and watched it bounce off the red brick and slam into an unused table then walked over to Ben.

Ben moved some windows on his screen and pulled up a website. "Cunningham Construction, same as the work shirts you found in the officer's apartments. I looked into contracts for work on the Capitol and they came up."

"What kind of work were they doing?" Grace said.

"Running wires to increase the network capacity," Ben said.

"So they'd have needed to tear into walls," Grace said.

"Likely," Ben said. "People usually don't want the network wires running along the wall and floor."

"What do we know about Cunningham?" Grace reached and pulled a rolling chair over and sat down on it backwards, leaning forward onto the back of the chair.

"They're based out of Linthicum, Maryland. Smaller company, maybe 15 employees," Ben said. "They mainly use individual subcontractors under their own project managers. They got their clearance for secure government work less than a year ago."

"Less than a year and they got a contract on the Capitol building?" Grace said. "That seems pretty lucky."

"Maybe they have some good connections," Ben said.

CHAPTER 23

Netty drove the van while Avery slept in back and Grace sat in the passenger seat, his eyes pointed out the side window not looking at anything. It had been 18 months since he'd lost a member of his team and before that it had been two years. It was the nature of the work. The inherent danger that draws people to it, but that could also be their ending.

"Didn't want the rest of the team?" Netty said.

"Hmm?" Grace said. "Oh, no. I don't think we needed everyone for this. I just want to get a look around."

The van left the toll way and merged onto the beltway headed north. She took the off ramp for the Baltimore-Washington Parkway and slipped into the left lane and matched speed with other traffic. Forty minutes later they exited into Linthicum Heights and made a few turns and caught one red light before pulling up at the edge of the parking lot to a business park.

Grace turned to look at Netty in her green combat pants and flannel shirt left out to cover her sidearm. In the back Avery wore a white tank top.

"Netty, you're with me," Grace said. "Avery, get up front and keep eyes out." Even in a seemingly safe environment it was standard practice to have someone keep watch. Being stuck inside an unknown building and having shooters come in after you is never a position you want to be in.

Grace and Netty left the van and walked across the parking lot to the front door of the offices of Cunningham Construction.

"What do you think we'll find here?" Netty said.

"I don't know," Grace said. "Sometimes staring at a computer screen doesn't work as well as knocking on doors. Just keep your eyes open for anything."

He opened the door and let her in first. A middle-aged female receptionist sat at a desk in the corner of the front room, a small television was on showing the ongoing news from the National Mall.

"How can I help y'all?" she said. Grace could see her trying to size them up. He hadn't tried to cover the Glock on his side. He pulled out a folded leather case and flipped it open to show a badge.

"We're with Homeland Security," Grace said. "We just like to have a look around."

The woman's head tilted as she took in the information and tried to process it.

"Why would you need to look around here, sweetie?" she said.

"We're checking out all the companies that had access to the United States Capitol over the last six months," Grace said. "Just routine based on, well, based on recent events."

The woman glanced at the television then back to Grace.

"Oh, it's horrible, isn't it?" she said. "My son is in the Army. Thank God he's at Fort Bragg and wasn't . . .. All those families of the boys killed this morning, I just can't imagine…"

"Me either," Grace said.

"Just let me know if you need anything. I'm Mattie," she said. "Nobody's really in today, due to the explosion. We're a Christian company, you know. The owner thought people should be with their families."

"What about you?" Grace said.

"My son is my only family I have left and he's in North Carolina," she said. "I figured someone might as well be here to answer the phones."

"Well, we're glad you're here," Grace said.

"Sure enough, sweetie," she said. "You two have a look around and let me know if you need anything. Nothing to hide here."

Grace nodded then glanced at Netty and they worked their way through the hallway. The first door on the right was a small conference room with nothing but the wooden table and a huge whiteboard on the wall that had been wiped clean. The next room was a small office and he motioned for Netty to check it as he kept moving.

"There's coffee made if you two want any," the receptionist's voice came down the hallway. "Just help yourselves."

"Thanks," Grace said. He passed the open door to the break room on the left and smelled the coffee and was almost tempted to stop for some but kept moving. The next door was closed and he turned the handle but the door didn't move.

He looked left towards the front room. "Mattie, this

door on the left is locked. Can I get in here?"

Her head poked around the corner to see where he was.

"Oh, sweetie, that one sticks a little. Just put your shoulder into it a bit," Mattie said.

He turned the handle again and leaned into the door and with a pop it swung open and he stepped in. It was a larger office with a big mahogany desk facing him, papers neatly stacked on top. The walls were covered with photographs in mismatched frames on wood paneling. Grace went to the desk and flipped through the papers and glanced in the drawers. Everything was too well organized to be hiding something. He sat down in the leather chair and leaned back as he scanned the office. He could hear Netty opening and closing file drawers across the hall.

On the desk was a color photograph of the owner of the office he was in, standing next to a tall woman in a red dress, red hair flowing down over her neck. In front of them were six children. He turned and looked at the photos on the wall then stood and began inspecting each one.

There were the standard snapshots of ribbons being cut and hands being shaken. A few were from company picnics and celebrations. He saw Mattie the receptionist dancing at what looked to be a wedding. The next frame to the right held a black and white image of a group of men. It was a grainy enlargement from a film negative and printed along with a newspaper article. Looking down the wall at more than 30 framed images, he stepped back to his left.

He pulled his phone out and tapped the icon to activate the camera, rotated it sideways and squared it up to fill the screen with the first photograph and pressed the button. He continued along the wall, capturing each framed photograph. Back at the desk he did the same with several of the contracts and documents stacked in the center of the blotter.

Back in the hallway he saw Netty come out of the other office and followed her to the front.

"Mattie, thanks for your time," Grace said. "As I said, just routine."

"Anytime, sweetie," Mattie said. "If you need to talk to Mason just let me know." She gave Grace a business card. "I'll get you an appointment whenever you need."

"Thanks," Grace and Netty left and walked back to the van.

"Find anything?" Avery said.

"Just this," Netty handed Grace a folder that had been tucked inside her shirt. "A copy of the contract for the work on the Capitol, including the names of all the subcontractors used."

"Well done," Grace said. "You know, for a woman."

CHAPTER 24

The grey Suburban picked up Arash Abbasi walking down Jones Mill Road, the green duffel over his shoulder, three blocks from where the white Range Rover was left on a side street. In the affluent neighborhood it would be days before anyone noticed the luxury vehicle didn't belong there. After two miles of driving, the Suburban was abandoned in a parking garage in Bethesda, a block from the metro station where the four men rode the escalator underground. They used paper tickets to enter the station, which would be discarded when they reached the other end.

They stood away from each other on the platform and stepped onto separate cars when the red line train arrived. Ten stops later they exited the train at Union Station and kept distance between each other through the large atrium of the building. Security was heavy but was concentrating on passengers entering the building rather than leaving.

Abbasi's family had left Tehran in the middle of the night when he was ten years old. His father, Hamid Abbasi, was an employee at the Teymour Bakhtiari mansion, the final holding area for the American hostages from November 1980 until their release in January 1981, and had worked with the Americans during the final months to help them plan a rescue. When the hostages were released, those loyal to Ayatollah Khomeini began to hunt down anyone who had aided the United States.

From then on they were a family with no country, disillusioned by their government's actions and left helpless by America's inability to protect the people that had helped them try to rescue the hostages. After a short time hiding in border villages in Iran they made their way into Pakistan and spent two years in Karachi. As tensions grew between Pakistan and India, Hamid moved his family once again, making the long trip south to Bombay. In the population of over 15 million, they were able to keep to themselves without being noticed.

At 17 years old, Arash joined the Indian Territorial Army, a branch similar to the National Guard. He learned basic weapons and fighting techniques during weekend drills but wanted more. When he tried to enlist in the Indian Army, he was denied for the inability to prove his nationality and the Territorial Army began proceedings to have him discharged. He chose to leave India before risking being put in jail.

His training gave him an opportunity to join a private security firm in Dubai where his nationality didn't matter. Over time the security work turned into covert operations for the huge oil corporations that owned everything. On an assignment when he was 24 years old he killed his first man when the team he was working with was discovered stealing documents inside the mansion of an oil executive in Abu Dhabi. The silenced nine-millimeter bullet had entered the heart of the surprised security guard who found them. A second bullet went through his forehead.

It wasn't long before he realized he had a talent for leading as well as planning. He began to take contracts and hired some of the same men who he had trained with to work under him and collected a list of experts in firearms and explosives he could call on when he needed them. He slowly became the name to call when you needed something done quickly and discreetly and when money was not an issue.

Union Station was busy as the men worked their way through. Arash stopped and ordered a coffee and kept from watching where his men were. He knew each of them well and had no doubt that they would be exactly where they were supposed to be. After paying for the coffee, he walked out the front door of the building and across the lane of taxis and buses then over to the rows of cars parked across the street. At the far end of the aisle on the right, close to North Capitol Street, he saw the taillights of an SUV blink twice and he walked to it. The hatch opened as he approached and he placed his duffle in on top of the bags his men had been carrying then sat in the front passenger seat.

The green Ford Explorer backed out and headed away from the Capitol and made a wide loop through the city to avoid closed roads until they were finally headed south toward Buzzard Point.

CHAPTER 25

Grace dropped the folder on the table beside Ben Murray with the list of contractors taken from Cunningham Construction. Beside it he sat a large cup of coffee.

"I want all those names checked out and full backgrounds run," Grace said. "Every detail you can find."

Ben opened the folder and scanned the list as Grace walked towards the door.

"I'm not going to find anything," Ben said.

Grace stopped and turned to look at him. "Why?"

"These aren't real names," Ben said. "I mean, they're real names, but I really doubt it's their real names."

Grace walked back across the room and read the list over Ben's shoulder. "What do you mean?"

"See," Ben said. "Rick Blaine, George Bailey, John Chance, Roger Thornhill."

"No, I don't see," Grace said. "Enlighten me."

"They're all names of movie characters. Rick Blaine was Humphrey Bogart in *Casablanca*. George Bailey was Jimmy Stewart in *It's a Wonderful Life*. Roger Thornhill was Cary Grant in *North by Northwest*."

"Are you shitting me?" Grace said.

"No," Ben said. "I can look them all up if you want, but I recognize most of them."

Grace grinned. "See. You're already paying off your debt."

"Debt?"

"For the honor of working in this shithole," Grace said. "Get into the Capitol security system and track down video during the time frame these guys were working there. We need good screen grabs of each of them so we can run them through facial recognition."

"We have facial recognition software?" Ben said.

"No, but the CIA does," Grace said. "That reminds me, hack into the CIA facial recognition system, too."

"Okay, that should be . . . easy," Ben said. "And I got a name off of one set of the fingerprints."

"Which set?"

"The ones for the guy locked up in the basement," Ben said.

"Really?"

"I had partial matches on three systems with different names until I got a full match through Mabahith," Ben said.

"You hacked into the Saudi Arabian Secret Police's system?" Grace said.

"Wasn't that hard," Ben said.

"For you, maybe," Grace said. "What did you find?"

"His name is Efraim Khouri," Ben said. "Served for the Mabahith for three years before being arrested and held at 'Ulaysha Prison."

"Now you have my attention," Grace said. "Most people

who go into 'Ulaysha don't come out."

Grace went down the stairs to the main level then unlocked the door to the basement and locked it behind him. At the bottom of the steel stairs he hit the switch on his left and a row of lights came on down a hallway. The moving company that had owned the building had used the sublevel as deep storage for clients' items of value that didn't fit in a safety deposit box. The steel doors would withstand most small explosions to breach them. He went to the third door on the right and looked through the six inch by four inch opening.

"Efraim Khouri," Grace said. The man didn't move. "Formerly of the Mabahith." He thought he saw a slight twitch.

He hit the buttons next to the door to start the video camera recording the cell, unlocked the door and stepped in then closed the door.

"Why were you trying to kill my men?" Grace said.

Efraim Khouri didn't say anything.

"How did you get out of 'Ulaysha?" Grace said. The man's eyes closed. "Ahh, now we're getting somewhere. That reaction was practically a full sentence. How did you escape?"

"I did not escape," Khouri said. "I was released."

"Strange. There's no record of that," Grace said.

"The Mabahith are notoriously bad at keeping records," Khouri said. "They are not much for paper trails, as you might say."

"I can understand that, what with all the illegal detentions and civil rights violations," Grace said. "One thing I don't know, why were you locked up?"

Khouri returned to being silent.

"That's fine, doesn't matter," Grace said. "I'm more

concerned with your activities since your release than those before your arrest."

"I have nothing to say to you, Mr. Grace," Khouri said.

"First of all, it's just Grace. Second of all, I don't believe I ever introduced myself," Grace said.

"You are not the only one who has information." Khouri sat up and looked Grace in the eyes. "You work for the Special Collection Service but operate as a rogue unit to do the work your government deems too messy for their SEALs and Special Forces. If you care to remove the shackles from my wrists and ankles, we could have a more interesting conversation."

"Nah, I think I'll leave them on," Grace said. "So it's obvious you've done your research on me. What's your end game? After you killed me, what was next?"

"Would it not be more fun to wait and see what happens next?" Khouri said.

"How many of you are there?" Grace said.

Khouri lay back down on the cement bunk. "I grow tired of this conversation."

CHAPTER 26

Derek Arrington stood beside President Abrams and CIA Director Leighton in the ETTF and watched the video coming across the satellite from Al Jazeera Network's Middle East broadcast. Over the course of half an hour, three terrorist organizations had claimed responsibility for the bombing of the United States Capitol.

"What the hell do we do with this?" President Abrams said.

"Langley is going through all three to see if any chatter substantiates their claims," Leighton said. "There was nothing leading up to it, but maybe there's talk now."

"I don't buy it," Arrington said. "Of the three, only one has ever orchestrated an attack on U.S. soil. Another is thought to have been disbanded 18 months ago for lack of funding."

"So you're saying you think it's Al Qaeda?" Abrams said.

"It's the most likely," Arrington said. "Not that ISIL doesn't have the backing."

"There's still the possibility it was none of them," Leighton said. "It's rare we don't have any intel leading up to an attack, even if it is vague and incomplete."

"Great. A new terrorist organization that isn't even on our radar, Director Leighton?" President Abrams said. "That isn't comforting. Get me something." She walked away and returned to the table with the cabinet members.

Arrington pulled his phone out and dialed and waited for the voice on the other end. "You have anything there?"

"We brought one tango in from the shooting," Grace said. "Interesting past and he knew who I was."

"What nationality?" Arrington said.

"Saudi," Grace said.

"You suspect he could be Al Qaeda or ISIL?"

"His history could make him a prime recruit, but I don't have any reason to think he is," Grace said. "No reason to think he isn't, either."

CHAPTER 27

"Efraim Khouri was one of the subcontractors at the Capitol," Ben said. "I have video of him on several dates wearing a Cunningham shirt through the halls." On the computer screen the faces of six men appeared in black and white.

"The surveillance video from the Capitol?" Grace said. "You went through all of it already?"

"I was here all night," Ben said. "I have images for 14 men, and have identified these six. I was hoping a few more would come in, but the system is running slow."

"Tell me who they are," Grace said.

"We have Khouri, of course. The rest are different nationalities, German, Russian, even an Australian. Varying ages, backgrounds, but the differences pretty much stop there," Ben said. "They're all on lists of known terrorists. All of them are explosives and firearms experts. And they're all freelancers. Confirmed kills, targets and operations all over the world. These are bad, bad men."

"Still no clues to a larger organization or country," Grace said.

"Not on the surface, but crosschecking known sightings and associates around the world, one name keeps coming up," Ben said. "Arash Abbasi."

"Who's that?" Grace said.

"Another gun for hire, but he sees himself more of an entrepreneur. After a quick start in the Indian Territorial Army, it appears he started his own little terrorist company."

"They responsible for anything big?" Grace said. "I haven't heard the name before."

"Again everything is rumors and suspicion, but mostly one-off assassinations," Ben said. "Their favorite weapon seems to be C4."

"Not a very subtle approach," Grace said.

"It works," Ben said. "They've used it for car bombs as well as bringing down buildings on top of targets."

"Do we know if anyone other than Khouri is still in the country?"

"They were all together overseas at the same time and entered back into the U.S. within a week of each other."

"Where were they before?"

"London," Ben said. "They began coming over about a month before the contract on the Capitol began."

"So in London they were probably getting instruction on the contract," Grace said. "Can we trace their movement there?"

"No record of them in hotels or rental cars," Ben said. "None of them have credit cards. They were probably all holed up together off the grid."

"But then went very visible on their flights over here," Grace said. "Why not hide yourself getting into the country?"

"Maybe it was just too much trouble," Ben said. "The risk of being stopped with altered identification is high, especially at Dulles. They boarded flights at Heathrow, then they had six hours in the air for every intelligence organization in the states to notice the anomaly of so many bad guys on the same flight and have feds waiting for them."

"But if they're known terrorists," Grace said, "they should have been on no-fly lists."

"They are known but not by us," Ben said. "INTERPOL has a few of them flagged for activities in Eastern Europe, but most of their activities so far have been against individuals or companies that aren't necessarily friendly with the United States, so I guess we leave them alone. And as far as I can tell, none of them has left the U.S. yet."

"We know a few have been killed. I'll get photos of them to compare to the video stills. If the rest are still here, then why?" Grace said. "Is there a second target?"

"That's not even funny," Ben said.

"No, it isn't," Grace said. "When did Cunningham finish at the Capitol?"

Ben turned to his computer and began typing, moving windows around the screens.

"Looks like about two months ago," Ben said.

"That's plenty of time to wire another building," Grace said.

"Or they were told to wait here for further instruction . . ." Ben said.

"In case the operation failed," Grace said.

"Which it did," Ben said.

"Does Cunningham have any active contracts in the area right now?" Grace said.

Ben turned back to his computer and began going through files he'd retrieved from the office of the Architect of the Capitol. "Not on Capitol grounds."

"Get me their number in Maryland," Grace said.

Ben pulled up the website for Cunningham Construction and read the phone number off as Grace dialed his phone. He greeted Mattie on the other end of the line and had a short conversation then hung up.

"They have one other contract in the area right now," Grace said. "Asbestos and black mold removal at Walter Reed Medical Center's Building 18."

"Isn't that the building that shut down a few years ago?" Ben said.

"It is, but before demolition, they have to get rid of any contamination," Grace said. "It was actually an out-patient resident dormitory, not part of the main hospital campus. Not many people want to step foot in there until it's done. Which sounds like a great place to hide stuff."

CHAPTER 28

With their two cars out of commission, the team loaded up in the black Mercedes Sprinter van with Netty at the wheel. They all wore their Kevlar vests and had filter masks ready for entering the former hospital building once they got there. The garage door opened and the van pulled out and followed the tracks through the field to the street then turned left.

"Did you see that?" Levi said.

"I did," Grace said. "Netty, circle back around but stay a couple blocks away from the building."

The van turned right while Levi and Grace watched out the side window at the green Ford Explorer they'd seen parked on the street across from their building. Just as they began to lose sight of it the driver's door opened.

"Step on it, Netty," Grace said. The van sped up and she made another right. "One more block then stop. We can't get too close in this whale. They'll see it a mile away."

Grace dialed his cellphone as they climbed out of the van, already dressed for battle. The phone rung four times before Ben Murray answered and Grace began talking to him.

The team checked their weapons as they left the van behind. Each had their Sig Sauer assault rifle and sidearm with extra magazines of ammunition for each. After a few short commands from Grace, the team separated and groups of two began running down the road. Holden and Corbin took the first corner while Levi and Avery were at a sprint to get to the next street. Netty stayed with Grace. She was still the newest and greenest of the team, and although Grace knew she could handle herself in sticky situations, he wanted to watch over her. They headed back the direction they'd come from in the van then turned left to head towards the building at Buzzard Point.

Netty and Grace reached the northeast corner of the lot and took cover behind a deserted car. He knew the other two teams would already be in position. Grace raised his rifle and used the scope to scan the exterior of their building when his radio popped to life in his ear.

"I count four," Avery said.

"Copy," Grace said. "Only have eyes on two from here. Looks like they have AR-15's."

"Same here," Holden said. "Definitely AR-15's. Nothing you can't get at a Virginia gun show."

As Grace watched the men through his scope he thought about Chip for the first time. He knew the sniper could have taken the targets out quickly and easily with no threat to the rest of his team. Most of them were proficient and long range but not with the speed Chip had of acquiring and firing on multiple targets.

"What's the play, chief?" Avery said.

"We watch and wait," Grace said. "Copy that?"

He received confirmation from the team.

"Tango has gained entry," Holden said. "Repeat, front door has been breached. All four tangos have entered the building."

"What about Ben?" Netty said. "He's still in there."

"He'll be fine," Grace said. "These guys only want one thing or they'd have come in while we were still there."

They waited.

It took only seven minutes. Four men had entered the building and five came out and made their way through the field and climbed into the Ford Explorer.

"Take cover, they're passing."

The three team members dropped to the ground behind cars and trees to be blocked as the green SUV sped past them then turned and went out of view.

"Netty, get to the van but don't come back home until I tell you," Grace said. "Holden and Corbin, you're in first. Watch for anything suspicious, these guys like to make things go boom."

As Netty turned and began to run back to the van, Grace moved towards the building and in his peripheral vision saw the other two teams come in to view. As they reached the door, Holden went in first to look for explosives the terrorists may have left behind. Grace went in after him. At the back of the garage bay Grace found the door to the downstairs detention area open and the lights on. He continued upstairs where the secure door to the workroom was open and all of the lights still on.

He worked his way through the room watching for

tripwires and saw only the tables with computers just as he'd left it with Ben.

"I'll huff and I'll puff . . . ," Grace said.

A five-foot wide section of the brick wall behind him began to move, swinging into the room on a hinge. Once it had opened Grace looked into the open area as the steel door to the panic room unlocked and opened inward to reveal Ben Murray standing there, a wall of video monitors showing all of the rooms of the building inside the safe area.

"Was that fun?" Grace said.

"Screw you," Ben said.

"Missed you, too," Grace said. "Guess you made it into the panic room in time?"

"Barely. I got downstairs and opened the door and turned on the lights to detention just like you said," Ben said. "I left the key on the hook at the bottom of the stairs. But as I was running up the stairs I heard them come through the front door. I wasn't even sure the brick wall was back in place."

Grace stepped into the panic room and looked at the wall of monitors. "You get them all on video?"

"Sure did," Ben said. "Audio, too. Clear enough to hear one of them call another Arash."

"Arash Abbasi was with them?" Grace said. "Dammit. Maybe we should have taken them down."

"Why didn't you?" Ben said. "These aren't nice guys."

"That would have been the short play," Grace said. "We don't know what they have planned next or where they may have planted C4. We stop them now and we might be leaving a building wired to blow with the dialing of a wrong number."

"And we still don't know what they're up to, because

they're gone," Ben said.

The rest of the team came into the room.

"Holden," Grace said, "Is the tracker in place?"

"Sure is," Holden said.

"Tracker?" Ben said. "You put a tracking device on their car?"

"Not only on their car, but while Efraim Khouri was knocked out from the sedatives we gave him, a tracker was put in the sole of his shoe."

CHAPTER 29

It was 9:30pm on the side street next to the old Walter Reed Medical Center. Grace and Levi had taken first watch and sat in a late 1990's model Honda Accord with tinted windows. The tracker placed on the Ford Explorer had led them straight to where they had expected to find Arash Abbasi, Building 18. The notorious structure had been the end for the hospital complex. In 2007 newspapers and news channels began reporting on the horrendous conditions inside the facility, with black mold and rat droppings found everywhere. Congress saw to the closing of the building and the reestablishment of the medical center up the road in Bethesda in new facilities. Since then the buildings had sat unused and empty, waiting to be cleared out for demolition.

Building 18 sits just across the street from the main entrance to the Walter Reed complex and had been outpatient military housing. Once cleaned out and torn down the lot was to be used for a new fire station for the District of Columbia

"We can't see a damned thing from here," Grace leaned his head back against the headrest in the drivers seat while Levi sipped coffee and stared at the building. A black box sat on the floor between his feet with the dimmed screen showing the location of the Explorer only a couple hundred feet away in the parking garage below the abandoned building.

Grace's early days with the NSA had been spent infiltrating foreign government buildings and embassies to put eavesdropping equipment in place, the primary purpose of the Special Collection Service. Derek Arrington always had other ideas for him and once he'd proven his abilities he moved him into a new role at the agency, one they hadn't ever officially had before. By nature the NSA is a peacekeeping organization. They listen to our enemies, and even our allies, to ensure the safety of Americans. But sometimes things are heard that require action, things that aren't right for the military to handle. Smaller, discreet operations are necessary to take down a threat even before it can completely materialize: a suspected coup in a third world country that could destabilize an entire region the United States has ties to or the black market purchase of plutonium by a combatant country that isn't known to have a nuclear program. That's where Grace's team came in. Fast, quiet resolution to a problem.

While taking lives wasn't always their mission, it was a side effect of their work. In a perfect world everybody was left standing on both sides. But their world wasn't perfect and the enemies tended to shoot first. His team was the best at what they did, but Grace worked to insulate them from the inner workings of the NSA and CIA. Still, the entire team accepted their fate when they signed on. Histories, and criminal records, were erased. Your past was no longer your own. If captured in an incriminating position, their orders were to kill or be killed.

"I think my coffee just froze," Levi said. The engine was off to avoid the warm exhaust alerting anyone to their presence. Plenty of cars were parked along the street with numerous apartments and townhomes in the area. They both wore cold weather gear that would keep them alive to negative 20 degrees but was designed with the idea that the wearer would be in motion and creating body heat. The cardboard ring around the coffee cup did nothing to help the liquid inside from becoming solid.

"Then lick it," Grace said.

Levi put the cup in the cup holder between the seats then looked back out the window. "We have movement."

Grace lifted his head and watched as the green Explorer pulled out from the alley where the ramp to the garage was located and drove past them headed south on Georgia Avenue.

"We gonna follow them?" Levi said.

"No. It looked like there were only two people in the car when they went under the streetlight," Grace said. "They could be looping the block to see if they're being watched. The other three men might be watching for any cars to follow. Hand me the tracker."

Levi picked the box up and handed it to Grace, who tapped a button to switch sources.

"Khouri, or at least Khouri's shoe, is still in the

building," Grace switched back to watch the tracker from the SUV and gave it back to Levi.

"It stopped a few blocks down," Levi said. He pulled his cellphone out and opened the maps application and scanned the area for businesses. "Looks like they're on a pizza run."

"Makes sense. You don't call for delivery when you're hiding out in an asbestos lined deserted government building," Grace said.

They sat and watched the stationary blip on the screen as each exhale of breath fogged the air.

"It's moving again," Levi said. "U-turned on Georgia and should be coming past us in a few seconds."

The two men waited until the lights passed them and watched the green Explorer turn back into the alley behind the condemned building and the taillights faded from view as it went underground.

"I don't know about you, but I'd really like to see what's going on in there," Grace said.

Levi raised his arm and checked the time on his Ironman digital watch. "9:42. I believe Corbin is the big winner tonight."

"Everyone bet on how long before I'd go in?" Grace said.

"We did," Levi said. "I lost 30 minutes ago."

"Nice," Grace said. "We only got here 40 minutes ago. They're going to be busy eating. It's the best time to get in." He opened the door.

Earlier in the day when they'd taken the car from the impound lot in Northeast DC Avery had disconnected all interior lights and put in a quick kill switch for the brake lights. Grace opened the trunk and pulled out a small pouch and put it in his coat pocket.

"Am I coming with you?" Levi said. "Or are you a loner tonight?"

"What's the Lone Ranger without Tonto?" Grace said.

"One of these days I'm going to human resources. I swear it, white man," Levi climbed out the other side.

Grace tapped out a message on his phone to Ben to watch the trackers from the office to make sure nobody went mobile while they went in to take a look. The temperature was in the teens with no wind as they worked their way across the street, avoiding the arcs of the streetlights on the pavement. Levi fell in 20 feet behind Grace, leaving enough distance to see what went on in front of him to have time to react. They didn't have their radios and relied on hand signals to communicate. Grace had his Glock and Levi had his Walther P99. Both had silencers mounted to the barrels.

Grace watched Levi go around the corner at Butternut Street then stopped to watch the perimeter for any motion. With only five terrorists inside he felt they didn't have the manpower to have a watch on the whole building and the streets surrounding it. Seeing nothing he continued and went into the alley. He knew Levi would go all the way around the building and they'd meet at the far corner. It wasn't anything they had to discuss or plan; they both just knew that was how they'd approach the urban building.

Grace kept to the far side of the alley away from the ramp to the underground parking for Building 18 in case anyone saw him. In this neighborhood it was not uncommon for people to cut through side streets and even yards. As he approached the back end of the building he saw a shadow at the corner of the building and paused. Levi stepped out of the narrow opening between the building and a house built feet away from it.

Grace turned and headed back towards the ramp, staying close to Building 18 now to cut the chance of being seen from a window. Levi now followed him from 20 feet back. At the short wall above the ramp he looked down to watch for any lights and saw none. He motioned with his left hand that he was going down. Levi went around the outside of the retaining wall then did a 180 and proceeded down into the darkness below the building. Grace waited ten seconds and when he heard nothing followed him down.

The lightless garage was the top of three levels. No electricity ran to the building and the stillness of the structure was palpable. There are noises that buildings make, that you generally don't pay any attention to, humming of air conditioners, the buzz coming from florescent lights. They both reached up and pulled the black balaclavas down over their faces to keep their faces from reflecting any light that might reach them, possibly giving them away. Once all the way down the ramp they made the left turn into the garage. A small amount of ambient light filtered in from the streetlights above through the metal grates at ground level that let exhaust fumes escape. Levi went left and Grace right as they worked themselves through the garage, feet moving slowly to keep from tripping over cement parking medians or accidentally kicking a discarded soda can. Once they both reached the far wall and the steel door that would take them to the stairs they regrouped.

Grace motioned he'd go in first and Levi didn't argue. Grace grabbed the handle and slowly pushed the heavy thumb latch down. A quiet "clunk" was heard as the bolt slid back into the door. He pulled and Levi grabbed the edge of the door with his gloved left hand to make sure it didn't slam shut. Once open enough, Grace slipped through the gap. Levi went around the door and came in behind him and kept both hands on the rusted metal until it was rested back against the frame.

They followed their process of moving through the darkness, opening doors and closing them and pausing regularly to listen for noises until they reached the first floor then stopped when they heard the first signs of life. Voices came from one floor up, and flashes of light from a battery powered lantern splashed across the wall to the stairs. They both knew that as long as they could hear the voices, the chances of being heard were lower. It was when everything went silent they needed to really worry and pull their weapons.

The two men looked at each other and nodded. Grace began the ascent up the stairs, keeping his back to the wall to avoid casting shadows from the dancing light. With each step he could hear the voices more clearly and he knew that the five terrorists were not far away. He reached the point where his head would come up above floor level and moved very slowly, keeping his chin tucked to his chest to stop light from reflecting off his eyes, the only part of his face not covered by the balaclava. His head broke the plain of the stairs by five inches and he got his first look at the men on the second floor.

They sat on upside down plastic work buckets and the floor. The LED lantern was on the floor in the middle of their circle. Grace could smell the pepperoni and cheese pizza and the distinct odor of cheap domestic beer.

Good, he thought. Their reactions are slowed from drinking.

He went shape to shape, counting the bodies to account for all of the men they knew of.

He put his hand into his pocket and carefully brought out the black pouch he'd taken from the Honda, opened it, and pulled out a two by three inch square box that Holden had built out of high impact plastic then covered with duct tape and dirt. Grace leaned forward onto his knee on the third step down from the second floor and stretched his body out then reached his arm out and placed the box on the floor just around the corner from the stairs. He moved back down the stairs and the two men made their way back through the building, the parking garage and to the street.

"Did you just put a mic in there?" Levi said.

"I did. Holden put it together for me earlier," Grace said. He sent another message to Ben to begin monitoring the cellphone-based bug.

"There were more than five men in there, weren't there?" Levi said.

"Yup," Grace said. "I counted at least eight, could have been more in the shadows or sleeping."

CHAPTER 30

The morning light came through the east window of the third floor of Building 18. Arash Abbasi was already awake and going through the day's plans in his head. It had only been two days since he considered leaving the contract behind and getting on the next flight out of the country. In his opinion the mission had gone according to plan. He'd been hired to infiltrate the United States Capitol and plant the explosives that would be used to bring the House of Representatives to the ground. He wasn't hired to kill the president or Congress or the Supreme Court. His job was done. He'd handed the code to the detonator to his client in person. He stayed with his team in D.C. only to confuse the investigation that would follow. The first thing the FBI would do was search airline manifests for any foreign nationals that had left the country in the days and weeks preceding the explosion.

But his client didn't see it the same way and 50 percent of the money due to him was still in a holding account in the Cayman Islands. Nothing else would be transferred to him until the client was satisfied. The rules were changing and he had no choice but to follow if he wanted the rest of his money. He had eight men left that he had to pay, though he'd several times considered killing them and keeping the money for himself. It would be safer, cleaner. Eight men is a lot of opportunity for secrets to be spilled.

He heard heavy footfalls running up the cement stairs. He stood up from his blanket spread on the cold, linoleum floor to be ready for whatever news was so important to bother him. Efraim Khouri came to the door along with Ormand Baasch, a German mercenary Abbasi had come across while working a contract in Russia two years earlier. They stood outside the doorframe, waiting for him to speak first.

"What is it?" Abbasi said.

"We found something," Khouri said. He glanced to the tall man beside him. "Ormand found something."

"And what did you find, Ormand?" Abbasi said.

The German's English was flawless, having perfected the accent in his teens watching American television shows. The team came from six different countries so they spoke English to each other. "A bug. It appears to be a microphone hidden inside a taped up box."

Arash Abbasi turned and looked out the window, multiple layers of dirt and grime filtered the winter light. He had seen the shadow on the stairs the night before as his men talked and laughed and ate their pizza and the non-Muslims drank their beer. He had seen the shape of a head looking out over the edge of the stairs at them, the light from their electric lanterns casting enough of a glow to silhouette the shape against the slanted stairwell ceiling behind the figure. At the time he wasn't sure if it was a vagrant looking for his sleeping place for the night, a respite from the cold D.C. sidewalks, or something more nefarious. The thought had crossed his mind that it was the man who had taken his second in charge, Efraim Khouri, but he believed if it had been that man he wouldn't have come in and left quietly. Guns would have been fired and blood would have been shed.

He'd not alerted his men to the intruder, truly believing it had been one of the District's many homeless and not wishing to kill a man already at the lowest rung of the society in this country. To him it was better to leave alone the counterpart to the excess that America craved, an eyesore to the luxury car driving heathens. Though he didn't consider himself an Iranian anymore, choosing instead to relate as Persian, he did find truth in some of the Ayatollah's rhetoric.

"Thank you," Abbasi said. "Speak quietly to the rest of the men and inform them to keep their voices low. I'll be down in a moment."

The men left, confused at the lack of concern over being bugged. Abbasi had more important things on his mind. Breaking with every unwritten rule of their trade, he was to meet, face to face, with his client again. It was not something he wanted to do but it had been made clear it was a requirement of receiving the rest of his funds. Abbasi intended to demand more money if there was to be another act to their mission. If the increased fee was refused, he had decided to kill the client right there and be on an airplane out of the country within an hour. He grew restless, as did the men who followed him, sitting in hiding.

He turned from the window and went down the stairs where the men were staring at the small, duct taped box that sat on the floor beside the top of the stairwell to the next level down. Abbasi motioned to Khouri who joined him directly above the bug, and spoke in Farsi, a language he knew he had in common with Khouri.

CHAPTER 31

"Have you been up all night?" Grace walked into the workroom to find Ben Murray sitting at his desk, a row of empty paper coffee cups lined up to the edge.

"Most of it," Ben said. "I started getting the signal from your bug. Picked up several voices. I listened for a while but they weren't talking about anything of interest so I set up a voice activated recorder to kick on whenever there was anything other than ambient noise."

"Did it get anything?" Grace said.

"Shows activity a few times then more consistent at about six o'clock this morning for 20 minutes," Ben said. "But it sounded like Farsi so I haven't listened to all of it."

"Get it on a drive and I'll review it," Grace said. His training with the NSA and CIA had given him a level of comfort with understanding Farsi though he couldn't speak it well at all.

"I got ID's on a few more of the faces from the video, too," Ben said. "Their backgrounds are all in line with what we already have."

"I doubt you're going to find any tax accountants on there," Grace stopped to look at the faces matched with the details of their pasts. "That one," he pointed. "Saw him last night. Maybe some of the others. It was pretty dark."

A red light began to blink on the wall by the door and was accompanied by a buzzing sound.

"We have company," Grace said. "Pull up the exterior cameras."

Ben tapped some buttons and brought up the feed from the security system on the outside of the building. A black GMC Yukon was coming down the dirt drive from the street.

"That's unexpected," Grace turned and left the room and went down the stairs and hit the red button to open the garage door. The GMC pulled in and he closed the door behind it. With his hand on the grip of his Glock he stood behind the SUV as the back right door opened and Derek Arrington stepped out. Grace let his gun go and walked up to his boss. "What the hell are you doing here?"

"Nice to see you, too," Arrington said. "I needed out of the ETTF for a while and wanted to see what you've come up with. Looks like you haven't done much with the place."

Arrington began to follow Grace and saw Holden and Avery cleaning and packing weapons into large black cases.

"What are they up to?" Arrington said.

"Moving day is coming," Grace said. "Can't stay here anymore."

"Why?" Arrington said.

The men went upstairs and Grace and Ben briefed the

NSA director on the events of the last 24 hours, the men they had identified and the infiltration of their building by the terrorists.

"Arash Abbasi was in this building?" Arrington said. "And you let him go?"

"Yup," Grace said. "That's why we gotta leave Buzzard Point. The building is burned."

"Abbasi is wanted on at least a dozen charges in six countries," Arrington said. "And is obviously behind the attack on the Capitol, and he just walked in and out of your building?"

"He did," Grace said. "But we tracked him and have eyes on him as well."

"You should have apprehended or killed him," Arrington let his usual coolness fade while he paced the room.

"That would have slowed things down, not stopped them," Grace said. "If he's still here, and still has as many men with him as we think he does then there's another act. If we'd nabbed him yesterday we'd still be in the dark about what's happening. A man like Abbasi doesn't talk."

Arrington shook his head, his back to his top operator. "What have you gotten?" he said.

Grace knew Arrington was under pressure to show progress to the president.

"I was just about to listen to this morning's conversations, but what I do know is we have at least eight terrorists all holed up in DC. I don't know if they're awaiting orders or have already implemented them."

"Just find out," Arrington said. "Langley is at least ten steps behind you. We have a chance to shine on this one. Richard Graham is breathing down my neck and keeps pushing the president to shut you down."

"What? Why?" Grace said. "Did I ruffle his feathers that badly?"

"No idea. I think he's just trying to stay visible in the commotion to be noticed for a better placement in the future. I overheard him pushing to get read in on all security updates."

"You think he wants the CIA?" Grace said.

"CIA?" Arrington said. "Leighton is doing just fine."

"Yeah, but he's looking to retire by end of the year," Grace said.

"Where'd you hear that?" Arrington said.

"He told me a couple months ago when I was having dinner at his house," Grace said. "His wife wants them to relocate down to the coast in North Carolina."

"You had dinner at his house?" Arrington said.

"Sure. The salmon was incredible," Grace said.

Arrington just stared at Grace then moved on. "I don't know what Graham wants, I just know he's annoying the hell out of everyone."

"The Explorer is moving," Ben said. Grace and Arrington stepped over to watch the tracker on the large computer screen.

"What are you up to now?" Grace watched closely then dialed Netty's phone and she answered. "Anything else going on at the building?"

"The SUV left. Looked full," Netty was sitting in the Honda with Holden watching Building 18. "Several other guys left on foot and got in a white work van that was parked a block up Georgia Avenue."

"Sounds like everyone is on the move," Grace said. "If you can, follow the van and keep us updated. We're tracking the Explorer. If you even begin to feel like they've spotted you, abort and get the hell out of there as fast as you can." he hung up.

"So we have at least eight terrorists driving around Washington DC right now," Arrington said. "With no idea what they're planning."

"I call that job security," Grace said. "And I don't want to be sitting here if something goes down. Ben, get on comms. We're going mobile in the van." He turned to leave the workroom.

"Hey," Arrington said. "I'm coming with you."

"Nope. Can't put you in a situation that might turn dangerous," Grace said. "You should get back to Herndon."

"It wasn't a request," Arrington said. "You're in charge. I just want to be there."

Grace turned and looked at him. The man's black suit was tailored to fit perfectly. "Then you'd better change. Hit Holden's locker, you're about the same size."

The van left ten minutes later with Avery at the wheel and Corbin beside him. In the back sat Grace, Levi and Netty on the first row. Behind them Derek Arrington sat in green combat pants, shirt and bulletproof vest with his two security agents sitting on either side of him in their black suits.

"Well, this is fun," Grace said. He turned in his seat to talk to the men behind him. "If anything goes down, you three stay back. I don't care what your training was—this isn't what it was for. You two stay with him," he pointed at Arrington. "And keep him safe. Anything happens to him and I'm coming after you."

"I know how to handle myself," Arrington said.

"I'm not saying you can't. I'm saying you're not going to have to handle yourself on my watch," Grace said. "This is self-preservation. I don't want to break in a new boss."

CHAPTER 32

Avery listened to Ben over his earpiece and worked the van through the city to get within two blocks of the moving Ford Explorer. After the event that took the life of Chip Goodson he had no intention of putting the large black van where it could be spotted and targeted. Netty and Holden were staying well behind the work van, which was on a different route than the Explorer but headed the same direction.

"They're going to converge somewhere," Grace said. "And I'll bet you it's the target. No other reason to put them all in the open at once."

Ben's voice came through the earpieces they each wore. "The Explorer stopped on Connecticut. Netty reports the work van is on Beach Drive. They're on opposite ends of the zoo."

"Weird time for sightseeing," Grace said. "Avery, cut down Cathedral."

"The Explorer is on the go again," Ben said. "Traffic camera at the crosswalk showed two men exiting the vehicle and walking towards the zoo entrance."

The van turned sharply as Grace checked his pistol then grabbed a Seattle Seahawks jacket from below the seat and pulled it on over his bulletproof vest and zipped it up.

"Seahawks?" Arrington said.

"Yeah. Nobody pays attention to a Seahawks fan," Grace said. "If I wear a Redskins jacket then I look like a local. I wear a Cowboys jacket and I just look like an asshole."

Avery turned left and pointed the black van into a no parking zone as Grace jumped out the side door. "Stay moving but nearby." And he turned and jogged towards the zoo.

"What's he going to do without backup?" Arrington said.

"How long have you known Grace?" Avery said.

Grace slowed to a quick walk as he entered the zoo and watched the tourists ahead of him for signs of Arash Abbasi. Even in the middle of winter the free attraction brought in plenty of foot traffic during the day, which gave him enough people to blend into, but also made it harder to find someone.

"Grace, Netty said two men got out of the van at the other end of the zoo and are headed in," Ben said. "According to the tracker, one of them is Khouri."

"Thanks," Grace said.

"He knows what you look like," Avery's voice came through.

"Yeah, I know," Grace said. "The more the merrier. It's easier to spot four grown men walking around the zoo together than two and at least we have the location of one of them. Just keep an eye on the tracker."

"I can be there in three minutes," Avery said.

"No, you stay with the van and Arrington. I don't want to draw any added attention," Grace said. Ahead of him he saw two men disappear around the bend in the main walkway of the National Zoo. "I think I have visual." He went into a jog to close the distance since he knew the two men couldn't see him.

He got to the bend and regained a sightline to the two men and fell in 50 feet behind them, ready to stop if they turned to check if they were being followed. As he passed the next trash can he paused and looked in and pulled out a zoo map a tourist had thrown away then continued walking while holding the map in front of him.

Anyone paying attention would notice the two men walking along Olmsted Walk through the zoo without ever stopping to see any of the animal enclosures along the way. But everyone else there was too busy watching the zebras and elephants to see Arash Abbasi and his fellow terrorist. Grace kept up with them and closed the distance to thirty feet just as the two men made a left down one of the trails off the main route.

"Ben, where's Khouri now?"

"Still showing him standing still at the entrance to the zoo," Ben said.

"Good. Let me know if he moves," Grace said.

Abassi and the other man turned right onto the sidewalk that led into the great cats exhibit, the only entrance and exit for that area. Grace moved forward quickly to see which way they went around the circle then followed them to the left. He was now 20 feet behind them and stopped at each enclosure to lean on the railing and look at the lions and tigers as they were sleeping among the trees, showing no interest in entertaining the visitors. He would glance at the animals then to his left and keep moving.

More than halfway around the circle he saw the two men step into the small cat-themed café. Grace kept going to get to the corner just as they stopped at a table where a man wearing a hat sat with his back towards the entrance.

"Hey, asshole."

Grace turned at the voice behind him to see Efraim Khouri and another man standing there. The other man grabbed Grace's left arm as Khouri took his right and turned him away from where Abbasi was and walked him back the way he'd come. A hand went up inside his Seahawks jacket and pulled the Glock from its holster. He felt the barrel of the gun jam into his ribs.

"Come on, guys. I just wanted to see the tigers," Grace said. He struggled to keep his feet under him as they dragged him. A few tourists slowed down to look then kept moving.

"Trust me. You're gonna see the tigers. Shoulda killed me when you had the chance," Khouri said.

The man shoved Grace against the low wall of the tiger enclosure. A metal and wire screen was built up over the cement wall to avoid having people fall into the animal's area as had happened at several zoos around the country.

Khouri pulled Grace's hands behind his back as the other man grabbed his feet and they raised his 190 pound body and dead lifted it to head level then pushed him over the top of the screen. Grace grabbed the wire with his left hand as he fell, his feet dangling 15 feet above the water that separated the wall from the tiger's home. Khouri began to walk away and Grace noticed he wasn't wearing shoes, his thick grey socks dirty from the asphalt paths within the park.

The other man still stood facing him and pulled a knife from his pocket and jammed the point of the large blade into the back of Grace's hand. His fingers opened and Grace fell down into the dirty, freezing water. It was deeper than he could stand up in and his clothes and jacket were quickly absorbing water and pulling him down. He pulled the jacket off then swam the dozen feet to the cement edge and pulled himself out of the water and rotated to sit on the bank just as he heard the first scream.

Looking up he saw the woman through the screen pointing behind him. He didn't have to turn to know what was happening. The four large tigers that lived in the enclosure had finally found something of enough interest to raise them from their 16 hours of daily sleep. Each of the great animals slowly climbed to their feet and looked down from the top of the three tiers at the new arrival in their private space.

Grace had faced down countless men with guns aimed at him, jumped out of airplanes and had once run across the border from Iran into Turkey with 20 members of the Armed Forces of the Islamic Republic of Iran chasing and shooting at him. But he'd never faced down an adult tiger.

He reached down and pulled his right pants leg up and retrieved the small backup Glock G26 he kept strapped to his ankle almost every minute he was awake, barring showers and the occasional tryst with a willing woman. As he turned to face the cats he pulled the slide back to load the first of fifteen bullets. Three of the animals were still on the top level, but the largest one had jumped down to the middle tier and was eyeing him from no more than twenty-five feet away, its giant tongue licking its lips.

Grace raised the gun and aimed it at the majestic creature; not wanting to take its life but valuing his own life more.

He wondered how much effect the nine-millimeter would have on the large beast and if he'd have time to get enough shots off before it could jump the short distance to him. They stayed there, locked in the moment of who would flinch first, survival of the fittest at its purest. He knew he would have barely two seconds to react before the animal's teeth would find their way into his body. His finger was still stretched out on the trigger guard although he knew the threat was imminent. These animals had been raised in captivity, but their DNA still had the encoding for being killers. He felt he might possibly be able to take one down, but the other three cats were now moving to the edge of the top tier.

They stared at each other in a primal game of chicken, one where one loser might possibly be eaten. Their moment ended and the cat jumped down to his level of the enclosure in a smooth motion, defying its 450 pound weight. The distance was down to 20 feet and closing quickly.

Grace hesitated on the trigger until he knew he couldn't wait any longer. As his finger moved from the guard to the trigger he heard what sounded like a series of silenced pistol fires from behind him and the tiger stopped, its eyes still locked with his, then its back legs gave way forcing it to sit down then its front legs buckled. Finally the large head dropped to the ground, the large eyes still trying to focus on its prey until the eyelids drooped down and closed.

Grace looked up at the other three cats, his gun following his gaze, to see them retreating to the far corner of the top tier. He then turned around and saw two park employees with tranquilizer rifles aimed through the mesh fence. They fired again, bringing two more of the beasts to their knees.

CHAPTER 33

In the commotion at the tiger enclosure next to the café, Arash Abbasi carried out his short but tense meeting with his client. As predicted, there was more work requested and his demand for more money was met first with laughter. He held firm, staring the client in the eyes without saying another word. The client's hands finally rose in agreement. The outcome meant more than the money.

Abbasi stood and walked away, out of the great cat exhibit and exited from the near end of the zoo. The work van pulled up and he climbed in the back and slid the door closed as it pulled away.

Grace was sitting in the zoo security office with half a dozen guards lining the walls while two District of Columbia police officers questioned him about how he came to be inside the tiger enclosure and why he had a gun with him. He gave them as little information as he could while still trying to be helpful. When the cops changed positions for the third time, the smaller of the two men taking over the questioning again, the door opened and another officer walked in, spoke quietly to the men, then left. Not sure what had happened or who the man they were questioning really was, they simply told him he was free to go and handed him back his gun and the radio unit that powered his earpiece.

Once clear of the security office he turned on the radio. "Where are you?"

"Take a left, we're on the street outside the main entrance," Avery said.

Grace followed the directions and found the black Mercedes Sprinter and climbed in the back, avoiding looking his boss in the eyes. Avery put the van in gear and pulled into traffic.

"I'm guessing that was you?" Grace said.

"Uh huh," Arrington said.

"Thanks," Grace said. "We have any eyes on them?"

"The Explorer was dumped," Avery said.

"Of course it was," Grace said.

"Netty followed the work van until it ran a red light," Avery said. "She caught up with it four blocks later, abandoned on a side street."

"Perfect day to have your boss riding along with you."

CHAPTER 34

The afternoon sun had warmed the air to the low thirties, enough for kids to be out on the playground, climbing the structures and creating new games by the minute. First they were mountain climbers, summiting the highest peaks. In the blink of an eye they were in a battle with invisible warriors, swinging their arms around in swordplay.

Next to the playground were three new soccer fields with games being played by corporate teams, likely including the parents of some of the children on the playground. The neon colored uniforms of local business teams competed for not much more than the benefit of knowing they'd played.

Arash Abbasi sat on the metal bench inside the playground fence, watching the children play. There were enough parents around that he didn't stand out. A newspaper was folded beside him and he drank coffee from the closest Starbucks, barely stomaching the acidic fluid only to blend in. The game had changed again as his mind wandered; now the boys were spinning the small merry-go-round as fast as they could with two girls sitting in the middle.

He watched the two girls, their high pitched voices screaming in the still air, hoping at least one of them would get sick and propel the vomit out with the momentum of their spinning onto the boys. But the boys grew tired of the game and moved on to something else, leaving the girls behind.

Abbasi turned his head slightly to the right, taking in the shape of the six-story building beyond the playground with his peripheral vision. He'd counted 11 cameras mounted on the roof so far and knew there were likely more that he couldn't see. A second building sat to the right with the same design. To the right of that one was the smaller, windowless mechanical building, which provided electricity and pumped hot and cold air for the buildings on the campus that was surrounded by large stones and a tall security fence with razor wire along the top. The near buildings held his interest because he knew they were the weak points in the system. It was the third building, 200 yards further away, that most concerned him. That was the one he needed to fulfill his contract, to get his money: the Homeland Security Building in Herndon, Virginia. And far below it, buried deep in the soil beneath the building, the Executive Terrorist Task Force control center where the president of the United States had settled in to track down the people who had destroyed the Capitol.

A mission like the one they were about to undertake would usually take months of planning, reconnaissance and most importantly, gaining access to the buildings. They didn't have that luxury now. A clock had been started and they had to succeed before time ran out in order to be paid. Abbasi did not like having such ridiculous parameters put on him and it was more than just a passing thought to kill his client once the money had been transferred. The client had seen his face on more than one occasion and eliminating the threat would make Abbasi feel safer. But more than that he just wanted to do it.

They would have to breach without having put an inside man in place. Usually they would find an employee to slowly gain trust then coerce into aiding them, but there wasn't enough time for that kind of long play. The access cards and random order keypads were too difficult to bypass. The fact that the ETTF was two stories below ground made things more interesting as well. Detailed instructions had been given on how the task was to be carried out once inside, but getting in was solely on him, so that at least gave him some room to be creative.

CHAPTER 35

Grace stood and stared at the map of Washington D.C. that hung on the wall of the workroom at Buzzard Point. He wasn't able to focus on it, upset about losing Abbasi. He rubbed the bandage wrapped around his left hand. The knife had gone through clean, piercing the muscle along the strands rather than across them. He would have limited use for several weeks but should regain all movement. Netty and Holden had returned to Building 18 and there was no sign of the terrorists after 12 hours. They entered the abandoned structure and found the bug sitting out in the middle of the empty room, resting on top of a stack of eight empty pizza boxes. Grace had seen Khouri's shoeless feet at the zoo and knew they had discovered the tracking device in the sole.

"I might have something," Ben Murray said.

Grace turned to him from across the room. "What?"

"I got access to the video surveillance from the zoo," Ben said. "And I found Abbasi."

Now interested, Grace moved through the room to the analyst's desk. "Show me."

Ben played the clips he'd extracted from the video that showed Abbasi and another man walking through the zoo from various cameras mounted above the walkway. In one shot he saw the men turn left then saw himself follow and moments later Efraim Khouri and a tall dusty blonde man fall in behind him.

"Amateur move. I was so fixated on Abbasi that I never saw them," Grace said. "I put too much trust in the tracker's information and didn't think anyone else was near."

"Get's better," Ben played the next clip.

Abbasi could be seen glancing back towards Grace then stepping into the small open air seating area of the café in the Great Cats exhibit. He then walked up to a table in the far corner, the morning sun casting a shadow across the area.

"Is he talking to someone?" Grace moved closer to the screen. "There's someone sitting at the table."

The edge of a head wearing a fedora and a left shoulder were barely visible. Grace stepped back, still staring at the monitor.

"This wasn't a mission. It was a goddam meet up with a client. It makes sense. Abbasi is a gun-for-hire. He doesn't mastermind anything."

His thoughts tripped over each other as he considered what had gone on just yards from him as he had been thrown into the tiger enclosure. The person behind the attack on the Capitol had been there and he missed him.

Grace was excited at the find. "Retrace the video back from there. Let's find that man."

Ben loaded the multi-camera video, which showed 28 frames in a grid on his monitor then put them all in slow motion rewind. The man at the table had been there for eight minutes before Abbasi arrived and had brought his own coffee cup. As the video rolled in reverse the man stood up and moved with his back to the camera, the wide brimmed fedora on his head, his body concealed inside a long black coat.

"We have to get ahead of him, see his face," Grace said.

"Working on it," Ben said. "It was right after the zoo opened and the sun was low so everything is in shadows."

As the video ran in reverse he enlarged a second video of the man walking backwards through the entrance to the cat exhibit. The sun struck the man from behind and rendered his face into dark tones. They continued through the videos, one by one. Each time the man was obscured by shadows or tourists, and several times was outside the frame of the camera.

"He knew what he was doing," Grace said. "Wherever possible he followed a line that kept him blocked. Let's try the other way. Go back to the café and let's watch him leave."

The images reloaded and they traced the man's steps again. The sun was higher by then so the black coat was getting lighter, but the face was hidden in shadows of the hat. As the man stood from the table, just as the light would hit him, he kept his chin down, further obscuring his face.

"Dammit, come on," Grace said. "Nobody is that good or that lucky."

On the sixth video tracking the man he went into the visitor's center. Ben sped the playback up and ten minutes later he still hadn't come out.

"Inside, get inside," Grace said.

"I don't have that video," Ben scrambled through the feed he'd accessed and searched for the cameras inside the building. "It's not here. If there's cameras then they're on a different system."

"Park police monitor the outside cameras," Grace said. "The one's inside may be for local access to watch for shoplifters. Get down there and find that video."

In his years with Homeland Security, Ben Murray hadn't stepped outside of a secure government building for work purposes once, barring a team-building event his boss had insisted everyone attend at a ropes course in rural Virginia. After talking to Grace, he went to Netty and asked her to take him to the National Zoo.

The Honda Accord was filthy inside, littered with coffee cups left over from the surveillance of Abbasi's men. Ben sat in the passenger seat, holding the door handle with his right hand, the seat belts having long been broken, as Netty drove them through the city.

"You ever want to be a field agent?" Netty said.

"What? Well, yeah," Ben said. "Who didn't want to be an agent at one point in their life? I never really had the physical presence for it but had the analytical down so I went that way."

"You ever shoot a gun?" Netty said.

"No. Except for a bb gun my best friend had in fifth grade," Ben said.

"You want to?"

He looked out the side window as two police cars passed them with lights and sirens on in the right lane. "Yeah, sure."

"I'll take you sometime," she said.

"Really?" He turned his head to look at her. "You'd do that?"

"Don't get any ideas," she said. "Just trying to be nicer to you than they were to me when I joined the team. Plus Grace wants to make sure you can take care of yourself."

"Yeah. Thanks. I appreciate that," he said.

Netty pulled into the parking lot at the zoo and took a ticket from the machine. It was late in the day so there were several spaces available. Ben got out and closed the door and stood beside the dirty beige car. When Netty still hadn't gotten out a minute later he looked through the window to see her wiping down the steering wheel, gearshift and any other surface in reach with a microfiber cloth. She got out and walked around to his door, opened it, and wiped the handle on the inside down then on the outside. She tossed the keys onto the seat and bumped the door closed with her bottom.

"Are we not driving this back?" Ben said.

"It's burned," she said. "Used it too much already. Plus it's a piece of shit."

"Then how are we getting back?" Ben said.

"We'll find something," she said. "All else fails, there's metro."

They walked into the zoo to the visitor's center. On the left was a gift shop and straight ahead there were three steps with a chair lift on the right side that led to the hallway back to the bathrooms. On the right was a security door.

"In here," Netty said.

"Hold on," Ben looked down the hall past the stairs then started walking. He went up the stairs and down the hall towards the bathrooms and stopped. Netty came up behind him.

"What are you doing?" she said. "The security office is back there."

"Wait here," Ben pushed through the door into the men's room leaving Netty standing in the hallway. She stared at the door, hands on her hips. A few seconds later the door opened and he came back out.

"If you had to piss you coulda just told me," she said.

Ben looked down the hall. Nobody was in sight. "Come here," he grabbed her arm and pulled her into the bathroom.

"What the hell?" she said. "I could shoot you, you know."

"Look," he walked past the two wall urinals and three stalls. In the back corner of the restroom was a dented grey steel door with scratches and rust marks and a faded sign that said "Do not enter."

"So?" she said. "It's probably where the janitor keeps cleaning supplies."

Ben kept his eyes on Netty and reached out with his left hand and pushed the door. It swung open away from him then he turned and walked through.

"Where the hell are you going?" Netty pushed the door open as it swung back on her and saw Ben standing a few feet away, a stairwell going down behind him. "What the . . . ?"

"High school field trip," he said. "Jerry Larson said he got a hand job from Melody Maddox on a secret stairwell behind the men's restroom at the zoo. Nobody believed him. Melody was a prude and Jerry was a nerd."

"More of a nerd than you?" Netty said.

"Way bigger nerd than me, and that's saying a lot," Ben said.

"And you remembered this?"

"Not until we walked into the visitor's center," he said. "I bet you this is why we never saw our mystery man come back out of the building."

CHAPTER 36

The metal folding chair barely held Ormand Baasch's six foot five frame. Across the desk from him sat a rotund government employee. A picture frame sat on the corner of the desk with a 30 year old wedding photo mostly obscured with photographs of children and grandchildren. The man's hair had left him at least a decade earlier. Baasch watched as the man turned and used his hand to wipe powdered donut crumbs off of the desk blotter calendar onto the floor, most of them ending up on the right leg of his thick blue work pants. A nameplate on the edge of the desk said "Larry Ferguson."

"You got any experience?" the man said.

"Been in construction for a long time, Mr. Ferguson," Baasch said. "I've installed a lot of large HVAC systems. I'm certified in most of the major brands to maintain them as well."

"Shit. That's more experience than most of my men have. And call me Larry. Mr. Ferguson was my father and he was an asshole. I'm just impressed you're sitting here and can actually speak f'n English. Get so sick and tired of havin' to explain 20 times to these guys what to do and they still don't understand a word of what I'm sayin', no matter how loud I say it."

Baasch laughed with him and imagined what it would be like to reach across the desk and strike the obscenely large man in the throat with his fist then watch him struggle to breathe.

He'd grown up in the era that his country brushed past their history in school, but the atrocities his nation had committed were known and to most people were a dark blotch in their memories. He had read everything he could about the genocide of the Jews and it repulsed him. His own grandfather had worked in the infamous Auschwitz death camp in Poland and had been assigned to clean the showers used to delouse the detainees which actually sprayed the cyanide based Zyklon B pesticide on their naked bodies, killing them in brutal, painful deaths. His grandfather had died from the chemicals himself, though in a slower, more drawn out process as his body, organ by organ, succumbed to the effects over the 20 years following the war.

"Yeah," Baasch said. "Pain in the ass, isn't it."

"Well, you'd be a supervisor, obviously," Larry said. "Sure as hell can't promote one of them."

Baasch nodded, his eyes still trained on the oversized neck. "Appreciate that. Sure wouldn't let you down. I know a bit of Spanish, too, so I can tell when they're talkin' back."

"Oh, man, I'd love that," the man leaned back in his chair. Baasch was surprised it handled the weight. "Make sure not to let them know." He leaned back in and shuffled some papers on the messy desk. "There's security checks, of course. Forms to fill out."

"I've worked in secure facilities before," Baasch said. "I was with Cunningham up in Maryland for a year or two. Did some time on the Capitol before, well . . . "

"Shit. Don't even talk about that," Larry said. "F'n tragedy."

"Sure was," Baasch said. "So, the forms?"

"What? Oh, yeah," the man opened his desk drawer and pulled out a cluttered folder. He flipped through it and took out six pages and put the folder away. "Not much they don't ask about, hope you aren't shy. But I guess it's the world we live in today."

"Sure is," Baasch said. He took the forms and without thinking about it squared the pages up and folded them cleanly in half. "I'll get these back to you as quick as I can."

"Yeah. I got a couple people interested," Larry said. Baasch could tell he was lying. Nobody who interviewed with this man would actually want the job unless they were desperate. "They usually like to go through an agency, but the pricks they send over never last more than a few months before they take a job somewhere else."

"Well I'm looking for something long term," Baasch said. "I live out in Aldie and this would sure be an easy commute."

"I hear that," Larry said. "I drive in from f'n Winchester everyday. At least an hour each way and that's on a good day."

"You should get an earlier start home," Baasch said. "Beat the traffic." He glanced over at the brown metal time clock on the wall and vertical row of cards beside it then back at his interviewer, a slight smirk on his face. "There's ways to make sure you get your time in." He knew the lazy American likely left early every day, presenting the option to help him clock out long after he'd left would be very tempting.

"You get it," Larry nodded. "So, any questions?"

Baasch looked around the small room in a trailer that had been made a permanent structure on the government compound. "Would it be possible to see the equipment?"

Larry Ferguson looked at him with no expression, hands on the edge of the desk in front of him and he didn't move for several seconds. Baasch was sure he'd gone too far, sent up a red flag that triggered some little bit of the security training the government employee had been through, when the fat man finally spoke. "Shit. You do like what you do, don't ya? You probably get a hard on for HVAC. Supposed to have your clearance first, but you said you worked for Cartwright before?"

"Cunningham," Baasch said. "In Maryland."

"Right, Cunningham," Larry said. He pulled open the top desk drawer and took a key ring out and slammed the drawer shut. "Good enough for me. No harm in a little tour." He stood and worked his way out from behind the desk.

Baasch hadn't yet seen Larry Ferguson standing up. He'd already been settled in behind the gunmetal grey desk when Baasch was escorted in by a security guard driving a base model Chevy Cruze with Homeland Security Police written across the side. The size of the facilities manager surprised him and he briefly wondered where clothes that size could even be purchased. Baasch stood up as Larry came around the desk and towered over the short but very round man.

"Shit. You're a big son of a bitch, aren't you?" Larry said as he stopped in front of Baasch. "Sure wouldn't want to f' with you."

"Never really been in a fight," Baasch said. "Can't say I'd even know what to do."

"Right," Larry nodded his head, not believing the tall man in front of him.

CHAPTER 37

"So you think our guy disappeared down a stairway behind a door in a men's room?" Grace looked at the door. A yellow mop bucket had been placed in the door to the main hallway to keep tourists from entering the restroom. Avery and Holden stood outside the door as extra incentive for nobody to come in.

"Yes," Ben Murray said.

"I guess it's possible. We never saw him come out of the building. Where do the stairs go?" Grace said.

Ben had made a phone call to a friend at the Smithsonian offices while waiting on Grace to arrive. He pulled up schematics on his tablet of the underground tunnels. "There's a whole network of passages under the zoo, not too different from a big amusement park. Most of the entrances to the tunnels only connect within the park, but one provides access outside the zoo. The stairs from here go down to the zoo tunnels, but there's a door to the subbasement of the apartment building behind the visitor's center."

"Why would that even exist?"

"Those apartments date back to the same time the tunnels were built. Maybe it was designed to allow a zoo director to live close by," Ben said.

"Are there any traffic cameras with a view of the front of the apartments or the buildings parking garage?" Grace said.

"There isn't," Ben said. "The closest camera just gets the corner of the building from the opposite street corner, nothing usable."

"Netty, grab Avery and walk the area to see if you spot any private surveillance that might pick up the front of the building," Grace said. "Holden and Ben are with me. We're going into the tunnel."

"Me?" Ben said.

"You found it," Grace said. "You get to explore it."

The stairs made three turns at landings until they arrived at the cement block passageway thirty feet below the National Zoo. A single row of fluorescent lights lined the ceiling of the eight-foot wide tunnel, with many of them burned out.

"Which way?" Grace knew just by having glanced at the maps but wanted to give his newest team member the opportunity to lead.

Ben looked each way down the tunnel then glanced at the diagram on his tablet then started walking. "This way."

They hadn't walked long in the winding tunnel until they came to a large metal door with a deadbolt lock. Ben reached for the knob when Grace grabbed his arm. "Hold on."

Grace knelt down and looked at the scratches around the keyhole. "Been picked, and recently," he said. "Someone who didn't know what they were doing." He stood and grabbed the knob and turned it then pulled the door open. "And luckily for us they didn't bother to lock it again."

Beyond the door the hall opened up into a wider area. "I think we're under the apartment building now," Ben said.

There were two doors. One was locked, the other opened to the parking garage under the building.

"And here's where he left from," Grace said.

They walked into the garage. Most of the parking spaces had cars in them. Holden walked off to the left to look around.

"I don't see any cameras," Grace said.

"What about those?" Ben pointed at the two parking spots with the green illuminated electric car charging stations. "I know the chargers at the mall have systems in place to make sure non-electric cars don't park there and to track who uses them."

"Sounds awful Big Brother," Grace said.

"Says the man who works for the NSA," Ben said.

Grace turned and looked at Ben. "True."

"Hey, might want to check this out," Holden called from around the corner and they went to find him. He stood beside a green metal trashcan and had removed the plastic top.

They walked up and looked into the can and saw a wadded up piece of black wool. Grace reached in and grabbed it and let it unroll. "It's the coat," he said.

As the coat opened up a grey fedora fell to the ground.

"You have a bag?" Grace said.

"Sure do," Holden pulled a clear trash bag from his

pocket on the side of his green combat pants that he wore every day.

"I want these bagged and every test in the book done on them," Grace said. "Whatever you have to pay your contact to get it to the top of his to do list. I want to know where every hair, fiber and speck of dust came from."

Holden got the two items in the bag then turned and left.

"I'm going to walk the whole garage," Grace said. "Find out what you can from the charging stations."

Over the next hour Grace methodically moved through the parking structure, between every car and dropping to the ground to look below each vehicle.

Ben found him in the far corner. "There's no camera on the chargers, just a license plate scanner. You have to use a credit card to access the station. If it sees you aren't in an electric, you're charged for parking."

"Sneaky," Grace said. "But doesn't help us."

"Probably not. Still, I got a list of all cars that parked there over the last 12 hours," Ben said.

CHAPTER 38

Grace hung up his phone and set it down on the table. Derek Arrington was back at the ETTF and getting restless. The FBI was pushing to get access to everything they'd found. Once it got turned over it would change the rules of engagement for Grace and his team. They operated outside the confines of the Department of Justice, generally resolving issues without a single person ever getting arrested or going to trial. But once DOJ got involved, everything had to be done by the book to ensure they could prosecute or at a minimum work with the state department to have those responsible detained and extradited back to the United States.

There was no way Grace was going to let that happen. He'd been within feet of Arash Abbasi and had purposely let him walk in and out of his building at Buzzard Point in order to identify the next target and his plan had failed. He had to get results soon or he'd be pushed out of the way.

Ben Murray sat at his computer a few tables away, churning through data he'd downloaded from the electric charging station company. Holden was due back anytime with test results on the suit jacket and hat. Everything was taking too much time and when it was done, wasn't driving them forward.

"Shit," Ben slammed his hands down on his desk, startling Grace.

"What?" Grace said.

"It's just been, it's been crazy. Too much information coming in from so many directions," Ben said. "I shouldn't have missed it."

"Missed what?" Grace was up and walking over to his new analyst.

"I'm sorry," Ben said. "This is days old now." He handed Grace a stack of printouts with columns of numbers and names lining the pages.

"What am I looking at?"

"Call log from Tuesday," Ben said. "I put in a request through Homeland Security to all cellphone carriers in the area to get a list of calls around the Capitol during the time of the takeover."

"That's a lot of calls," Grace flipped through the pages. "Don't beat yourself up. The phone companies are notoriously slow on delivering."

"It wasn't them. It was me. They had the data over to me in a few hours. I ran it through a program that would put names with numbers as well as access any GPS data for the call," Ben said. "It takes a long time for this much data."

"You can feed thousands of numbers in and it does all the work?" Grace said. "Where'd you get that software?"

"I wrote it," Ben said. "It was the basis of my master's thesis."

Grace nodded, staring at the young man. "So, what did your program come back with?"

"It finished its routine a couple days ago, but I had it running on a cloud server," Ben said. "I simply forgot about it."

"So this is running outside the Homeland Security firewall?" Grace said.

"Yeah," Ben said. "It's not an approved piece of software. It was just a list of phone numbers. I figured nothing would come from it and I'd delete the results."

"What did come from it?" Grace said.

Ben stood and took the stack of papers from Grace and sat them on the empty table beside his desk then flipped through them quickly until he found the page with the highlighter markings. "This," Ben said.

Grace read the line of information. "Richard Graham," he said. "He made a phone call. I'm sure I'm on here as is everyone else in the city."

"No, you wouldn't be unless you called somebody near the Capitol," Ben said. "The numbers I had were calls sent or received from towers closest to the building."

"Graham is a Cabinet member. I'm sure there's a hundred reasons he'd be calling someone at the Capitol."

"But who? Everyone on the Hill was either locked up in the Capitol or had been evacuated from the office buildings. Plus he didn't call someone. At least nobody answered," Ben said. "In the thousands of numbers, he shows up once. And that one call was made to a cellphone at the Capitol. It rang, but nobody answered."

"We know there were cellphone jammers, so even if he

was trying to call someone being held there, nobody could have answered."

"Right, but the call wouldn't have found the phone it was looking for," Ben said. "It would be a different record, an error. This found the phone and made it ring. Look at the time of the call."

Grace looked back down at the list and read it again, tracing the lines with his fingers. His hand froze and he looked up at Ben. "This is real? This data is accurate, without a doubt?"

"Yes," Ben said.

"Can you show me where the phone was that he called?" Grace said.

Ben sat back down at his desk and dug into the software, finding the line displaying Richard Graham's phone call and clicked in to place the signal on a layer over an online map system. "Right there."

Grace looked at the time on the paper again then at the satellite view of the United States Capitol. "I gotta get to Herndon, and you're coming with me."

Netty had brought back a new Dodge Charger sedan in black with the overpowered HEMI engine. It was more than she usually went for, generally opting for vehicles that would blend in or that weren't new enough that insurance companies would try to find the car before paying out to their client for the stolen vehicle. The Charger had been low-hanging fruit, left at the end of the circle drive in front of the Hamilton Hotel with the engine running. The rumble of the 370 horsepower engine had been irresistible to her. She'd sent Ben to distract the hotel doorman with typical tourist questions and then picked him up from a metro station eighteen blocks away then they'd returned to Buzzard Point.

Now the Charger was across the bridge and onto Interstate 66 and Grace had it doubling the speed limit. Every few seconds he reached for his phone to call Arrington, but he didn't want to discuss this on an open line. Ben sat beside him, white knuckling the handle above the passenger window. The car exited onto Route 50 and rolled through two red lights, barely missing being hit from the side by a Fairfax Connector commuter bus at the second light. A right turn onto Centreville Road and a half-minute later he made the turn to the gate for the Homeland Security building. It had been 24 minutes since he'd stood talking to Ben in the workroom.

The elevator to the sublevel was slow and Grace was tapping the door with his fist until it opened. The lone security guard that had been there days before had been replaced by several Secret Service agents in their suits and wires coming out behind their ears. He raised his credentials and they passed through the door into the ETTF.

Derek Arrington saw him enter and Grace looked around the room to find the least populated area and pointed then headed in that direction. His boss came over to the two men.

"What's up? I didn't expect you out here," Arrington said. "Monroe is getting really itchy. He's pushing the president and the Attorney General hard to take over."

Grace opened his mouth to speak then stopped and looked at Ben Murray. "Ben has some new information."

Caught off guard, Ben fumbled through the folder he'd brought with him and laid the papers out on the desk in order. "Uh, yes, sir. I've come across some data that, well, let me start from here, from the beginning."

"Yes, please do, Mr. Murray," Arrington said.

Grace watched as the analyst went through everything he'd shown him back at Buzzard Point. Arrington asked almost the same questions he had and Ben answered clearly and kept the presentation moving while the NSA director listened.

"1:38pm. The call was made the precise minute the explosion started. The location of the receiving phone was here," Ben pulled the final paper over, a print out of the Capitol building, with a red circle he'd drawn over the top of the House of Representatives. "The phone was above the cell phone jammers. It was the only phone on that end of the building that registered any calls, incoming or outgoing, for the duration of the siege."

Derek Arrington took a half step back and looked at Grace.

CHAPTER 39

Grace closed the door to the secure meeting room as Murray, Arrington and FBI Director Jim Monroe took their seats. While he still planned to take down Arash Abbasi in his own way, any accusation against a member of the president's cabinet had to go through the feds. He would just be careful what information he shared in order to keep his hunt for the Persian terrorist alive.

"What's up, Derek?" Monroe said. He glanced at the analyst and over at Grace. "You guys finally ready to play nice and share intel?"

"We're not just going to share intel," Grace said. "We're going to give it to you on a silver platter."

The meeting went mostly as Grace expected, the FBI director listening intently, asking minimal questions and taking in everything he could. He was one of the modern era's directors who had never served as an agent but came from a law background.

As the young analyst finished, leaving the image of the Capitol in the middle of the table, Jim Monroe leaned back in his chair then looked at each of the other three men in the room one at a time then back to the print out.

"What else?" Monroe said.

"What else?" Grace said. "Doesn't this say it all?"

"So what you are trying to tell me," Monroe said "is that the secretary of transportation blew up the United States Capitol?"

"We think—or at least I think—that this call detonated the device, yes," Grace said. "That Graham is involved, if not in charge of, the attack. He obviously couldn't have worked alone."

"That's a huge accusation based on a phone call," Monroe said. "Couldn't the number have been spoofed from a different device?"

Ben was caught off guard. He hadn't even considered the idea. "Technically, yes," he said.

"While the Capitol was locked down, Graham pushed to send in Special Forces, over and over," Arrington said. "He resisted any other options, even though we all said that could trigger a response from the terrorists."

"He was scared shitless of becoming president. He wasn't trying to kill nearly a thousand people to take office," Monroe said.

"Perhaps, but what about the phone call?" Grace said. "There were cell jammers inside the building keeping all of you from communicating with the outside world. The GPS puts the receiving call directly over the south wing of the Capitol where the mother lode of C4 was."

"It's thin," Monroe stared at the document. "This isn't

a liquor store robbery here. It's murder and treason at the highest level. We need more." He leaned forward. "Did you know Graham ran for Senate in Illinois?"

"No, I didn't, but still—" Grace said.

"He lost to Rebekah Abrams," Monroe said.

"All the more reason," Grace said. "He's probably held contempt for the woman since then."

"So much contempt that he jumped at the chance to be within her inner circle of advisors?" Monroe said. "He's a man that's fumbled his way up the food chain. How could Graham even orchestrate something like this? He's barely capable of keeping his own job."

"What do you mean?" Grace said.

Monroe shook his head and looked away for a moment.

"There's talk of him being asked to step down," Arrington said. "Frankly, his office is in deep shit. The FAA is bleeding money with all the new security measures he's pushed through. And the only highway projects that have been approved in the last two years have directly benefited his home state of Illinois."

"If this isn't a desperate man, then who is?" Grace said.

"There's a wide area between desperate and treason," Monroe said. "Bring me something concrete or even better, drop it altogether. I know this man. To think he was behind the biggest attack on our government since the Revolutionary War is ludicrous."

Monroe stood and nodded to his equal at the NSA then left the room.

"Something concrete," Grace said.

"He's right," Arrington said. "If we want it clean, it has to be done his way."

"I could just nab Graham and interrogate him," Grace said.

"Not funny," Arrington said. "Find something else. I'm with you on this, but watch your back. We don't want Monroe and DOJ coming down on us for following a lead they don't believe in."

Arrington left and Grace sat down across the table from Ben.

"What now?" Ben said.

"How can we know if the number was spoofed?" Grace said.

"Only real way is to get a look at the phone, see if the call shows up in its history," Ben said.

"You think we're right?" Grace said.

"My job is all about data," Ben said. "And numbers don't lie, whether it's cellphone tracking or offshore bank accounts. It's like they say: follow the money. We have numbers telling us one man's cellphone made a call that could only have been for one purpose."

Grace looked at the young man. "You're right, so right. We haven't considered who was bankrolling this. We're talking millions of dollars if not more. Does Graham even have that kind of money?"

"Let's find out," Ben said.

Ben sat at his desk in the ETTF poring through every financial record he could find on Richard Graham while Grace sat beside him, watching the screen.

"This might take a while," Ben said.

"Nowhere to be," Grace said.

CHAPTER 40

It was too fast and too sloppy. Abbasi knew that. But he also had no choice. He'd developed a plan, but there were too many variables and far more moving parts than he liked. Simple works. Simple is good. This was going to be complicated.

Ormand Baasch had gotten a look at the large heating and ventilation system and the underground channels that carried the air over to the three buildings. Once into the industrial building, security was low and there were only a couple of cameras to deal with. But to get to the machinery building required passing through a double-gated entry system with armed guards 24 hours a day as well as all the rooftop cameras watching everything that moved.

After the building in DC had been compromised, Abbasi had moved his team closer to their new target. Hiding in the suburbs was more difficult than urban settings, so he took a new approach. He paid $2,400 for an old, beat up former U-Haul moving truck that became their mobile office and home.

The president had stopped coming to the ETTF daily, working from the Oval Office and keeping communication channels open with the teams working on the investigation. He was to keep the men ready. When she was to return to the building the client would signal him. It would be their only chance.

There was too much to do, so preparations were underway, hiding what they could as they worked. They only had to get one man in at first to set the plan in motion. Then everything would begin rolling downhill so quickly they had to be ready for anything. Ormand Baasch was the only one who knew what it looked like inside so he'd make the primary entry. The next phase could take anywhere from five minutes to five hours and the clock would be running on how long the president would stay at the ETTF.

The international team leveraged their European members to make face-to-face contact when necessary, to reduce any suspicion of dark skinned men that so many assumed were terrorists just by the shade of their complexion.

CHAPTER 41

"What are you doing back here?"

Grace spun in his chair at the voice, putting himself as casually as possible between the assistant director of the FBI and the analyst's computer monitors. He didn't need anyone, no matter how much he trusted them, knowing what they were doing.

"Had to brief Arrington on a few things," Grace said. "Thought we'd hang out a while."

"You wanna," she bit her lip and glanced at Ben then back to Grace. "You wanna go outside and talk for a minute?"

They stepped into the elevator and Grace reached to press the button for the first floor when her hand grabbed his. She pulled it back and pressed the top button.

He glanced over and saw a smirk on her face he hadn't seen since the night they'd first met at a bar in Bethesda. He'd recognized her, but she hadn't known what he did until the beginning of this mission. That first night was spent in a hotel room on Wisconsin Avenue and involved a lot of room service and no inhibitions.

He still didn't know if they were dating or if he was just a physical thing for her, but he had no intention of asking. They provided releases for each other, her from the daily routine of helping run the largest crime fighting organization in the country, and him from the stress of never truly knowing if he was coming back from a mission.

He had no time to date, to get to know anyone, and he feared getting to know anyone too well. The closer someone got to him the more chance there was they could be used as leverage against him. He kept an arm's length with his team as much as possible, though it was hard not to become friendly with the men and women you go into battle with.

The elevator stopped at the roof and he followed her out. The sun was low in the sky over the airport and the wind was whipping around the stairwell exit. She pulled him around the corner, sheltered from the wind. She pushed her body against his and he pulled her in tight. As she reached her face up to his he glanced around and noticed it was perhaps the one blind spot in the building's security system.

He put his lips to hers and felt the warm, wet sensation of her tongue against his and then her burgundy fingernails pushing through the thick cotton shirt that was stretched across his back. Her right hand came around his waist then reached down inside the front of his black combat pants. Her fingers wrapped around him and he forgot to breathe for a moment.

He pulled his face away. "Here?"

She smiled. "Here."

CHAPTER 42

Grace pulled the chair up next to Ben Murray and sat down and Ben glanced over at him. "You okay?" Ben said.

"Yeah, great," Grace said. "Why?"

"You just look, I don't know, flush," Ben said.

"I was outside for a few minutes. It's a bit chilly," Grace said.

"Right. That's probably it," Ben said. "So, while you were . . . outside . . . I came across something."

"What is it?"

"Going back through Graham's financial history I found regular payments from Cunningham Construction."

"What?" Grace said.

"So regular, in fact," Ben said. "That it looks like he worked there."

"How can that be?" Grace said.

"Well, he had to be doing something before now, right?" Ben said.

"True, but working for the company that planted the explosives in the Capitol?"

"It appears he left the company about six years ago," Ben said.

Grace leaned back and stared up at the ceiling. "This is far more than a coincidence."

"Is it enough, though?" Ben said. "You probably only have one more chance with Director Monroe."

"I want more," Grace said. "Keep digging."

The men sat at Ben's computer and went through every public record they could find, as well as many that weren't public. Once they began looking, Graham's past easily spilled out before them. He'd started Cunningham Construction in Illinois with his best friend 20 years earlier and had helmed it as CEO for most of that time. A few years later a larger company bought control but let them run their own business, except for moving them to the Washington D.C. area where government contracts began to flow.

"Small jobs, mostly, but they've done well working for Uncle Sam," Ben said. "They built up a good reputation quickly, so once they got their clearance to work on secure facilities they began getting more work."

Grace watched the screen. "This plan was in the works for a long time."

"They look like a legitimate company. How would they even pull off something like this?" Ben said.

"Of course they're legitimate. They had to be to get the job. They then used that strength to infiltrate the Capitol without suspicion, hiring the contractors," Grace said. "I need to talk with Arrington." Grace stood and walked away, finding his boss talking to two men he didn't recognize.

Arrington excused himself from the men. "What do you need now?"

"Just want to talk," Grace said. "More info is coming in and I need to run through it."

Arrington glanced around the room. "Well, not here. Too many ears. How about the roof?"

Grace paused. "No. Let's just walk and talk."

They left the ETTF and moved through the hallways of the building above them, talking in low voices and standing still only when no other people were in sight.

"If you think Graham is behind the Capitol bombing, to what, become president? Then what is his play now?" Arrington said. "It almost made sense in a sick way when he was set to claim the throne, but now he's way down the line of succession."

"That's the only thing bugging me," Grace said. "There's no reason for it, not for personal gain at least." He looked down the hall at a man and a woman talking outside a restroom door. By their body language Grace guessed they'd slept together and the woman wanted to cut it off. "Unless it was to cover up the first attack."

"What do you mean?"

"If we look down a list of people who had something to gain from the first attack, his could easily slide to the top," Grace said. "But if a second attack happened in which he'd have no potential for climbing the ladder, then his name would drop off the list of suspects."

Derek Arrington shook his head. "That's a lot of time, money and effort to clear yourself, especially when the entire country and every intelligence agency is looking at foreign terrorist organizations, not the secretary of transportation."

"Still just a working theory," Grace said.

CHAPTER 43

The old U-Haul truck's vinyl seats were torn and the springs poked through into Arash Abbasi's back as he lay with his head resting on a rolled up moving blanket, another one covering his body. It had gotten down to 17 degrees in the night, but now the sun was hitting the windshield and warming the cab up. The truck was parked on the edge of a construction site not far from the Homeland Security compound in Herndon. He'd been awake for an hour, just listening to the sounds of traffic building up as rush hour began. He knew the sound of the diesel pickup truck the site foreman drove. As soon as it went past, Abbasi would sit up and drive the truck away and park it in a grocery store parking lot to prepare for another day of waiting.

Just as the knocking sound of the diesel Ford two-ton pickup rolled past, the cell phone in his pocket vibrated then stopped. He didn't have to look to know that it was finally time after three days of waiting. The phone would have a simple message on the screen, a single number. That would be the time that the president was scheduled to arrive at the ETTF for a briefing by her intelligence and military leaders. His men would begin an hour before that to be ready.

He pulled the phone out and looked at the screen, then glanced at the time on his watch. Two hours until they carried out their last mission for this client. And perhaps, he thought, tomorrow he would find and kill the client once the funds had cleared in his account.

The engine groaned to life as Abbasi sat up and put the truck in gear and drove away. He was ready for a warm bed again, a good meal, perhaps in his favorite restaurant in Caracas. *I can be there in 24 hours*, he thought.

His men would be waking up in the back of the truck, still in darkness, as it bounced over the curb onto to the four-lane road. He was excited to tell them that it was time, that soon they would part ways. He knew some of them would not survive the mission. It was a given based on the plan. He had not shared all of the details with them as he was sure it would have created dissent. At the next intersection he turned right then left into the parking lot of an abandoned Walmart, a newer and larger building having been built a block down the road, and parked the truck behind the store. He got out and slid open the back door.

"It is time, warriors," he said. "Today we strike. Tomorrow we are rich."

He saw the men look out of the darkness at him and knew none of them believed they were warriors in this mission. They were all guns-for-hire and nothing more and were all tired of sleeping in abandoned buildings and rusted moving trucks. Only he knew that most of them would likely be dead before the day was over.

With time before they needed to move into position, they split into small groups to feed themselves at the various fast food restaurants that lined the street, making sure no more than three of them were seen together. When it was time, they arrived back at the truck.

Khouri would stay with Abbasi, the only two of the men who couldn't blend in as easily. Ormand Baasch was already wearing the thick blue work pants and grey shirt with the name Francis embroidered on the name patch. His work would be the most difficult and the most dangerous. If he failed, the entire mission would fail.

With no words shared, Baasch walked off across the parking lot to the street, pulled the plastic metro card out of his pocket, and waited for the next bus to come past and carry him down the road to the target.

Abbasi watched after him, knowing it might be the last time he saw the man even if the mission went well. The chances of him carrying out his tasks and getting out of the building were slim.

Two other men of European descent, Gerald Moline from the UK and Alexandre Fortier from France were the next to move out. They'd spent the last few days doing surveillance on a business down the road and were anxious to do something more than sit all day.

The remaining four men had carried out the majority of their job two days earlier and would now be on hand to aid in the recovery of the rest of the team. The plan didn't require all of them in the building, but they were going to be close by in case they were needed and Abbasi had plans ready for them as well.

Glancing at his watch again, Abbasi smiled. *So close*, he thought. *Soon it will be done.*

CHAPTER 44

Grace woke up in his apartment and went to the kitchen to find sour milk in the refrigerator and not much else. He'd barely been there since arriving home from the mission in Russia and there'd been no time to shop. He wandered around the small apartment deciding where to head that day, not really feeling like being under the microscope of the ETTF but also wanting to avoid Buzzard Point. The rest of the team was going to the memorial service for Chip Goodson near the ocean in Maryland. It wasn't that he didn't want to go; it was just best to avoid any unnecessary questions about his relationship with Chip. The team was under orders to avoid interactions outside their group and to get out as quickly as they could. Mourning is important, but he needed them ready.

He found one clean pair of khakis and pulled an Army Rangers tee shirt on, his way of honoring Chip that day, then a striped and untucked dress shirt over the tee. The pants easily covered the small Glock he kept on his ankle and the shirt somewhat obscured the nine-millimeter pistol on his side. At the door he stopped to see the repairs the landlord had done to the lock after Arrington's bodyguards had smashed their way in four days earlier.

Outside he walked to the far edge of his apartment's parking lot to his car. It had sat unused for two weeks, a layer of dust covering the shiny black paint of the twin turbo BMW M5 sedan. He'd bought the car used and had some work done to it at a shop in Wheaton, Maryland that specializes in armoring personal vehicles. He never drove the BMW on missions, but still felt safer knowing that nothing short of a .50 caliber shell could penetrate the glass or sheet metal that surrounded him. The engine had been modified to handle the extra weight.

The engine came to life with a light tap of the start button to the right of the steering wheel. Grace turned on the stereo and spun the volume knob up as the mp3 player in the glove box pushed the song "Vicarious" by Tool to the speakers. He threw the shifter into first gear, let out the clutch, and let the rear tires spin for a second as he launched from the parking space. At the exit onto the street he considered heading out on a drive to clear his mind, cruising the high-powered car towards the Shenandoah Valley or even West Virginia, but decided to save that for another day and took a right to head to Herndon.

The drive didn't take long enough for him that morning and as he cleared the security gate he wished he'd opted for Skyline Drive instead, but he parked the car and went in.

The ETTF was busy for eight in the morning and he looked around at the constant motion of suits and uniforms. He then saw Ben Murray sitting at his desk and went over to him.

"Thought you were going with the rest of them," Grace said.

"Didn't know him that well," Ben said. "And I wanted to get back to work."

"I understand," Grace said. "Find anything new?"

"Not much. A few photos of Graham with his cofounder of Cunningham," Ben said.

"Oh, wait," Grace pulled his phone out and handed it to Ben. "When Netty and I were at their offices I took a bunch of photos of the CEO's walls. Something else to go through."

Ben plugged the phone in and glanced through the images stored on the internal card and copied them to a folder on his desktop. "I'll see if there's anything there." He stopped, looking past Grace.

Turning, Grace saw Richard Graham and his partner walk into the ETTF and over to the growing group of Capitol Hill dignitaries.

"Why's William with him?" Grace said.

"Didn't you hear?" Ben said. "Graham made him his chief-of-staff."

"What?"

"Yeah. Fired his old one in cold blood over the phone," Ben said. "Had a press release out five minutes later."

"Ballsy," Grace said. "Guess he wanted to make sure they never got separated again."

Derek Arrington emerged from the group in the middle of the room and came over. "Been talking to Monroe," he said.

"Yeah?" Grace said. "How'd that go for you?"

"Better than you might think," Arrington said. "He thinks the Cunningham connection is too big to ignore.

He isn't putting any weight behind your theory yet, but he wants to cover his ass just in case."

"So . . . "

"So, we're going to talk to Graham," Arrington said.

"Incredible," Grace said. "I'll do it."

"No way," Arrington said. "I've seen how you talk to people. Five minutes in and you'll be waterboarding him. This needs to be handled by Justice. We're going to get him to a room without causing a stir. Monroe will do the talking. You can be in the observation room."

"What about William?" Grace said. "I think he's permanently stuck to Graham's side now."

"We'll have Amanda distract him," Arrington said. "Tell him he needs to complete some new security checks as Graham's chief-of-staff."

Arrington and Grace went down the hall and opened a private room then went next door and got set up to record. On the monitors they saw Monroe lead Richard Graham into the room and ask him to sit down as he closed the door behind them. Graham looked at the cameras mounted in the corners then to Monroe as he sat down.

"What's this about?" Graham said.

"Just need your help with something," Monroe said. "You were president of Cunningham Construction, correct?"

"Cunningham?" Graham said. "We're in the middle of a national security crisis and you're asking me about Cunningham?"

"Just a few questions, Richard," Monroe said. "We're following up on a few things and feel you're the best person to talk to. Why did you leave Cunningham?"

"I started the company. I left when Abrams asked me to run transportation," Graham said. "I'm very confused here.

Why are we talking about Cunningham right now?"

"Did you know they had a contract to do work in the south wing of the Capitol a few months ago?" Monroe said.

"No, I didn't," Graham said. "But good for them. I wasn't sure they'd amount to much after I left."

"No faith in your co-founder?" Arrington said.

"Plenty in him, not much in the company that bought them a while back," Graham said.

Monroe glanced at his handwritten notes in the brown leather book he kept in his suit pocket at all times. "So you were president when Cunningham was purchased by Whitlock?"

"CEO, and yes, I was," Graham said. "We were struggling and got a good deal. Whitlock put some money into the company and turned it around. At first they really just wanted to absorb our assets and take over our clients, but I convinced them we had a name, a reputation."

Jim Monroe looked up to watch Graham as he continued, wanting to gauge his reaction. "Cunningham is suspected to have been involved in placing the explosives in the Capitol," he said.

"What?" Graham looked at the cameras again. "Is this why . . . ? Are you interrogating me?"

"Not at all. When we saw your connection to them we thought you might have some knowledge of the inner workings of the company that could help us out," Monroe said.

In the next room Arrington and Grace watched as the conversation was being recorded.

"They were the only firm with access in the areas the explosives were known to have been located," Monroe said. "The type of work they were doing would have given them all the access they needed to hide the C4."

"You're delirious," Graham said. "Why would they do that? And how? Their employees have been with them for years. It's just impossible."

"They used contractors to do the work, so very few company employees were on site," Monroe said. "This could have allowed them to bring in explosives experts."

"Even still, what does this have to do with me?" Graham said. "I have nothing to do with the company anymore."

"Again, just some groundwork before we dig deeper into them. I appreciate your assistance," Monroe started to stand up then stopped. "Oh, you ran for Senate a few years ago, right?"

"Ancient history," Graham said. "Lost by six percent."

"Who'd you lose to?" Monroe said.

"The way you're asking I get the feeling you already know," Graham said. "Rebekah Abrams."

"That why she appointed you to her cabinet?" Monroe said.

"I guess," Graham said. "The call surprised me when it came. She promised in her campaign to reach across the aisle so I figured she picked me because she thought she could control me. But I don't hold a grudge and in politics you just don't turn down a Cabinet position."

"True," Monroe said. "One more thing. Can I take a look at your phone?"

"Excuse me?"

"Totally voluntary," Monroe said. "I'd just like to take a look."

"Why?" Graham reached into his inside suit jacket pocket and set the phone on the table.

Monroe picked it up and tried to access it. "Would you mind unlocking it for me?"

"0812," Graham said.

Monroe tapped the four digits in and it gave him access.

"Really, can you tell me why you want to see my phone?" Graham said. "This is feeling more and more like I'm about to be accused of something."

Going through the menus on the Android based phone, Monroe found the outgoing calls list.

Grace turned to Arrington in the next room. "What's he doing? I thought he wasn't on board?"

Arrington shrugged. "Beats me. He must have seen something we didn't in his reactions."

After looking through the call history Monroe turned the phone to show Graham the screen. "Can you tell me who this number belongs to?"

"I have no idea," Graham said. "I make a lot of calls and can't remember who all the numbers belong to."

"This call was made at 1:38pm on Wednesday," Monroe said.

"I don't know. I don't recall making a call," Graham said. "But I have been a bit busy."

"Richard," Monroe said. "The Capitol blew up at 1:38pm on Wednesday."

Graham sat back in his seat and grew quieter. "What are you saying?"

"This number belongs to a burner phone that was located at the top of the south wing of the Capitol, above the House of Representatives."

Graham stared at the FBI director.

"Do you understand what I'm saying?" Monroe said. "We have reason to believe your phone made the call that caused the explosion."

"That, that's just impossible."

"Anything you want to say?" Monroe said.

"No. I just—" Graham's voice faded. "It's not possible."

"I'm going to need you to stay in here," Monroe said. "You aren't being arrested at this time, but we're going to detain you until we have more facts. If at any time you decide you have more to tell me, let the guard at the door know."

Monroe stood and left the room as Richard Graham sat still, his eyes staring down at the table in front of him. The FBI director came through the door of the observation room.

"What the hell, Jim?" Arrington said. "I thought you were just going to talk to him."

"I was a prosecutor for nearly twenty years," Monroe said. "You learn to tell when people are lying. And he's lying."

Grace pointed at the monitor still recording the room next to them. "Look at him," he said. "He's freaking out."

"He should be," Arrington said. "Okay. Now you'd better lock this down and get the rest of the proof. We can't hold him forever."

CHAPTER 45

Ormand Baasch got off of the commuter bus and walked down the street to the security entrance of the Homeland Security campus. His chances of being stopped right here were high, but it was the plan Abbasi had set in motion and their only option for quick entry into the machinery building. He stepped up to the guard booth with his wallet already in his hand and watched as a uniformed officer stepped out of the sliding door. Baasch could tell the solidly built black man was strong, even though he stood several inches shy of six foot tall and the bulletproof vest was tight around his abdomen. He had almost a foot on the officer but knew he wasn't someone to get through easily in combat. The Sig Sauer seemed like an afterthought on the officer's waist, almost unnecessary. He knew he could take the man down but hoped he wouldn't have to that day.

"Where are you coming from?" the guard said.

Baasch motioned back toward Centreville Road. "Bus. Don't have a car right now." He handed his driver's license to the officer. "It's my first day, trying not to be late."

The officer looked at the name on the license and glanced at the list on a clipboard hanging just inside the guard booth. "I don't have you on the list."

Baasch shook his head and looked across the parking lot. "Shoulda known," he said. "He's probably sitting there eating a box of donuts, not even remembering I'm supposed to be here today. The placement agency warned me about him."

The officer looked at Baasch's blue workpants and grey shirt with his name embroidered on it. "You're talking about Ferguson, right?"

"Yeah," Baasch said. "Couldn't stand the guy but its good work. He's a bit of a, well . . . "

"Racist asshole?" the officer said.

Baasch laughed. "You've met him, I guess."

"I see the looks he gives me when he rolls through here in the mornings, usually half an hour late," the officer said. "I haven't even seen him yet today."

"Shit," Baasch said. "What am I supposed to do now?"

"Hold on," the officer stepped inside the booth and picked up the phone receiver.

Baasch readied himself. If he acted fast enough he thought he could disarm the officer then shoot him with his own weapon, push him inside the booth and make the run across the parking lot to the machinery building within 60 seconds. It would take him at least five minutes to carry out his task but as soon as the officer was found the entire compound would be placed on lockdown. As he continued to consider his options the officer stepped back out.

"Head on over," the man said. "I'm sure Ferguson will be here soon. Just wait for him there." The same small white car that transported him a few days earlier for his interview pulled up inside the fence and the officer gave the driver a wave. "Carlos will drive you over."

Baasch nodded as he took his license back. "Thanks. Really appreciate it."

"We're all just workin'," the officer said.

The gate rolled to the right just wide enough for him to walk through. The three large posts that lowered into the ground to stop cars and trucks from smashing through stayed raised. As he stepped through, Baasch was stiff, waiting for them to try to grab him. He got into the passenger door of the small Chevy and it drove him across the lot and dropped him right outside the machinery building then left him.

Up the three metal stairs to the trailer that housed the office, Baasch pulled out his cellphone and sent a message to Abbasi, letting him know he'd actually breached the compound. The door to the trailer was unlocked and he went in. A Latino man sat in a chair beside the coffee maker on the other end from Ferguson's desk.

"Hola," Baasch said. "Como estas?"

"Bien," the man said. "And I speak English."

"Whew. I'd reached my limit on how much Spanish I know," Baasch said. "Coffee any good?"

"It's shitty," he said, "Ferguson buys the cheapest stuff he can for us. While he has that thing." The man pointed to a small table behind the foreman's desk.

A large black coffee maker that took single serve containers sat there, with a metal rack full of name brand coffee pods beside it.

"Yeah. He seems like a dick," Baasch said.

The man walked past him and patted his shoulder on the way out of the trailer. "You'll do just fine here."

Baasch looked around. He hadn't seen any cameras on his first trip to the trailer but wanted to make sure. When he didn't see any he went around to the other side of the desk and pulled the top drawer open. Just inside sat the key ring. He took the keys and was about to close the drawer when he saw the edge of a clear plastic case and he pulled it out. It was an ID badge with Larry Ferguson's face on the front and the black stripe across the back. He grabbed it and left the trailer.

Around the corner was the secure door to the main machinery building. He held up the ID and swiped it across the pad to the right of the door. After a series of beeps he heard a click and pushed the door open and walked through. He had expected to have to disable an employee and use their badge to gain access. Ferguson's laziness had made his job easier.

The top end of the huge heating and air conditioning unit was in front of him. He stepped forward to the metal railing and looked down to the lower floor where the six huge boilers sat, pushing hot water through miles of tubing to send warm air through the vents to keep the three large office buildings heated. He had seen a couple of cameras on the lower level and kept them in mind as he worked his way around to the backside to the stairs, keeping his head turned away from the cameras. He jogged down the stairs and jumped down the final two steps and landed on the concrete floor. It was much louder with the machines in front of him and he wouldn't be able to hear if someone came in up above.

He moved quickly, looking at the gauges and controls lining the metal box, knobs and levers and a row of red switches. Though he wasn't trained in maintaining the large beasts as he'd told Ferguson, he was very familiar with them. He'd used the heating and cooling systems as a means to drive people from buildings he wished to rob or to pump poisons through the air as a simple weapon. The heating was working hard to warm up the buildings as staff was coming in for the day. At night they let air get cooler to save energy, only having to overcompensate in the mornings to heat it all back up. Flipping switches wasn't enough. Even Ferguson would figure that out quickly.

From his pocket he retrieved a thin carbon fiber screwdriver that wouldn't have shown up on a metal detector if they had bothered putting him through one at the gate.

He identified the primary control panel and had the four screws off and lowered the cover to the floor. The different colored wires were all organized and simple to trace. Each of the six boilers was designed with a backup system in case the internal computer sensed something wasn't working correctly. The load that boiler was carrying would be transferred over to the remaining tanks. Tracing the wires, Baasch found the green line that carried the signal to switch the boiler's load. He pulled the small black plug at the end of the wire out of the circuit board then used the tip of the screwdriver to bend the contact points back enough to where they wouldn't have a connection anymore. It was a small break in the system, but one that would have maintenance workers scrambling for hours to figure out.

Having found the proper wire, he performed the same

task on the other five boilers quickly, replacing the control panel covers afterwards. From his left pants pocket he pulled a plastic zip lock bag full of playground sand. He unscrewed the side of the motor for the water circulating pump and poured most of the sand onto the drive axle of the motor then replaced the cover, then again carried this out on the other machines with less of the abrasive grains on those.

He estimated it would take at least twenty minutes for the first motor to burn out, which would stop the flow of circulating hot water that the system required to work. The other motors would take longer to burn out.

The hard part was done. Now he just had to wait. He had to come in unarmed and unprotected. Though he was used to working alone quite often, it wasn't usually on such high security facilities and he would always have a weapon. He followed the venting down the cement hall and stopped in front of the large steel door to the passage to the other buildings and placed his hands on it.

CHAPTER 46

"We have an hour until the president arrives," Arrington said. "Are you going to have any additional information to provide on why her secretary of transportation is being detained?"

"Working on it," Grace said. "The team is picking me up in a minute and we're heading over to his office to look around."

"You think he'd keep anything there?"

"Gotta look," Grace said. "We've gone through his phone, and except for the one number to the burner, it's clean. He's got to have another phone he uses to make contact with Abbasi."

"You don't want to ask him about Abbasi yet?" Arrington said.

"No. We need proof in front of him of their connection so he can't just deny it," Grace said. "Next time Monroe sets foot in that detention room, Graham is going to lawyer up."

"Okay, go," Arrington said. "I'll call ahead and get you cleared to search."

"You already did," Grace said.

"And I don't even remember doing it," Arrington shook his head. He began to turn away just as raised voices could be heard across the room.

Grace turned around to see William confronting Director Monroe. Grace and Arrington walked over to them and William turned to them.

"Where is Richard?" William said. "This asshole won't tell me anything."

"That asshole is the director of the FBI so I'd watch what you call him, if I were you. Richard is working with us to provide some information that may be helpful for our investigation," Arrington said.

"You sound just like him," William shoved his finger in Monroe's face.

"Let's calm down and keep in mind who you're talking to," Arrington said.

"Where the hell is Richard?" William said. "I'm his chief-of-staff and have the right to go everywhere he does."

"We've told you, he's helping—" Grace was cut off.

"I don't want to hear that again," William said. "Take me to him now!"

"I'm sorry, we can't do that," Monroe said. He turned and motioned for Amanda Paulson. "We're going to get you a ride home. Richard is going to be tied up the rest of the day then we'll send him home."

Paulson walked up and Monroe turned to her.

"Get a car here to take him home and make sure he has anything he needs," Monroe said.

"What I need is Richard," William said.

"And as soon as we can we'll have him home," Monroe said. "Right now we just need your cooperation. Assistant Director Paulson will get you taken care of."

Grace rode in the back of the black van. Netty was driving and Avery was beside her. They were all quiet, having just driven back from the memorial service, and all were dressed in suits, including Netty.

"How was it?" Grace said.

"Nice. He'd have hated it," Corbin said. "Not a lot of people."

"Anyone ask you about how you knew him?" Grace said.

"We kept our distance," Holden said. "If anyone came too close, I growled at them."

"At least you were respectful," Grace said. He caught the team up on what had happened at the ETTF, that Graham was being detained.

"Knew he was a dick, but didn't think he had that in him," Avery said from the front of the van.

"We need more to lock it down, but so far we think he's good for it," Grace said.

"What about Abbasi?" Levi said. "He in the wind?"

"Not that we know of. There's still a chance of a second attack," Grace said.

Netty had taken the GW Parkway down to 395 and across the 14th Street Bridge into the district. Traffic was still slow from the roadblocks near the Capitol and the Navy Yard so she exited and cut over to M Street then east towards the department of transportation building. Grace's phone rang.

"What is it, Ben?"

"The pictures from your phone. I've been going through them trying to ID the faces," Ben said.

"And?"

"I got to one that didn't need to be ID'd," Ben said. "Just texted it to you.

Grace took his phone from his ear and tapped to look at the photo that had just come in. He stared at the man's face. A thin moustache lined the upper lip and wavy blonde hair rose from the top of the head. Glasses with large frames rested low on the nose. Still the face was easily recognized. He put the phone back to his ear.

"That who I think it is?"

"It is," Ben said. "The caption on the photo said Bill Whitlock. Guess he started going by William sometime after that."

"Wait, Whitlock?" Grace said.

"Exactly," Ben said. "His father owns Whitlock Development and William was a VP there when they bought Cunningham Construction."

"Is he still in the control center or did they take him home?" Grace said.

"I haven't seen him in a while but I haven't been looking for him either," Ben said.

"Thanks, Ben," Grace said. He hung up and dialed another number.

"Arrington," the voice came through the phone.

"We need to get William back in," Grace said. "He's connected to Cunningham also."

"Shit, Grace," Arrington said. "Make up your damn mind. Is it Graham or is it William?"

"Why can't it be both? Either way I think it's best to have him secured just in case," Grace said.

"Amanda Paulson and a couple of agents took him home right after you left," Arrington said. "I'll get Monroe to bring him back in." The phone line went dead.

Grace stared out the window as the van pulled up to the parking area behind the building on 4th Street SE. He tried to connect the dots to see where William fed into the plan.

"What does William get out of it, except for being the first "First Gentleman" of the country?" Grace said.

"You actually asking questions or just talking to yourself?" Netty said.

"A little of both," Grace said. "If you have any ideas, chime in anytime. What sense does it make to go through so much in order to become president? It doesn't mean you'll get re-elected next time around."

"It sure didn't work out for Gerry Ford," Netty said.

"Check you out on the history," Grace said. "But it did work out for Johnson and there's still some wackos who think he was involved in the JFK assassination. Still, I don't know why any sane person would want the job in the first place."

"I don't think we're dealing with anyone sane, here," she said.

"True," Grace said. His phone rang again and he answered.

"Just talked to Monroe and they can't raise the agents watching William," Arrington said.

"Give me the address," Grace listened and began tapping it into the GPS then hung up. "Turn it around, we gotta get to McLean fast."

CHAPTER 47

The tires squealed as Netty threw the van in reverse and punched the gas pedal. "GPS has it at 33 minutes. I'll get us there in twenty," she said. Traffic heading out of the city was lighter and she went back over to the GW Parkway and up towards McLean.

Grace turned in his seat to take inventory. "Everyone gear up. We're flying blind on this one. I don't have any information on the house. Holden and Avery, you take the sides and back. Netty and Levi are with me through the front door. Corbin, you're sweeper."

"What are we up against?" Holden said.

"Nothing, hopefully," Grace said. "As far as I know William is at home with two FBI agents and the assistant director watching him. I'm getting Ben to send us whatever he can about the house."

The team pulled on holsters and vests over their black

suits and sat calmly in the back. There was a silence that happened before going into combat. Each member of the team focused their thoughts and raised their alertness to be ready for anything. The weight of having just come from the funeral of a friend who had died in a firefight was not lost on any of them. Netty was the least experienced but had still been through the door many times. She would be pulling on gear as she got out of the van when they arrived.

"Four minutes out," Grace said.

The van was on Georgetown Pike approaching the intersection with Balls Hill Road. Cars were backed up ten deep in all four lanes where they had to make a right turn.

"Go around," Grace said.

"Around?" Netty said.

"Around," Grace said.

Netty cranked the wheel left as she laid on the horn with her elbow. The left two tires jumped up onto the narrow grassy median as she kept honking and watching for oncoming cars. A red minivan swerved as it came straight at them.

"Clear from the left," Avery said. "Go for it."

Netty hit the gas and the right tires came down off of the median into the oncoming lane and she sped out into the intersection and began to make the right turn as a taxi screeched to a stop from their left.

"Thought you said it was clear," she said.

"Clear-ish," Avery said.

She punched the gas and sped across the four lanes with multiple cars and trucks honking behind them.

"We may get company after that move," she said.

"What, police?" Grace said. "We're in Fairfax County. You're pretty much expected to drive like that."

The van leaned far to the right as Netty took the turn on the smaller two lane road that would wind them around through the multi-million dollar estates.

"Left here," Grace watched the map moving on the dashboard. "Then it's just down on the left." His phone beeped. "Okay, three stories, over 12,000 square feet. There's going to be a lot of places to hide. Be ready."

The homes on the road were larger than the ones they'd passed and had more land around them. Netty pulled to a stop one house over from Richard Graham and William Whitlock's residence. Trees formed perfect lines separating them from the neighbors. A black Ford Explorer was backed into the driveway.

"The agent's SUV is empty," Grace said.

The sliding door opened as men and guns came pouring out. Avery and Netty left the front as she pulled on the black bulletproof vest over her fitted black suit that showed more cleavage than one would usually show at a funeral. The teams broke into groups as they had been instructed. Grace took point while Levi flanked to his left and Netty took up the rear, scanning the windows. Grace and Netty had their pistols out and raised while Levi was still using the Sig Sauer assault rifle Chip had handed out in the tunnels under DC.

"Quiet in back," Avery's voice came through Grace's earpiece. "This place is a monster. Looks like we'll be coming in a level down than the front."

"Copy that. We're at the front. Breaching in five . . . four . . . ," Grace said. He continued the countdown silently and as he hit "one" he went through the unlocked front door.

Grace went left into the open floor plan. A huge suspended staircase ascended up to the second level 20 feet above them. Somewhere below them he heard glass shatter as the other team breached on the lower level. He motioned with his hand for Netty and Levi to move left and he went right as they came around the stairs into the ballroom sized living room. The back wall was all glass looking out over a small yard down below and the Potomac River flowing past at the bottom of the hill.

He came into the kitchen and beyond that a formal dining room with a chandelier the size of a Volkswagen Beetle. As he turned to go into the dining room his earpiece came on.

"Man down," Levi said. "Looks like one of the agents."

Grace stopped and turned at a sound behind him. Holden came up the service stairs into the kitchen. They moved towards the living room and stopped behind a sofa and looked at the body on the floor across from him.

"Big pool of blood," Grace said. "He's been down a while." He turned to go to the back stairs to the second floor. Holden followed as Netty and Levi met Avery coming up from the main stairs and continued on up to the open walkway suspended above them.

"Second agent down," Netty's voice came through. "Right through the heart."

Grace turned off the stairs and could see her standing in the hall, the feet of the downed agent coming out from around the corner.

"Everyone stay still," Grace said as he stopped and listened to the house, his Glock still up and ready. It was 30 seconds later he heard a quiet thump from down the hall. He ran towards Netty and jumped over the dead body of the FBI agent then circled left into the large master bedroom and stopped just inside the door.

"William, it's Grace. I know you're here." He scanned the room through the sights on his pistol. "Time to come out and tell us what happened here."

There was silence for a few moments then a muffled voice. "In here."

Grace moved to the closet door and swung it open slowly. It was larger than the living room in his apartment. Custom mahogany shelves were lined with dark suits. In the center was a tall table lined with silk ties.

Amanda Paulson stood at the back of the closet, her arms raised in front of her with a small Glock aimed at the door Grace had opened.

"Amanda?" Grace said.

She lowered the weapon then let if fall to the floor. Grace stepped over to her and she collapsed into him.

"How do you do this?" she said.

He helped her out of the closet as Avery's voice came into his ear. "Chief, we have another one down. Looks like it's William."

Grace stopped beside the king sized bed and let Amanda sit down. "Status?" he said.

"Dead," Avery said.

Grace turned away from Amanda while he thought for a moment then turned back to her.

"I need you to tell me exactly what happened here," he said.

She wiped her eyes with a tissue from a box on the nightstand, her mascara running down her ivory skin. "I'll try," she said.

Grace turned as Avery walked into the bedroom. "Would you get a glass of water?" he said. Avery walked back out.

"We arrived at the house and William said he'd make

tea. He'd finally calmed down and seemed to understand that Richard was just helping out and couldn't be disturbed," she said. "He went into the kitchen to put the kettle on and I followed him. We heard the first gunshot and William dropped the kettle on the floor. I pulled my weapon and directed him to hide. When I came around the corner to the living room I saw Special Agent Jeffers on the floor."

Avery walked in and handed her the glass of water. She took a sip and sat it down on the nightstand.

"I heard the next shot from behind me in the kitchen, I guess that's when he killed William," she said. "I ran up the stairs and heard someone running after me. I got to the end of the hall then turned and took aim and waited. As soon as Special Agent Barrow came around the corner I began pulling the trigger. Once he fell to the floor I ran in here and hid in the closet."

"Did you try to call for help?" Grace said.

"My phone was downstairs," Amanda said. "It wasn't very long before you got here, maybe ten minutes. I was too scared to come out. I'm still shaking."

"I understand," Grace said. "Let's get you out of here."

Grace led her through the house and down the stairs to the front door. Three FBI cars were pulling up as they came out the front door.

"You have three down in there, two of them are agents," Grace said. "We need a full work up on the scene."

The arriving agents saw the assistant director and nodded as they began to set up the perimeter.

CHAPTER 48

Grace walked into the ETTF and found Arrington and Monroe. He told the men the story Amanda Paulson had given him.

"Good God," Monroe said. "Looks like I picked the right assistant director. We're not agents, but she acted like one out there today."

"She's a tough girl. That's for sure," Grace said. "But what we don't know is why this went down. Seems to clear William and just puts more light on Graham."

"But why would he kill his own boyfriend?" Arrington said.

"Maybe to make himself look innocent," Grace said. "He knows the heat is on him."

"Just that you can say that tells me how differently we think," Monroe said.

"Maybe William was indeed involved and wanted to come clean," Arrington said. "Graham got nervous and ordered the hit."

"Definitely an option, but all we have now is William's photo hanging on a wall at Cunningham Construction," Grace said.

"Where did you get the photo?" Monroe said.

"It was on the wall at Cunningham's offices," Grace said.

"How'd you get in there?" Monroe said.

"Mattie the receptionist let me in," Grace said. "Sweet lady."

"So no warrant," Monroe said.

"No. She said we could look around all we wanted," Grace said. "Only thing we took out was a folder with the names of all the contractors who worked on the Capitol."

"You really aren't used to working within the confines of the law, are you," Monroe said. "None of that is usable. Thankfully we can back up his connection to Cunningham through public records."

"Want me to talk to Graham?" Grace said. "See his reaction when he find out William is dead."

"No," Monroe said. "You're not to step foot inside that room," he glanced at his watch. "The president should be here soon. After I check in with her I'm going in to talk to Graham again."

Monroe walked away and Grace turned to Arrington. "Nope," Arrington said.

"Dammit," Grace said.

CHAPTER 49

Arash Abbasi had the truck parked across the street from a business park. A row of matching trucks with a company logo plastered across them lined the curb facing him. It hadn't been too difficult to find out which companies had contracts to service the large heating and air conditioning system two miles down the road at the Homeland Security building. He'd searched help wanted ads for HVAC service people and ruled out any that didn't require active government clearance, which in the DC area wasn't rare for any business. From there, he just had to see which ones were certified in the brand Baasch had seen on his field trip to the machinery building. It left only two. Instead of trying to figure out which would be called first, he decided to create an emergency big enough that would require as many technicians as possible.

He was ready to be done, to get on a plane and fly away. Collect his money and be done with Washington DC. He hadn't decided whether he would kill the client yet, but he did know he wasn't going to take a contract in the United States again. There was enough good money to be made in Europe and the Middle East.

He looked at the time on the dashboard radio. 10:00 am.

CHAPTER 50

President Abrams arrived at the building with her Secret Service detail in tow. The guards at the gate were only informed a few minutes before the caravan of black cars pulled up. Most of the agents lined the exterior of the building, checking all of the entrances. The hallway inside had another dozen men as well as a few who were working their way through the six-story building. Four agents stood outside the thick steel door to the ETTF along with the guards. The man in charge of her security detail, Agent Rick Haggard, was the only one inside the room and he stayed within a few feet of her at all times as he had since she'd been sworn in.

All conversations that had been taking place came to a stop as she worked her way through the room. CIA Director Leighton was sitting at the head of the long conference table and promptly stood, stacked up his papers and moved to a seat three down on the left side.

"We'll begin in five minutes," the president said. "In the meantime, would someone please bring me some coffee? It's chilly in here."

"Yes, Madam President," her personal aide scampered off to find her a hot drink.

Grace heard her request as he walked past the group to Ben Murray's desk and pulled up a rolling chair beside him.

"We gotta get more on William," Grace said. "Just because he's dead now doesn't mean he wasn't involved."

"It could just be coincidence," Ben said. "His father owns the company that bought Cunningham, so of course he was around them. Probably where William and Graham met."

"Doesn't smell right," Grace said. "Keep digging." He turned and saw Jim Monroe get the president's attention and speak to her for a few minutes. She was shaking her head.

"Wish I could be a fly on the wall for that one," Grace said.

CHAPTER 51

Jim Monroe stopped and took a deep breath outside the locked door. He turned the handle and stepped in.

"When am I getting out of here?" Richard Graham said. "I have meetings in DC."

"You're in here for your own safety, Richard," Monroe said.

"Quit the bullshit," Richard said. "You're detaining me."

"Do we have reason to?"

"No," Richard said.

"You have meetings scheduled when the president is getting briefed by her cabinet?" Monroe said.

"I just found out about the briefing last night. I already had meetings on my calendar that couldn't be rescheduled," Richard said. "I was going to get face time in here then get back to my office in time for an 11 o'clock appointment."

"You might as well just forget about your meetings. Would you like some coffee?"

Richard leaned back and glared at the FBI director then his shoulders lowered. "Yes."

Monroe looked up at the camera and nodded then turned back to Richard.

"Before we begin," Monroe paused. He wanted to be ready to receive the reaction but still was hesitant to tell a man his boyfriend had been killed. "William Whitlock was taken home by two agents and the assistant director. Sometime after they arrived at your residence--" he paused again.

"What?" Graham said.

"Richard," Monroe said. "William is dead. He was killed in a shooting at your home."

Graham stared at Monroe as if he was waiting for some warped punch line, to hear it wasn't true. When he realized that wasn't coming, he leaned back in his chair and crossed his arms across his chest and squeezed himself tightly, shaking his head.

"How?" was all Graham could get out.

"It appears to have been similar to the attacks on the Capitol, a coercion of one of our agents," Monroe said. "We're looking into it to find out exactly what went on there."

The door opened and a guard carried in two cups of coffee in paper cups, set them on the table then left the room. Monroe let a few moments pass. He had learned from his time as a federal prosecutor that questioning people in the wake of learning about a lost loved one can be one of the most productive interrogations. Their guard is down, they are weakened. As bad as it felt to continue, he knew he had to.

"You founded Cunningham Construction," Monroe said.

"That's not a crime," Richard said. He was answering on autopilot, his eyes drawn down to his coffee cup.

"In itself, no," Monroe said. "Whitlock Development purchased Cunningham Construction years ago. William Whitlock's family owned company."

"Again, no crime," Richard said. "It's how we met. Sure, it was a bit of a hostile takeover of my company, but we were barely treading water. We'd bidded too low on several big contracts in order to get the business. Whitlock put up a lot of capital to keep us afloat."

"Was this before your Senate run?" Monroe said.

"A few years," Richard said. "Don't know why I ever tried that."

"Really? You didn't want to be in politics?"

"Never had the drive to. I liked construction, owning my own company," Richard said.

"Why'd you run then?" Monroe said.

"I don't know. I think William put the idea in my head," Richard said.

"Did he push you to run?" Monroe said.

"I wouldn't say he pushed," Richard said. "I don't think. Maybe. He certainly seemed far more into it than I was. Probably why I lost. Nobody's going to vote for the guy who acts like he doesn't want to be there."

"True," Monroe said. "How was William when you lost?"

"He said we'd try again, and again if we had to," Richard said. "I didn't have the heart to tell him I didn't want to. Plus it was the 90's. Being an openly gay politician wasn't quite accepted yet. Harvey Milk proved that in 1978 and things hadn't changed. Not sure they have now, either."

"But you aren't out, are you?" Monroe said. "You still hide it from the public."

Graham looked up at Monroe then turned and stared at the wall.

"No. I'm not," Richard says. "And it kills me everyday. Parading around with women to put on an act."

"Why do you do it?" Monroe said.

"Abrams. She told me she thought it was best that I kept it secret," Richard said.

"Really?" Monroe said. "She's pretty liberal."

"Confused me, too," Richard said. "But I was happy to get the posting. Things at Cunningham weren't going well and my business partner Mason was always better at running the place than I was. It gave me an easy out."

"So, speaking of Cunningham again," Monroe said, "we've discussed the tie to the explosion."

"I can't believe it," Richard said. "I won't believe it until you show me solid proof."

"We're working on that, but so far it's a working theory," Monroe said. "And how about your phone being used to trigger the explosion. Any thoughts on that?"

"I told you before, no," Richard says.

"You insist on your innocence. Do you think William could have been involved with the attack?" Monroe said.

Graham sat silently and ran his finger around the rim of his coffee cup.

"Richard?" Monroe said. "Do you think William could have been involved?"

"No. I really don't," Richard said. "I've known him for years, loved him for years. I don't see any way he could have been."

"Seems like you're holding back," Monroe said.

Graham slowly shook his head. "He's gone and we're talking about him like he isn't. He joked once, maybe twice. He joked about making me president."

"After you lost the election?" Monroe said.

"Yeah. Right after I took over transportation," Richard said. "He made up a big story about how he could make me the first gay president."

"Did he say how he'd do it?"

"He was joking around. It wasn't real. We were just lying in bed and he was making up a story. He said he'd use his connections in DC to get me selected as designated survivor, then he'd--"

"What, Richard," Monroe said.

"Then he'd blow the Capitol up," Richard said. "It was a joke. It was a goddam joke," he looked up at Monroe. "Wasn't it?"

CHAPTER 52

Larry Ferguson sat at his desk in the trailer connected to the machinery building, a chocolate croissant on a napkin in front of him. His phone rang, pulling his attention from the pastry.

"Ferguson," he answered then listened. "Don't see any signs of malfunctions here," he looked around the empty trailer, knowing the person on the other end of the phone had never stepped foot near the workingman's area of the campus. "Oh, she's in the building? Yeah. I'll check it out."

After hanging up he eyed the croissant then grudgingly covered it with a napkin and struggled to his feet. For 12 years he'd listened to his doctors warn him of diabetes and gout and never gave it a second thought after walking out of their offices. His right foot was now swollen and turning black starting from his big toe.

He pulled open the desk drawer to get the keys to the boiler building and couldn't find them. He turned to the lockbox on the wall and keyed in the four-digit code, retrieved the master keys and left the trailer. A blast of wind hit him as the door opened. He used the master to open the machine-building door then saw his key ring on the floor and picked it up, swearing under his breath. It wasn't the first time he'd lost them.

The stairs were a chore to work his 350-pound frame down. The last time he'd made the descent was when he'd taken the man interviewing for the maintenance position down. After resting at the bottom he worked his way over to Boiler #1 and looked at the gauges. His head cocked to the side and he tapped the glass cases surrounding the needles that told him the pressures and temperatures inside the boiler.

Everything was wrong. The output temperature was down by eight degrees and the incoming water was registering at zero pressure. The motor that drove the pump was sitting silent, the smell of burning oil and metal in the air. With five more boilers and automatic rollover, he wasn't worried. It's why they built the redundancy into the system. As long as the other systems were working he could get a repairman in and nobody would notice that the huge machine had failed.

At the second boiler he was relieved to see the temperatures and pressures correct on the gauges. As he walked back to the stairs he heard a grinding noise. He turned around to see smoke begin to swirl out of the metal casing surrounding the motor on Boiler #2.

"Shit." He pulled his phone out and went through his contacts then dialed. "Yeah, hey, it's Larry Ferguson over at Innovation Square." The campus had a generic name to obscure the government agencies that operated within its fences. "I got one boiler down and a second on the way out."

He jumped as a loud popping noise came from Boiler #4. "Make that two on the way out. I need everyone you got right now. We have, uh, some VIP's here. Gotta get these things up and running fast," he listened. "Yeah, I'll alert the gate."

After hanging up he dialed the number to the security office for the campus to inform them that repairmen would be coming.

The phone shoved into his pocket he moved down the row of huge machines. As he approached Boiler #5 the motor burned out, sparks flying out of the vents.

"Goddam, this is bad," he turned to go to the stairs and stopped and looked up at the man standing in front of him. "What the f' are you doin' down here?"

Ormand Baasch looked down at the man's bulging face with contempt, not at his size or sloth, but at the man inside. "You should really be nicer to your employees."

"Wha?" Ferguson said. "How did you get in? my keys . . .. Did you steal my f'n keys?" His right hand fumbled into his pants pocket and tried to grip his cellphone. "You've made a huge mistake, asshole."

As the man pulled the phone out of his pocket Baasch slapped it out of his hand and it slid across the cement floor, the glass face of the touchscreen shattering.

"Jesus H . . . What do you think you're doin'?" Ferguson said. "I don't wanna do this, but you leave me no choice."

Ferguson thrust his right arm out, his hand in a fist, aimed for the German man's chest. Baasch took a slight step to the right and let the punch catch only air.

"My turn," Baasch said.

Ferguson raised his face to see Baasch's eyes. The powerful strike hit him square in the throat, cracking the hyoid bone and crushing his trachea. He immediately began to struggle for air, his windpipe reduced to a quarter of its normal size.

Baasch watched the man fighting to catch his breath, knowing it was a losing battle. He'd pass out first from a reduced flow of oxygen to the brain and would likely fall to the ground and further compress the area, fully blocking the airway. As the large man began to take a step forward, Baasch backed up and watched him fall to his knees, the sound of his left patella cracking on impact to the cement floor under the huge weight, a strained and gurgling scream of pain lost in the gasping. Baasch grinned.

Larry Ferguson fell to his side on the floor and Baasch listened to the breathing become more and more labored. Looking around, he saw there was a clear line of sight to the upper level. He grabbed the man's feet and dragged him to the back corner behind Boiler #6 and walked away with the fading sounds of the man asking for help behind him.

CHAPTER 53

Four men came out of the brown building across the street and began to climb into two of the white work vans. As the vehicles began to pull out Abbasi put the U-Haul in gear and turned to enter onto the road. Timing it right and cutting off one car from the left, he had the truck in front of both of the HVAC repair vans at the red light to turn left onto Centreville Road. He reached out the window and slapped his hand two times on the side of the metal above the cab of his truck.

Inside the cargo area, the rest of his team prepared. The next few minutes were the most exposing of the operation outside the campus.

Abbasi turned left when the light turned green and he watched the vans behind him in his mirror as they both swung wide into the right lane just as he had. It was only a quarter mile to the turn for the Homeland Security campus. He kept his speed low to catch the next red light, watching to make sure the vans didn't try to pass him. At the next intersection the light turned yellow and he hit his brakes and watched the vans come to a stop behind him. He reached out the window and slapped the cargo area two more times.

The rear gate of the truck rolled open. Two men came out wearing grey repairman uniforms and carrying Beretta's held down by their legs to hide them from other cars. The Brit Gerald Moline stopped at the passenger door of the first van as Alexandre Fortier went to the second van. They both opened the van doors and raised their pistols, telling the men in the passenger seats to move over and they climbed in.

The light turned green and Abbasi hit the gas and pulled away, the vans following him with their drivers at gunpoint. They went past the campus then turned left onto a side street and into the parking lot of a church with no cars on a Friday morning.

Abbasi got out of the truck wearing one of the work uniforms. As he approached the first van the driver jumped out and looked at him then turned to run. Abbasi raised his pistol and fired twice, the silenced rounds striking the man in the back and he fell to the ground. The rest of the men complied, arms up, and got out of the vans while watching their dead coworker with a pool of blood forming around him. Khouri and Fortier rounded them up and raised the door on the back of the U-Haul and told them to get in.

As the three remaining workers climbed into the truck they looked up and saw two other men waiting for them, silenced nine-millimeter pistols aimed at them. Six shots later they fell to the floor of the cargo area. Khouri and Fortier dragged the dead worker and loaded him in the back. They gathered the men's licenses and maintenance security ID's which would be handed out to each of the team members.

Abbasi pulled the door down then put a padlock through the holes and slammed the lock shut. They transferred the weapons from the cab of the truck into the work vans, hiding them deep under the tools in the back.

Moline and Fortier drove the vans, their western European complexions allowing them to be less scrutinized by the guards at the gate. Abbasi rode in the passenger seat of the first van and Khouri in the second. The vans pulled out of the parking lot leaving the U-Haul with the remainder of the team to clean up.

Abbasi had grilled his men about the security checkpoint. They had perfect American accents but hadn't lived in the states. He'd instructed them to stay relaxed and not act in a hurry about getting in to work on the machines, to mimic what he described as the laziness that infected this country.

The first van pulled up to the security gate. Abbasi picked up the oversized Styrofoam cup from 7-11 the previous occupant had left in the van and sucked the watered down soda through the straw. The taste was vile to him but he showed no sign of it.

"ID's," the officer ordered, no sign of asking.

Moline handed over the badges Abbasi had given them the day before, forged clearance badges with their faces. Inside the plastic cases they'd slid the RFID loaded badges from the dead workmen. The officer gave a cursory glance at the photos and compared them to the men then handed the badges to the officer inside the guard shack with the black tinted windows.

Inside the shack the other officer placed the badges against the sensor, the RFID tag supplying the data from the dead men's security clearance files and loading it onto the screen. He never stepped out to compare the photos on his computer monitor with the men in the van.

"They're expecting you," the officer said as he handed the badges back. "You know the way over?"

"Yeah. I helped with the install," Moline said. "The guys in the next van haven't been to this facility so I'll pull up and wait for them."

The officer nodded then the ten-foot tall gate with razor wire at the top began to slide to the right and the metal posts disappeared into the ground in front of them. Moline put the van into gear and rolled through, turned right and came to a stop to wait for the second van to be cleared.

Abbasi pulled the Beretta from under his seat and watched in the side mirror. Fortier was talking then the officer walked around to the passenger side and tapped the glass for Khouri to roll his window down. Arash put his hand on the door handle. In most cases he would leave a man behind if they became compromised, but he was already inside the secure gates of a government compound. His only option was to shoot his way out.

He watched as Khouri motioned too much with his hands while talking and knew they were going to get caught. Then the officer put his hand up to the radio clipped on his right shoulder, listened, then spoke. After finishing he walked back around the van, retrieved their ID's from the guard in the shack and opened the gate. Fortier pulled through and followed Moline around the perimeter of the parking lot and parked beside the trailer that housed the machinery building office.

"What happened?" Abbasi walked up to Khouri as they exited the vans.

"The name on my badge was too American," Khouri said. "The man had been a Marine and spent time in Riyadh. He recognized me as Saudi."

"What did you say to him?"

"I was telling him I took an American name so I could get work, that it was hard with the hatred towards my countrymen," Khouri said. "Then he was called on his radio, a man asking if the repair vans had arrived yet."

"You're welcome," Ormand Baasch stepped around the corner. "You were taking too long to clear security. I called and told them we were waiting on you, that we had an emergency situation."

Abbasi nodded, approving of the German's initiative. He hoped for a moment the details of the mission went better than he was planning for, and that he might be able to use Baasch again in the future.

CHAPTER 54

"We can't keep him much longer," Monroe said. "Unless we're sure he's involved."

"I just don't know right now," Grace said. "We need more information."

"You heard him talking about William, right?" Monroe said. "Seems like he suspected him but couldn't accept it."

"With bodies still dropping he's safer locked up in here, if nothing else," Grace said.

"Except for his constitutional rights being trampled on," Monroe said. "Better figure it out quick. I'm cutting him loose at the end of the day unless you have something concrete. The man lost his partner today. Unless we know he's guilty, we need to let the man out so he can grieve and begin making arrangements."

Amanda Paulson walked up and put her hand on Jim Monroe's arm and spoke to him quietly then walked away.

"I'm needed in the briefing," Monroe said. "Find something." The director walked away.

Arrington turned to Grace. "What about Abbasi? Any sign?"

"No," Grace said. "We've totally lost him."

"And you still think there's another strike imminent?"

"I do," Grace looked across the room. "I'd be worried right now if Graham weren't in the building. Seems like the perfect set of targets over there."

"Graham wasn't supposed to be here," Arrington said. "At least not all day. He told Monroe he has an eleven o'clock meeting in DC."

"What?" Grace looked at his watch. "That's half an hour off."

"There's dozens of Secret Service agents in and around the building," Arrington said. "The regular security detail has been doubled while the president is here. Nobody is getting in that gate unless they're pre-cleared."

Grace watched the president listen to the briefing. "You're right. I hope."

"The worst thing that's going to happen in here today is a few people are going to put jackets on to stay warm," Arrington said. "What the hell is up with the heat in here anyway?

Ben Murray stood up from his computer a few feet away. He handed Grace a folder. "Not much, but some basics on William Whitlock."

Grace scanned the page and paid special attention to the section about William's military service.

"Six years in the army. Looks like he was trying to join the Rangers when his career abruptly ended."

"Why'd it end?" Arrington said.

"Doesn't say here. Seems odd he'd get caught that flat footed in a hostile situation. He was on the ground in Iraq," Grace said. "Hey, when Graham gave Monroe the code to unlock his phone, what was it?"

"0812," Ben said.

Arrington and Grace turned and looked at the analyst.

"What, I transcribed the video," Ben said.

"Already?" Grace said. He looked at the first page in the folder. "William Whitlock's birthday is August 12th. 0812. So William would easily have known how to get into Richard's phone."

"Not surprising. I know how to unlock my wife's phone," Arrington said.

"Does she know how to unlock yours?" Grace said.

"No. But that's different. I use mine for work," Arrington said.

"Don't you think Graham uses his for work?" Grace said.

CHAPTER 55

After blocking the door to the boiler room and chaining the doors shut from the inside, Abbasi and his men moved downstairs and through the gate Baasch had opened that led into the tunnel that carried the air vents to the three buildings on the campus. With four of his men with him, four more were still outside the campus to carry out the exfiltration once the mission had been completed, if any of them survived.

The walkway was narrow beside the pipes and vents and the men walked single file, Baasch in the lead. They'd brought sound suppressed AK-47's into the building inside the toolboxes and several magazines of ammunition for each man, as well as .40 caliber Beretta PX4 Storm pistols.

A single row of LED lights illuminated the hallway ahead of them as they walked. After five minutes underground they came to a junction that split three ways. A sign on the wall directed them to the left for the long walk to the farthest building.

The strides of the tall German kept putting him ahead of the rest of the men. He would stop and wait a few moments for them to catch up then continue. It took another ten minutes to get to the steel door to the building. Baasch looked at the door. It opened out into the next room and had only a metal rectangle to push on rather than a handle or knob. A steel plate covered the area over the bolt and locking mechanism.

"Can't pick it from this side. We'd have to blow it," Baasch said. "Would be too loud."

"I was prepared for this," Abbasi turned to the large air vents and placed his hands on the cool metal. "One man will go in through here."

Efraim Khouri produced two pairs of sheet metal pruners with eight-inch blades from his bag and handed one to Baasch. "Get cutting, my friend," Khouri said.

Abbasi motioned to where the opening should be and stepped back to watch the men work. Baasch had a hole punched and the top edge cut before Khouri could get started. The space would be tight, but whoever went in would only have to move ten feet then cut himself out of the vent on the other side of the wall.

Once the hole was big enough, Abbasi looked at the four men and nodded at the smallest, Alexandre Fortier. All of them were experienced in breaching any type of lock. The Frenchman handed his Kalashnikov assault rifle to Moline, checked that a round was in the chamber of the Beretta on his hip and the silencer was mounted properly, then climbed into the opening of the vent head first, Baasch and Moline helping his legs up. Once in, Khouri handed him a pair of the metal cutters.

Moline watched through the opening in the vent as the man moved slowly to avoid creating excessive noise through the ventilation system. He would reach forward and place the cutters down then inch his way along until he was on top of the cutters then repeat.

Baasch listened with his ear to the door and heard the initial pop of the pruners going through the metal to make a hole to start the cut. There was silence as Fortier looked through the hole to make sure nobody was waiting for him. Then the sounds of the cutters slowly slicing through the metal, an awkward task while inside the vent. Once three cuts were made, Fortier pushed the aluminum down towards the floor to give him room to climb out without gashing his skin open on the rough edges he'd created.

"He's out," Moline pulled his head out of the hole.

"Let us be ready," Abbasi said.

The men had their weapons out and lowered as they heard the clicking of the lock picking tools Fortier had carried inside his jacket pocket working the tumblers of the lock. The clicking stopped and another man's voice was heard, then the snap of a bullet leaving the barrel and suppressor of the Beretta. There was silence for another minute then the clicking began again.

The final tumbler rolled with a thud inside the steel door and the men heard the sound of the thumb latch being pushed down then the door opened in front of them. They all had their rifles up and aimed at the door in case someone other than Fortier stood on the other side.

Fortier stepped back, the body of a security guard on the floor behind him, a round hole in his forehead with blood draining onto the grey cement floor.

"Unavoidable," Fortier said.

Abbasi simply nodded, trusting the combat reflexes of all of the men he chose to work for him.

On a contract in Brussels one of his men killed two unarmed people who had just been at the wrong place rather than debilitate them. At the end of that mission, Arash transferred the contractor's payment to his account then wrapped a garrote wire around the man's throat as he sat and drank with the rest of the team and felt his life leave him.

They entered into the small room in the basement of the Homeland Security building and closed and relocked the door. They left the body of the dead guard where it was. The pool of blood on the floor was too big to hide or clean.

Moline opened the door to the hallway and looked out both directions. "Clear," he said.

They moved out with Moline taking point and Baasch in the rear. Twenty feet down the cement block hallway was the access point for the elevator shaft but no buttons or sliding doors, just a simple handle to slide the large door open to the right for access to the shaft for maintenance.

"The elevator to the secure room does not stop here. It only goes from the lobby to the sub-level," Abbasi said.

The men slid the door open and looked down then up the shaft.

"The elevator is at the top," Khouri said. "It's clear."

"Very good," Abbasi said. "Prepare yourselves. There will be guards at the bottom, but once into the room it should be less protected. You must eliminate all of guards before any have a chance to put the door into safety mode. Once that is done, we will not be able to gain entry."

Baasch reached around into the elevator shaft and grabbed the nearest rung to the ladder built into the wall and swung his body in then started down. Khouri followed, then Moline and Fortier. Finally Arash Abbasi went into the shaft and worked his way down. His four men got to the ground, which was four feet below the level of the floor outside the shaft, and Abbasi stayed up on the ladder, out of the line of fire until they cleared the next room. He had no intention of dying before completing the mission.

Baasch and Khouri gripped the edges of the elevator door and prepared to slide them open and step out of the way as Moline and Fortier set up on the back wall of the shaft in the shadows, their bodies protected from oncoming bullets by the floor in front of them.

"Now," Abbasi said.

The two men pulled the sliding elevator doors open. A row of armed guards and Secret Service agents stood along the wall and in front of the large metal door to the ETTF. The agent's weapons were all under their jackets and holstered. The guards had their rifles in front of them on straps.

The guards and agents watched the door open, not comprehending at first why the elevator wasn't on the other side. The first round of bullets came out from the dark shaft, the two shooters sweeping from opposite ends in towards the men in the center. One agent was able to pull his service Sig Sauer P229 and get two shots off as he fell to the ground. After several seconds the room fell silent with 11 dead men on the floor.

"Get to the door before they secure it from the inside," Abbasi ordered.

Baasch and Khouri swung around from the edges of the door and into the room. Moline and Fortier were up onto the floor and behind them checking to make sure none of the guards were alive to shoot at them. Baasch grabbed the guard nearest the door and lifted him to his feet easily, grabbed the key card that hung on a lanyard around his neck and swiped it across the sensor until it beeped. The red glass panel lit up below it and he took the man's still warm hand and placed it with the fingers spread and watched the laser move from top to bottom, reading the fingerprints, palm impression and body temperature from the hand.

After scanning the hand, the red light turned off and the panel went dark. Just as he thought it hadn't worked, the bolt on the door slid open and Baasch dropped the man to the floor.

Moline and Fortier were through first, rifles raised and moving to the sides. Baasch and Khouri came in next moving up the middle.

Agent Rick Haggard was already in position after hearing the gunfire, his pistol out and aimed as the men entered. Gerald Moline was closest to him and received the Secret Service agent's first shot through his chest, piercing a hole through his heart that began to bleed out inside him. The second shot struck his right cheek, removing the back half of his skull. The former British army officer turned terrorist collapsed to the ground.

Haggard already had his aim moved to the right to pick off Fortier as Baasch came through the door. The AK-47 fired off a three round burst, all striking the agent in the chest. He was thrown backwards onto the ground.

The three-dozen occupants of the room, consisting of most of the president's cabinet and half of the Joint Chiefs of Staff were all on their feet as Abrams was moved towards the back to be blocked by as many bodies as possible.

"Bring me the president," Arash Abbasi said. "Or my men begin shooting."

CHAPTER 56

Grace had dropped to the floor behind the row of analyst's desks when the sounds of gunfire erupted on the other side of the steel security door, dragging Ben Murray with him.

He'd seen Haggard stand up and move into the open and called to him to take cover, but the Secret Service agent held his ground and paid the price when the terrorists breached the doorway. Grace's hand went to his back and pulled the Glock from its holster. He knew the first round was already in the chamber and he didn't have to check it, for this very reason. The shooters would have heard the sound of the slide being pulled back then released to load a bullet and he'd be dead before he could get a shot off.

He heard Abbasi's voice demand to see the president and knew it wasn't a bluff. There were only moments before bullets would begin taking people down.

Grabbing his phone he made sure the ringer was off and typed in a fast message and sent.

Motioning to Ben to stay still and quiet, Grace inched along the ground, staying as low as possible to try to get a view through the rows of desks. At one point he could see the legs of one of the men but nothing more.

His phone vibrated and he hit the button quickly and looked at the screen. Holden and Netty had been in the observation room reviewing video from the interviews with Graham. With them coming from the far side of the room they would have the terrorists flanked. He continued crawling along the floor, moving to a position that wasn't straight across from the hallway to the detention cells so he wouldn't be in the line of fire from his own team. He moved close to the wall near the main door and would be able to come up behind the shooters.

"Let me through," Abrams voice came from the back of the room. "Let me through now."

Grace dropped his head to the floor and closed his eyes, waiting to hear the sound of Abbasi's gun as it killed the president. The clicking of her heels moved to the front of the room.

"Madam President, it is an honor. My name is Arash Abbasi." His gun was aimed at her head.

"What is it you want, Mr. Abbasi," President Abrams said.

Grace moved a few more inches and had a view from the back of the room. He saw the three remaining shooters with AK-47's trained on the group of suits and uniforms, Arash Abbasi standing in the middle, a pistol aimed at the president ten feet in front of him.

He ran the scenarios through his head and knew he could take one man down before the other two had a chance to turn and shoot. If Holden and Netty were in location and reacted quickly, they would have the other two handled, leaving only Abbasi to worry about.

"I am a contractor, Madam President," Abbasi said. "I do not kill for enjoyment or my own political gain. I kill for money, plain and simple. People hire me to do my job and I do it well. This is not personal. I have no loyalty to any nation or flag and am not an enemy to any nation or flag, only to men."

FBI Director Monroe had moved up beside the president in the absence of her lead Secret Service agent. He had never carried a gun and didn't have one now.

"Do you think you're going to be able to walk out of here alive?" President Abrams said.

"Yes, I do," Abbasi's thumb moved up and pulled the hammer back on the weapon.

"Do you have any demands?" the president said.

"Yes," he said. "Die."

Arash Abbasi pulled his finger and fired the pistol. As the bullet left the barrel, Jim Monroe jumped to his left, pushing the president to the floor. The gunshot struck him in the left temple and exited the back of his head. His lifeless body fell on top of the president.

Grace was on his feet and sprinted up behind the closest man, who happened to also be the smallest. He had his pistol but couldn't chance shooting towards the group of people. In a smooth motion he brought his left arm around the throat of Alexandre Fortier, shoving his chin up towards the ceiling and with his right hand grabbed the muzzle of the AK-47 and spun the man to his right, away from the group.

He counted on the man pulling the trigger on the

automatic weapon and hopefully taking out at least one of his own men. The terrorist's finger pulled back on the heavy trigger of the Russian made assault rifle. Three bullets exited the barrel as Grace continued to turn his body then throw him to the floor. His knee came down onto Fortier's forehead and knocked him out. He'd seen Abbasi duck and move forward as they turned and had heard the whispered snaps of the Sig Sauer rifles. He knew he would turn to see the other two terrorists on the floor.

He turned and froze. Abbasi was on his feet, his left hand holding President Abrams in front of him, his pistol to the side of her head.

"Put your guns down," Abbasi stared at Grace.

"Do you have him?" Grace said.

"I have him," Holden stood twenty feet away with his rifle aimed at the side of Abbasi's head.

Abbasi looked over at the tall black man with the gun pointed at him then back to Grace. He raised the Beretta into the air and released the hammer then threw the gun onto the floor in front of Grace. He then slowly let the president go and placed his hands on the back of his head.

"I wish to surrender and give my confession to the crimes I have committed in your country."

"Confession?" the president said.

"Yes," Abbasi said as Grace stepped in and yanked the man's hands down behind his back and tied them together with a zip tie Netty handed him. "I am responsible for the destruction of the United States Capitol."

CHAPTER 57

Holden and Grace held either arm of Arash Abbasi as they watched the black armored vehicle of the FBI SWAT team out of Quantico stop in front of them. There were two large SUV's with tinted windows with it, one in front and one behind. A well armed and armored agent climbed out of the back of the truck as half a dozen more came from the front seats as well as the SUVs.

Grace could feel Abbasi shivering as they stood in the cold. He'd thought about putting a jacket around the man's shoulders before bringing him up from the ETTF then chose not to.

Amanda Paulson was off to the side and met with the lead agent in the front vehicle. The convoy would transport Abbasi to the Federal detention center in Alexandria where he would be stripped and searched then dressed in a bright orange jumpsuit and put into the highest security cell in the building. He would stay there until his first court appearance in the Federal Courthouse across the street.

Two SWAT agents placed heavy handcuffs on the prisoner's wrists then clipped the zip ties off. A set of leg irons was wrapped around his ankles. He was then assisted up into the back of the armored vehicle and the door was locked from the inside.

"Seems kinda anticlimactic," Holden said.

"Yeah," Grace said. "I know what you mean. Would much rather have him in a bag. How'd you two miss the shot?"

"He was blocked by one of his own guys," Holden said. "I was going to double-tap, drop the guy closest to me then take him out with the second round, but Abbasi moved as soon as he fired at the president."

"Really?" Grace said. "No hesitation?"

"Not that I saw," Holden said. "Practically sprinted to grab the president."

"Hmm," Grace said. "How tall would you say Monroe was?"

"Couple inches shorter than me," Holden said. "6-2 maybe."

"And Abrams is five foot five in heels," Grace said.

"True," Holden said. "So how did he get a head shot on Monroe when he was aiming at her face?"

"Exactly."

The front SUV went into motion and the loud diesel engine of the armored truck revved and took off behind it. The final SUV rolled past silently in contrast. As the vehicles hit the street past the gate their lights and sirens came on to speed up their trip to Alexandria.

"Grace," Amanda walked up to him. "Good work in there. You and your team."

"Thanks. I wish we'd been a little better," Grace said.

"Don't give it another thought," she said. "The president is alive thanks to you."

"But your boss isn't," Grace said.

"No, but he died to protect the president," she said. "In the short time I got to work with him, I can say that his actions were fully in line with his personality. He wanted to give everything he could to his job and his country."

"Well, he did that," Grace said. "So what about you?"

"What about me?" Amanda said.

"You in charge now?"

She nodded slowly. "Yeah. The president asked me to step up as interim director."

"Congrats?" Grace said.

"Sure," she said.

CHAPTER 58

The used U-Haul truck sat in the right lane just ahead of the turn to the toll road that took traffic to the beltway, hazard lights flashing and hood up. The rear door was raised two feet. One man stood up on the front bumper staring under the hood.

The armored vehicle convoy transporting Arash Abbasi was moving faster than the speed limit, barely slowing for red lights. Cars were pulling out of its way as the three vehicles began moving from the left lane to prepare for the right turn onto the toll way.

As the lead SUV approached the U-Haul the first shots came out from the darkness of the inside of the box truck. Two sets of .50 caliber rounds came from the truck. The first weapon was set on disabling the lead vehicle, putting rounds through the radiator and front tires. The second shooter put a half-dozen shots through the front window killing the driver and front passenger.

The armored truck driver accelerated to move past the threat, forced to move between the disabled SUV and the U-Haul. The moving truck jolted forward with the wheels turned hard left and struck the front of the transport vehicle.

The man who'd been on the front bumper of the moving truck reappeared and climbed up on the hood of the armored truck and attached a hand grenade to a windshield wiper blade, pulled the pin, then jumped off the front of the truck. The doors flew open and the driver and passenger leaped to the ground as the grenade exploded. Two bursts of fire from an AK-47 cracked the air, killing both of the men before they could get off the ground.

The second SUV had stopped short and the three agents were out and had their rifles raised and were moving towards the U-Haul, putting distance between each other. Another grenade came through the air over the U-Haul and landed on the ground in front of the men. As it exploded, the agents were diving away from the blast. In the moment following, two men ran towards them and began firing with their rifles until there was no movement.

"Open up now," one of the terrorists banged on the back door of the armored vehicle. "You open the door, or we blow the whole truck."

The back door opened slowly to show Arash Abbasi standing in the opening. The men lowered their weapons at the sight of their leader then watched as he was pushed forward from the door, his arms and legs still shackled. Unable to brace himself, he struck the ground on his side, his skull crashing into the ground. The door of the truck slammed shut again and was relocked.

A Ford Explorer screeched to a halt beside the scene and the men helped Abbasi into the back seat and the truck sped off as a grenade taped to the back door of the armored vehicle blew.

CHAPTER 59

"They were waiting," Grace said. "Which means they knew he'd be coming."

"How's that possible?" Arrington said.

"I think the plan went exactly as he intended," Grace said. "He wanted to get into the ETTF, he wanted to shoot Monroe, then he wanted to get arrested and taken out."

"That would be a hell of a plan," Arrington said. "A man like Abbasi doesn't choose to get arrested."

"Unless he had someone inside," Grace said.

"Stop it. We already have a man detained that has essentially been rendered innocent by the actions that took place here," Arrington said. "Now you think someone else is involved."

Grace shook his head and looked away. "I don't know. It just doesn't make sense. Why did he go to all the trouble to get in here and then not kill the president?"

"You may be the only person not relieved by the fact that he didn't," Arrington said.

"Not what I mean," Grace said. "He had her in his sights, but ended up shooting a man more than a foot taller than her, with a head shot."

"Your point?"

"My point is he had to adjust his aim away from the president to get that shot," Grace said.

"Monroe was diving to protect Abrams," Arrington said.

"Even so, he was still taller than her," Grace said.

"Not everyone can be a perfect shot like you. Now I need to go get Graham released and hope he doesn't demand my head on a platter," Arrington said.

"He was involved. Or William was. At least one of them," Grace said. "I just don't know which."

"I can see motive in the first attack," Arrington said. "Graham had a lot to gain, though it still seems ridiculous that he would go through that. But what about this mess? What motive was there to attack the ETTF to assassinate the president?"

"Or Director Monroe," Grace said. "We don't know Abrams was his intended target."

"This isn't helpful," Arrington. "You want to be productive? Go find Abbasi before he disappears."

"I already have my team monitoring all possible exfiltration routes," Grace said. "If I'm right, he'll be out the U.S. within the hour."

"Great," Arrington said.

"Well, I think it is," Grace said.

"Why?"

"Once he's out we'll go after him the way we go after people," Grace said. "As long as he's still on our soil, my hands are tied."

Arrington stared at his lead operative then stepped in closer and looked him in the eyes. "Are you fucking crazy?"

"No," Grace said. "I'm practical. The American people will be far more relieved with a dead Abbasi than a long trial."

"Just go," Arrington said. "Do what you do. Just actually get some results."

CHAPTER 60

The Gulfstream G650ER was cruising at 525 miles per hour at 45,000 feet over the Caribbean Sea. The luxury interior of the jet was covered with tactical gear and weapons. The tables in the back of the cabin were lined with maps and Ben Murray had a laptop open with a secure satellite connection.

"At least it's somewhere warm," Avery said. "I'm getting sick of the cold."

"Tell you what, we get this done quick and there's a couple days R & R on any tropical island on the way home in it for everyone," Grace said.

"Don't you think Leighton wants his plane back?" Netty said.

"I'm pretty sure the CIA has other aircraft if the director needs to go anywhere," Grace said. "Or he can fly commercial."

The pilot's voice came through the speakers. "Thirty minutes to wheels down."

"Okay," Grace said. "Final checks. Once we hit the ground we don't stop until we're done."

"Think he'll know we're coming?" Corbin said.

"Maybe," Ben said. "But I registered a flight plan originating in Montreal and I hacked into the registry and reassigned the CIA director's tail number to a Canadian pharma company."

"That'll slow them down for a couple minutes," Levi said.

The plane touched down at half past midnight at Simon Bolivar airport just north of Caracas, Venezuela and taxied past the terminal. They approached a large unmarked hanger at the east edge of the airport and the wide door slid open and allowed them in.

After pulling to a stop and the door to the hanger closed behind them, Grace released the cabin door and stepped out. Two silver Mitsubishi Pajero SUVs were parked and waiting.

"You gonna take care of these cars?" a man stepped out of the office in the back corner of the hangar.

"We'll do our best," Grace jumped to the ground and walked over to shake the man's hand. "We appreciate the assist."

"When the call comes from as high up as it did, there's not a way to say no." The man looked up at the numbers on the tail of the Gulfstream then back to Grace.

"True," Grace said. "I've been there."

"I'm not so sure about that," the man said. "I know about you."

Grace looked at the man to take in his features. "Who's station chief here? Is it still Levin?"

"Levin left six months ago," the man said. "But I'm sure you knew that."

"Right," Grace grinned. "Slipped my mind. Will you be around if we need you?" He had no intention of relying on the man for anything.

"Sure," the man said. "Keys are in the cars. Try not to scratch them." He turned and walked back towards the office.

Corbin stepped up next to Grace. "Sheez. These CIA guys just get weirder and weirder, don't they?"

"Sure do. This is a hard post, though. Ever since some agency officers were accused of shipping cocaine up through Miami in the late 1990's, nobody's wanted the assignment." Grace said. "Okay, let's load the cars and get out of here."

The team began handing bags down through the door and placing them into the backs of the two vehicles. A few minutes later they left the hanger with Corbin behind the wheel of the first car and Avery the second. Grace rode beside Corbin and navigated them through the winding roads of the Venezuelan city.

"Nice place to hide out," Corbin said.

"He knew we'd expect him to go back towards the middle east," Grace said. "And with Venezuela having no extradition to the U.S. it's not a bad choice to hole up. Well, until we got here."

They drove just over an hour to the east, the ocean off their left shoulders, and passed through several small resort communities. The headlights of the vehicles illuminated the small shacks outside the towns where the underpaid employees of the resorts lived, traveling by foot or bus, when one came, to serve the wealthy people that came from all over South America to enjoy the northern coast of Venezuela and the warm waters of the Caribbean.

Grace looked down at his phone. "About a hundred yards on the right."

Corbin slowed and Avery followed suit behind them until they turned off the deserted highway onto a one-lane road that went up through the trees away from the water. A quarter of a mile into the woods they pulled into a clearing in front of a small house and parked the trucks. Most of the windows on the house were boarded up and the three steps up to the front door were all broken.

"You know, there's probably rooms at one of those hotels back there?" Netty said from the backseat.

"Later," Grace said.

They unloaded their gear from the two SUVs and went into the empty house.

"Get your gear ready. Check it, then put it away," Grace said. "We all know the plan," he looked at his watch. "Tonight we sleep, tomorrow we recon. Netty, we're getting wet in the morning."

CHAPTER 61

The sun had been up less than half an hour as Grace and Netty swam just below the surface of the southern shore of the Caribbean Sea. He wore dark blue shorts with black flippers and a red facemask and a snorkel poking out above the water. Grace caught himself glancing over at her as she moved just ahead of him in the water, her two piece green and white polka dotted bikini showing more skin on the young woman than he'd seen since she'd started working for him. Her mask and snorkel matched his.

Todosana is a quiet town that doesn't attract tourists with most of the homes being away from the beach. A few small estates face the water, owned by wealthier families from Caracas. The long beach is still as nice as the rest along the coast but is generally passed by in favor of the built up resorts with bars and restaurants a few minutes each direction from the sleepy village.

Grace gave two strong kicks to pull up next to Netty and got her attention then they stopped and let their heads come up above the water. He kept her between him and the shore so he could appear to be talking to her rather than surveying the cottage built up among the trees, thirty feet from the sand.

"See anything?" she said.

"Just the house, no movement," Grace said. "Wait, someone's sitting on the deck." He swam towards her and put his hands on her shoulders.

"And what are you doing?" she said.

"Someone's looking this way with binoculars," he said.

"So you're trying to give him something to watch?" Netty said. "Is it him? Is it Abbasi?"

"Can't tell," Grace said. He reached up and repositioned his facemask to place the small monocular mounted on the inside of the glass over his right eye. He cleared the mask of water then blinked to clear his vision and looked back over her shoulder to the house. "It's him."

CHAPTER 62

Grace was 26 years old when Derek Arrington recruited him into the NSA and 28 when he first killed a man. It had been from 60 yards out with a rifle as the target walked from his car to his home in a wealthy neighborhood of Stockholm, Sweden. Grace hadn't paused for a moment or ever stopped to consider if what he'd done, and what he'd do many more times, was wrong. It was just part of his job and became part of who he was. The man in Stockholm had been funneling money to terrorists in the Middle East through dozens of offshore accounts. Though the man never pulled a trigger or detonated a bomb, he was as responsible for more than 300 deaths as the jihadists on the ground were.

The night before a kill had become ritual. Early on he tried to avoid making it anything different, anything special, but eventually accepted the fact that it was different. Most men don't go to bed at night knowing they'll take a life the next day. He'd decided he should give more weight to the act than the people he was tasked with killing gave their actions.

He ate dinner with the team then retreated to the one room in the back of the small house with a door then sat on the floor, crossed his legs and closed his eyes. If asked he would say he didn't meditate, but that he cleared his mind and created the images of the kill in his head, going over that final moment of pulling a trigger, slitting a throat or however it was to be done, over and over until it became like an old movie he knew well. When the final event happens, the scenery may end up being a little different around him and the target, but the end result will be exactly the same as the movie in his head. In the end he would stand over the dead body of another man.

After he'd worked through the scenario until it was committed to deepest memory, he rolled forward onto the floor with his upper body supported by his arms and slowly lowered himself into a pushup, controlling his breathing as his biceps bulged under the stress. He would take 30 seconds to go down until his chest just touched the wooden floor then another 30 seconds to push back up. He repeated this ten times until his toned arms were screaming.

Flipping onto his back he rolled into a dozen sit-ups, again as slowly as possible to work his entire abdomen. He rested back onto the floor after the last sit-up and stared at the ceiling. He could hear his team in the other room, quietly talking about the mission over a couple of beers. They all knew not to drink too much, just enough to relax them for the night so they could be clear headed for the morning ahead.

Grace stood and wiped the sweat off his face and chest with the tee shirt he'd worn all day then pulled his shorts off and laid down on the thin cot in his underwear, closed his eyes, and let himself fade to sleep.

CHAPTER 63

Avery was with Netty in the water just as Grace had been a day earlier. They snorkeled 30 yards off the shore, stopping to splash each other and act cozy every few minutes until they'd worked themselves straight out from the cottage. Avery reached out under the water and grabbed Netty, making her squeal loudly then begin laughing, all the while watching over her shoulder.

"Nothing yet," Avery said. The radio earpiece was waterproof and worked off the vibration of your voice rather than the sound from your mouth so he didn't have to speak loudly.

"Do it again," Grace's voice came through.

Avery reached back towards Netty who was already glaring at him, having heard the order. As his hands reached her she was already screaming and laughing, splashing water into his face then began to swim away.

"Where are you going?" Avery yelled.

She stopped and waited for him to catch up and work into position for another visual check.

"We have movement," Avery said. "Can't confirm it's the target, but one person is standing outside and appears to be watching us."

"Keep it up out there," Grace said.

The dense woods surrounding the cottage were broken up only by the narrow drive that led from the highway to the house. Grace had been let out half a mile down from the driveway and disappeared into the trees. It took more than an hour in the darkness to reach cover just off the west side of the house where he hid to wait for sunrise and then for his team to draw attention out to sea.

Holden would be on the other side of the house but further out by now. Corbin had the car a mile down the highway. Grace traveled light, only his silenced Glock 19 and a hunting knife with a nine-inch blade. He didn't expect any security and so far had seen nothing to counter that thought.

He began to move from his position he'd held for ninety minutes to work around to the front of the cottage. Through the earpiece he continued to hear Avery and Netty frolicking in the Caribbean.

"Target is going inside," Avery said.

Grace froze. He was already out in the open and approaching the side of the building. "You need to draw attention. Do whatever you can."

Out in the water Avery looked at Netty and she just grinned and nodded. They turned and swam towards the beach until they were waist deep in the water then stood up and faced each other, taking their masks and snorkels off.

"You sure?" Avery said.

"It's just work," Netty said.

Avery reached behind her and pulled her body into his and kissed her, his tongue entering her mouth and being pushed back by hers. They had discussed the possibility of having to get creative. Avery had no issues with it and had thought Netty would. Her tongue surrounding his now out in the ocean made him think otherwise.

They turned so he could get a look at the house.

He pulled away from the kiss just enough to speak. "He's stopped and looks like he's trying to decide whether it's worth his time."

Netty pushed Avery away and turned around to face the beach and looked over her shoulder at Avery.

"Pull it," she said.

Avery hesitated briefly then grabbed the string on the back of her green polka dotted bikini and pulled. She lowered her shoulders and allowed the top to fall down her arms and off of her then tucked one string around the side of her bikini bottoms.

"Go for it," she said.

Avery stepped up behind her and brought his hands around to her tight belly. She grabbed his right hand and moved it up to her bare breast.

"Sell it," she said.

He glanced up enough to see the cottage.

"We have him," Avery said. "Damn perv has his binoculars out again."

"Whatever you're doing, keep it up," Grace said.

"Yessir," Avery let his left hand slide down her wet skin and Netty didn't stop him.

Grace went in motion. He decided to go through the

front to come up behind the target rather than approaching from the beach and risking being seen in peripheral vision. The front door was locked but the simple handle was easily picked in only seconds and he entered the cottage silently.

The house was small, only 18 feet front to back and thirty feet end to end to allow for more ocean views from the living area and the matching bedrooms on either end. He passed the small kitchen, which didn't appear to have been used. The living room had a few old pieces of wicker furniture with dated floral print cushions on top.

Through the wide glass windows in back of the cottage Grace could see Arash Abbasi standing on the deck, binoculars to his eyes. Grace's Glock was already in his right hand and ready. He got to the opening to the deck and paused. Glancing down at the old wooden deck he knew it was likely to creak when he stepped out. He raised the pistol and aimed at the man's head and stepped through the threshold. With his second step the wood below him groaned. He saw Abbasi's body become still, alert, then the man lowered his binoculars halfway.

Grace couldn't see a gun on the man and no bulge below his loose white shirt but he knew not to underestimate the terrorist.

"May I turn to face my executioner?" Arash Abbasi spoke.

"Slow," Grace said.

Abbasi let his binoculars fall to his chest and began to turn, keeping his arms out away from his body. Once he was facing Grace he stopped and looked the NSA operative up and down.

"I knew it would be you," Abbasi said.

"Yeah?"

"I saw you there, when I killed the FBI director," Abbasi

said. "And when they loaded me into that truck. I knew then it would be you."

"Happy not to let you down," Grace said.

"So, will you be taking me in for torture, or interrogation as your government prefers to say," Abbasi said. "Or will you simply be killing me here?"

"I'm not much for torture," Grace said. "But how helpful you are in the next few minutes will go a long way in determining whether you walk out of here today or someone finds your dead body in a week."

"Yes, of course. I know you have questions," Abbasi said. "Would you care to sit while we talk?" He motioned with his chin towards the faded outdoor furniture where a weapon was likely hidden.

"No, we're fine right here," Grace said. "Who hired you?"

"You must be more specific," Abbasi said. "I have many clients all over the world."

"Okay. Who hired you to destroy the United States Capitol?"

Abbasi nodded. "Right to the point, no desire for a longer discussion on the decision to accept such an assignment?"

"Nope," Grace said.

"I understand. The man who hired me for that assignment was William Whitlock," Abbasi said. "But I have a feeling you already knew that."

"I did," Grace said. "I just wanted to see how easily you'd give up your client."

"I am as committed to my clients as they are to me," Abbasi said. "But once a client demonstrates their lack of professional demeanor, I have no reason to protect them."

"What did Whitlock do?"

"It is what he did not do. He refused to pay the

remainder of his fee," Abbasi said. "He claimed the job was unfinished so I didn't deserve the rest of my payment."

Grace cocked his head to the side and sized up the Persian man. "Was the attack at the ETTF part of the contract?"

"No, it was not," Abbasi said. "That was negotiated after the destruction of the Capitol failed to achieve the results Mr. Whitlock desired, and after he withheld payment."

"Even after he didn't pay, you took another job from him?" Grace said.

"That I did not say," Abbasi said. "A second client stepped up with the remainder of the funds under the condition that I completed the second task."

"Who was the second client?" Grace said.

"That is information I cannot share," Abbasi said. "That agreement was fulfilled by both parties."

"So the president wasn't your target," Grace said. "If your client paid you then you must have achieved your goal."

Abbasi nodded in approval. "That is a fair estimation of the events," he said. "You are wiser than I expected."

"Thanks," Grace pulled the trigger on his Glock 19 pistol and the whispered nine-millimeter round flew from the barrel and entered the center of Arash Abbasi's forehead. The bullet shattered upon entering the man's skull and sent shrapnel throughout his brain.

Abbasi was dead before his knees buckled beneath him, dropping him backwards onto the wooden deck. Blood came down the side of his face from the single wound as his heart came to a stop.

CHAPTER 64

Grace stood facing the white door, a bottle of expensive Irish whiskey in his hand, then reached out and pressed the doorbell. He heard footsteps moving across the floor inside then the door opened to reveal Amanda Paulson.

"Wine is more traditional, but I'll take it," she stepped aside and let him in. "I was surprised when you called. You've been MIA since . . .." She wrapped her arms around his chest and kissed him then put her head on his chest. His heartbeat was slow and steady.

"Yeah, I had some work to do," Grace said.

"You don't get any time off after something like that?" she said.

"Usually just getting right back in is the best therapy," he said. "I try not to think about ops after they're done, when I do the reality of some of the situations can really hit you. You don't think about the danger you're in at the time."

"Tell me about it," she said. "What was the scariest part?" She moved him through the house towards the living room.

"I'd never say scary, but when I think back I guess what was probably the trickiest was when we were approaching Graham's house out near Charlottesville. There were Secret Service agents there, armed and ready to protect him. We came in totally off script and unexpected," Grace said. "I'm surprised Agent Foster didn't shoot me in the middle of the field."

She pulled away and looked at him. "I have dinner almost ready." She turned and walked through the living room and into the kitchen in the back of the house.

He sat down on the sofa. "This feels a bit more like a date than we're used to," he said.

She answered from the next room. "Is it weird?"

"Nah, I like it," he said. "Been a long time since I went on a date." He looked around the room. There was no television but several nicely framed art prints hanging on the white walls above the light green chair rail and wainscoting below it. The wide planked dark cherry hardwood floors were shining without a hint of dust. Everything was in its place and perfect.

He stood up and looked at the prints then to the corner where some more casual photos were framed. His eyes settled on one of an adult co-ed soccer team in their black shorts and red jerseys. He scanned the faces and stopped when he got to her.

"You play soccer?" he said.

"I used to," she called back from the kitchen. "Hard to find the time anymore." She came into the room behind him. "Let's sit down, that's ancient history."

"Aren't you a hot little one in your shorts and soccer shirt," he said. "The shin guards are kinda turnin' me on."

"I still have them upstairs, want me to put them on?" she stood and motioned towards the stairwell.

"Who's that guy beside you? He looks familiar," he said. "Wait a second, is that . . .?" He looked closer. "That's Agent Foster. I didn't know you knew him."

"Is he the one from Graham's house?" she said. "I never put it together, but, yeah, I guess it's the same guy. Now let's eat, foods getting cold."

Grace looked down the row of faces in the photograph and stopped again, letting his eyes rest on the narrow face at the end of the line with a thin beard and moustache. He heard a drawer open behind him and turned around.

Amanda Paulson stood with a Glock 42 aimed at him from ten feet away. "Why, Grace?" she said. "Why couldn't you just stop working?"

"What the hell, Mandy," Grace said. "I was just asking you about soccer."

"We both know you weren't," she said. "You saw the photo of Foster there and somehow in that twisted mind of yours tied everything together. I don't know how, but you did."

Grace looked over at the photo and back at her.

"True, it was kinda weird seeing Foster there, but it was more shocking to see William Whitlock in the photo," Grace said.

Amanda stretched her arms longer and gritted her teeth, her right forefinger already on the trigger of the pistol.

"Does this mean you're not going upstairs to get your shin guards?" he said.

"What did it?" she said.

"Everything out in Charlottesville made no sense; the SEAL trying to kill me, only one Secret Service agent dead from a shootout. Once Graham and William were suspects, it really confused me, until I realized it was a cover. There was never any threat against them, but it threw any suspicion against them away," Grace said. "I had a feeling about Foster when I was there. He was too easy to push over. No self respecting Secret Service agent would let some gang of thugs come out of the woods and take their asset out from under them without a fight. I also didn't buy that they were radio silent. I saw his radio on a different frequency before we left when he had no reason to change it from the secure channel we'd already communicated on. And I knew that Graham or William couldn't have pulled this off alone. I told Arrington I thought there had to be someone in the intel community involved."

"Why's that?" she said.

"Someone had to know the ins and outs of the security details, have access to the secure phones everyone carries, access their records to know who could be threatened," Grace said. "And Neurotomy, the college kids making the phone calls. That was your baby, wasn't it?"

She cocked her head. "Why do you think that?"

"We've gone through their data," Grace said. "They had access to all of the employee files for every agency they needed. Only someone high up could have arranged that. Tell me, what was Foster to gain?"

"A senior position in DC," she said. "Perhaps a move to the bureau."

"That's nothing compared to you," Grace said. "You were going to be the first female director of the FBI."

"Haven't you checked? I already am," she said.

"Interim director isn't the same," Grace said.

"It will be," she said. "Abrams told me she's going to appoint me. The Senate will have no choice to confirm me or come off looking sexist."

"I'm impressed. You've really thought this through," Grace said. "How'd you even get the money to pay Abbasi?"

"Whitlock," she said. "He knew I could still take him down, even if it meant my own career."

"And that's why you killed him," Grace said. "But you also had to take out the other two agents in the house. I had no idea you were that good a shot."

"Doesn't hurt when the two agents are misogynistic assholes and don't think lady assistant director can fire a weapon," Amanda said. "I picked them off clean. Whitlock was harder. He got to his gun but I fired first."

"You're the poster girl for feminism," Grace said. "And what about Monroe. Did you target him in order to get the appointment at the FBI? Was it similar to how we met? Did you use the same hotel in Bethesda?"

"It wasn't like that," she said. "It was more."

"It was more and then you blackmailed him into appointing you assistant director."

"Screw you," she said. "This is Washington. You do what you have to."

"Yes, you do," Grace said. "Like when I recognized you in that hotel bar when you were drunk and falling all over me."

"Bastard," she said.

"Opportunist," he said.

Grace made a motion to step forward. Amanda took a half step back. "Stop there, Grace."

"So, what, you're going to shoot me with that .380?"

Grace said. "I could take three of those to the chest and still have you on the floor before I come close to passing out."

"You wanna try?" she said.

He stared at her finger on the trigger of the baby Glock pistol.

"You have no more than seven shots to get me if I do, if you have it fully loaded," Grace said. "So, yeah, I wanna try."

Grace took a lunging step forward, his right foot slamming down onto the dark hardwood floors. Amanda Paulson pulled the trigger over and over. She stopped after five clicks and no bullets had fired.

Grace put his hand in his jeans pocket and pulled out seven .380 caliber bullets.

"You knew before you came here tonight?"

"I had a strong suspicion," he said. "Then right before I killed Arash Abbasi I knew."

"You found him?" she lowered her gun and her shoulders.

"Sure did. He sang about Whitlock, but he wouldn't give you up," Grace said. "But his bank accounts couldn't lie. You were pretty sloppy in your transfers to him, but I guess you were kinda rushed."

"So what now?" she said.

"Well, right now Foster is being arrested. The president has already appointed a new interim director, and Richard Graham will be resigning from his posting, a casualty of your little game."

"And what about me?" she said. "Are you taking me in?"

"No," Grace said. "They are."

The front and back doors of the house slammed in at the same time as a dozen heavily armed FBI SWAT agents flooded into the house. Grace stepped away as they pulled her arms to her back and roughly pushed her face forward onto the floor and began to put handcuffs around her wrists.

Grace glanced around the room then walked over to the end table beside the sofa and picked up the bottle of Jameson 18 he'd brought then turned and left the house.

Made in the USA
Middletown, DE
13 August 2016